W0114369

SUMMERHOUSE

SUMME

HOUSE

SUMMER HOUSE

YiĞiT KARAAHMET

Translated by Nicholas Glastonbury

Published by Soho Press, Inc.
227 W 17th Street
New York, NY 10011
www.sohopress.com

Originally published in the Turkish language under the title
Deniz Ne Kadar Güzel by Yiğit Karaahmet
Copyright © 2021 by Yiğit Karaahmet.
First Published in Turkish by 6:45 YAYIN, Altıkırkdört Basım Yayın Dağıtım Ltd.
Şti.
Published by arrangement with AnatoliaLit Agency.
English translation copyright © 2025 by Nicholas Glastonbury.

All rights reserved.

This is a work of fiction. Names, characters, places, and incidents either are the
product of the author's imagination or are used fictitiously, and any resemblance to
actual persons, living or dead, businesses, companies, events, or locales is entirely
coincidental.

Library of Congress Cataloging-in-Publication Data

Names: Karaahmet, Yiğit, author. | Glastonbury, Nicholas, translator.
Title: Summerhouse / Yiğit Karaahmet ; translated by Nicholas Glastonbury.

Other titles: Deniz ne kadar güzel. English
Description: New York, NY : Soho Crime, 2025.
Identifiers: LCCN 2024042064

ISBN 978-1-64129-586-4
eISBN 978-1-64129-587-1

Subjects: LCGFT: Gay fiction. | Thrillers (Fiction). | Novels.
Classification: LCC PL249.K36 D4613 2025 | DDC 894/.3534—dc23/eng/20241214
LC record available at https://lccn.loc.gov/2024042064

Interior design by Janine Agro

Printed in the United States of America

10 9 8 7 6 5 4 3 2 1

EU Responsible Person (for authorities only)
eucomply OÜ
Pärnu mnt 139b-14
11317 Tallinn, Estonia
hello@eucompliancepartner.com
www.eucompliancepartner.com

For the gurls

SUMMERHOUSE

PART I

When forty winters shall besiege thy brow
And dig deep trenches in thy beauty's field,
Thy youth's proud livery, so gazed on now,
Will be a tattered weed, of small worth held . . .

This were to be new made when thou art old,
And see thy blood warm when thou feel'st it cold.

Sonnet 2, William Shakespeare

OVERTURE

The storm had come.

The wind in all its violence had swept away every trace of happiness along the dirt path that led to the mansion, leaving behind nothing but rage, solitude, and betrayal.

He entered the garden where the fragrances of honeysuckle, jasmine, and rose had once mingled together in harmony. Their musky scents seemed now to smell like a corpse just beginning to rot. As he climbed the steps of the veranda, a few of the boards creaked. He hadn't noticed the sound before. But the wooden steps, at least as old as he was, had perhaps begun creaking that very same day. Everything was changing so quickly that he couldn't keep up with the pace of time itself.

He stood at the door of a house that no longer felt like his own. Though he knew every nook and cranny of this place by heart, it suddenly felt entirely foreign to him.

Trembling, his whole body shivering as though he'd been

left out naked on a cold winter night, he opened the door and entered.

Where was he? Whose chairs, paintings, and crystal glassware were these, whose photographs, harboring the hallowed memories of love in their silver frames?

He took one of the frames and looked at the face in the photograph. How happy he'd once been. How young, how handsome, how brimming with life. "Who is this?" he whispered to himself.

Whose face was this, far too happy to be his own?

He turned around in the half-dark. In the corner of the living room lay a shadow, immense and unmoving as a beached whale. He tiptoed to the ponderous shape.

The piano. The piano where, once upon a time, he had played the most beautiful of love songs.

This piano served no purpose now except to remind him of how old he was, how happy he had once been. Filled with loathing, he glowered at the piano, which seemed ever so briefly like a sealed coffin containing his memories. Now it was nothing more than a pathetic instrument, a piece of junk in the corner of an old house, waiting there to die.

"Was this the piano that played our song? It can't be. It mustn't be. It mustn't . . ."

In the heavy silence that filled the house he heard a voice. He crept to the foot of the staircase.

The voice was coming from upstairs.

He made his slow ascent up the stairs. He leaned on the railing with every step, trying to keep his breath, his anger, under control. When he reached the top, he stood and listened in the faint light of the hallway.

It was Deniz. Deniz's voice in the room at the end of the hallway. The bedroom.

And in that instant he heard *his* voice too.

Him. The man he loved. The man for whom he'd woven the most beautiful of tapestries. The other man smiling alongside his own young, happy face in the photographs downstairs.

That man. His husband. In the room too.

He crept down the hallway. Inside the room, their voices clamored in all their shamelessness. Dragging his weary feet along the hand-knotted rug, he reached the bedroom door.

Now he could hear every word, every groan, every gasp with ease.

In that moment he wanted so badly not to open the door; he wanted to turn around and run down the stairs, to leave that miserable mansion, to find a hollow in a tree and hide himself there, to slip into the ice cream shop on the square and buy a cone of strawberry ice cream, to sit until sunrise on the beach where they always swam. He wanted so badly to go back to two months ago, to return to a time when everything was peaceful, when everything was still normal.

But he couldn't.

So he took a deep breath and slowly opened the bedroom door.

Two months earlier

THE FORTIETH ANNIVERSARY

"Fehmi . . . Fehmi!"

Fehmi awoke in their bedroom, the dark blue velvet curtains still drawn closed. He took slow breaths, the double duvet pulled up to his nose, and looked at the clock on his bedside table.

8:15.

"Fehmi, darliiiiing . . ."

Şener stood on the landing at the bottom of the stairs, wearing a cotton shirt, heavily starched linen pants, and orthopedic walking shoes, massaging lotion into his hands and waiting for Fehmi to respond.

He craned his head around the stairway and called out again:

"My love. I'm headed out soon. It's time to get up already. We have to talk about tonight."

Fehmi sat up in bed and put on his slippers. He looked at the ceiling and wondered: *Talk about tonight?*

Even before he'd gotten out of bed, even before he'd woken up from that deepest of sleeps, he had known there would be nothing at all to discuss about tonight. No matter what he might have said every day of every year for the past forty years, things were always just how Şener wanted them. That had been the case on their first anniversary, and nothing would be different today, on their fortieth.

Fehmi knew that the topic of discussion—what they were going to eat for dinner—had been decided at least a month earlier by Şener. His knives were sharp as the sword of a samurai and his apron billowed like a glorious flag.

Today was Thursday, and the market was being erected on Büyükada.

Şener would first pick up the freshest vegetables, which he had long since ordered; he would look in his notebook to make sure he hadn't missed anything, leaving at least two check marks beside each item; he would go to the butcher or the fisherman he always frequented for meat or fish for whatever he had thought up for their main course, and, after a long process of ceremonial inspection, he would select exactly the cut he wanted; until, finally, he would come home to his kitchen. And as always, he would achieve something perfectly flawless, would present his work of art with well-rehearsed humility, would act as if this weren't their fortieth anniversary but any old Thursday, and would receive all the praise rained upon him with exceeding politeness.

For forty years now Fehmi had never felt included at any point in any plans, all of which always proceeded step-by-step in this manner. Fine by him; he didn't want to be included in the planmaking anyway. But Şener, who had an obsessive fixation when it came to celebrating special days, expected one single thing from him through these preparations: That he would get up early on the morning of their anniversary, that he would come downstairs before Şener went shopping, and that he would say a few things about the menu, which Şener had decided long ago even if he pretended he hadn't yet made any such decision.

It was an indispensable anniversary ritual for Şener, the starting point of a great many other rituals particular to this day. But above all else, it was also how Şener chose to be in a relationship: asking his husband what he wants to eat before he leaves for the market, and cooking him what he wants!

This was one of Şener's secrets to maintaining a happy family. Like the recommendations in women's magazines: "The way to keep your man is by cooking him up some delicious little treats!"

Fehmi got out of bed. He took the lounge robe hanging above his bedside and slipped it on over his gray pajamas. His right leg was numb from sleeping on it all night, so he stood on his left leg and clung to the wall. Though he'd only just gotten out of bed, he was already out of breath. At this age he felt exhausted all the time, even when he woke up in the morning. It had been this way for so long now he'd gotten used to the feeling. Aging was its name.

Aging was like the elderly husband he'd lived alongside for so many years now; aging was like an imaginary friend.

As the days passed it became less and less imaginary, its presence ever more tangible.

The sun stubbornly beat its way through the bedroom window, making itself felt despite the tightly drawn curtains. The room had been staged with great meticulousness and furnished with the utmost taste; only the bed was messy as Fehmi dragged his feet to the master bathroom. Şener had left the bedroom door cracked so he'd be heard more easily when he called out from downstairs. "I'm coming," Fehmi grumbled as he passed by the door.

Having finally heard the answer he'd been waiting for, Şener took the shopping caddy from the front closet. He took a turn around the living room, drawing back and straightening out the tulle curtains that let the sunlight gently filter in. With a contented smile he surveyed the room, ensuring that everything appeared flawless.

The freshly cut flowers had been placed in their vases, and the throw pillows on the chairs had been arrayed side by side with such symmetry it was discomfiting. Not a single speck of dust survived his morning assaults. The walnut furniture, a perfect picture of debonair refinement, shone in the first sun of summer on Büyükada. *A symphony of order*, Şener would call it. *I composed it myself. My most precious work.*

He paused for a second. His eye caught on a tiny spot on the black piano in the corner. He swished over to the piano and took a handkerchief from his pocket, blowing on the impertinent blotch, then rubbing it away.

Yes, now everything truly appeared flawless.

Refined. Elegant. Gleaming. Just like him.

"A perfect spring day," Şener said to himself as he returned to the kitchen. After the long winter, the freshness of the brand-new spring air always made him so happy. And because today was their anniversary, one of the most important days of his life, he felt even happier than usual. In His infinite generosity, God had given them this beautiful late spring day, filled with love, as an anniversary gift.

He entered the kitchen, where the cupboards were shabby but functional and the counters were festooned with practical little appliances, and crossed to the table, upon which fresh flowers had been placed not in a vase but an old pitcher. He had cut these flowers this very morning, placing them into the vases and pitchers around the house one by one with painstaking care and attention to the harmony and balance of their colors. If his life were a novel, its opening line would read, "Şener said he would cut the flowers himself."

He checked the placement of Fehmi's breakfast, straightening out the napkin and silverware. Since it was Thursday, Fehmi was allowed to have an egg. Şener had boiled the egg to perfection in a tiny pot and then covered it with a dish towel to keep it warm. He peeled away half the shell, placed it in an egg cup, and brought it to the table.

Fehmi was still in the bathroom, looking at himself in the mirror after rinsing his face and pawing at his sagging cheeks. It was time for him to shave; his beard made him look older than he was. He wet his thinning hair and combed it back, then dried his face with the soft towel Şener had put out for him that morning. He peed, though it wasn't easy. No matter how much care he took, it always hurt a little to pee. *I need to have my prostate checked again*, he thought, scowling at the prospect of an ailment as he left the bathroom and descended the stairs.

When Fehmi entered the kitchen, Şener stood at the counter checking his coin purse to make sure he had enough change. "Good morning, my love," he said warmly when he saw Fehmi, as though he hadn't been the one to wake him, as though Fehmi had thought, all on his own, to wake up early for once.

Fehmi walked straight past him with a cold "Good morning," offering less attention and warmth than Şener had expected in return.

"I see we woke up on the wrong side of the bed yet again this morning," Şener muttered as he returned to counting his change.

Fehmi sat down and picked up his egg spoon to dig into his breakfast. "And you're cheerful as ever. Where do you get all this energy so early in the morning? I don't get it. Normal people are usually grumpy when they wake up."

Şener zipped up his coin purse and put it in his pocket before sitting in the chair opposite Fehmi. "What else should I do, Fehmi dear? What do you recommend? Should I wake up in the morning crying like normal people do?"

Fehmi knew all too well he couldn't compete with Şener's flair for exaggeration. For Şener, there were only ever two paths through life. Black or white. Freedom or death. Waking up happy or waking up in tears.

Şener was the kind of person who chose to wake up happy. He had gotten up two hours earlier, spending the minutes he regarded as his "private time" working in the garden, doing his exercises, and having a light breakfast in preparation for his special day. He preferred this over waking up in the morning crying, and truth be told, it suited him quite well. His eyes sparkled like two bright stars shining side by side.

Fehmi met those sparkling eyes as he bit into his toast covered in fat-free butter. *Forty years together with this man*, he thought. Forty years and this man had never wavered in his attention, his love, his commitment to and passion for the life they'd built together; nor had he lost any of his mettle, his joie de vivre, his routine flawlessness. And today was their anniversary, their fortieth anniversary. "You shouldn't cry of course, darling," he said, this time sincerely, tenderly, lovingly. "Why cry? You look wonderful this morning, as always. I've always been jealous of your energy, that's why I'm picking on you."

"Don't be silly," smiled Şener, getting up to pour himself more tea. It had been so long since he'd heard the word "jealous." That word had long since exited his life. He felt a strange sense of relief, rather than disappointment, at the realization. Anyone who considered jealousy a form of love could not be more wrong. To the contrary, jealousy, lust, and obsession were poisonous feelings. Şener understood that long ago. When the two of them had first gotten together, he had of course been horribly jealous of Fehmi, but over time that feeling had faded away, had been replaced by other things altogether. Instead of jealousy, he preferred to know how Fehmi ate his eggs; instead of lust, he preferred having a man to bring him his sweater when he got cold; instead of obsession, he preferred to have command over how Fehmi drank his tea.

Şener dropped a wedge of lemon in his own cup of tea and returned to his seat. It had been years since he'd cut the feeling of jealousy, just like sugar, out of his life.

"Fehmi, darling," Şener said gingerly, "you know it's our anniversary today . . . You didn't forget, did you?"

Fehmi took his napkin and wiped the egg out of his mustache, which had gone almost entirely gray but was still full as ever. He looked at Şener, smiling. "I might have grown old, but I haven't quite lost my mind yet. Of course I remember. I think you're confusing me with yourself."

Şener let out a sharp, pleased laugh. "Oh, sweetheart. I'm not going to spend the morning of our anniversary arguing with you about which of us has lost our minds or is closer to having Alzheimer's. You're the one who usually forgets special days, that's why I brought it up. You remember, my birthday . . ."

Fehmi glared at Şener. Yes, he had indeed made the careless mistake of forgetting Şener's birthday once, just once, in their forty years together. Whenever something else had been forgotten over the years, that transgression was used as ammunition against him.

Şener understood from Fehmi's gaze what he was thinking right away and changed the topic. "Oh, yes. Pardon me. Don't worry, I'm not going to remind you of that business with my birthday anymore. I'm over it. I won't say another word about it."

But by now Fehmi had decided he wanted to be a brat. "That's right, you won't. In this house, what I say goes. I'm the man of the house, and if I tell you not to say another word, then there better not be another word out of you."

Şener cast a catty look at Fehmi as he stood up. He simply could not stand these jokes about their sexual roles, even though Fehmi made them specifically to push his buttons. "I'm the man here, and what I say goes." "You wouldn't understand, Şener, leave it to us." And especially on barbecue days: "Grilling is a man's job, Şener. Go make the salad." For this reason alone Şener had a particular resentment for barbecue. He hated it, and he hated making his famous salad, whose dressing their guests wanted to drink by the bowl.

He knew that Fehmi got a kick out of it when these jokes pissed him off, so Şener did his best to turn a deaf ear. But when these rebukes came out in the wrong time or place, they still pissed him off. On the morning of his fortieth anniversary, for instance . . .

Standing at the counter and in the most needling voice he could muster, he said, "I could throw a tantrum right now if I really wanted to, Fehmi dear, but like I said, I'm not going to argue with you about us losing our minds, nor do I have any interest in discussing which of us is more of a man. Nilgün

Hanım and her friends are waiting, and I mustn't be late to the market." He took his jacket from the chair and put it on.

Fehmi, nonplussed by Şener's threat, got to his feet and smiled, coming up to his man and straightening out the collar on his jacket. "Look how chic we are. The prettiest girl on the island," he said fondly. "Careful the coachmen don't steal you away."

Şener slapped Fehmi's hand. "Oh, Fehmi, enough already! I don't know what's gotten into you this morning. Stop it for a second. Tell me, what do you want for dinner tonight?"

Fehmi thought. "Hmmm . . . You haven't made your ragout for a while. What if you made ragout?"

Şener stared blankly back at Fehmi for a moment before snapping back into their conversation. "Ragout? Maybe. But . . . I had been thinking fish . . . Red meat isn't good for our cholesterol, darling. You're always cheating on our diet. Light starters, fish, and cold white wine . . . Perhaps a salad of spring vegetables . . . Well, we'll see what they have at the market."

Fehmi put one hand on his hip and the other on the counter. "Sure, fish is fine. Doesn't matter to me."

"But if you really feel like ragout, that's fine too," Şener said, double-checking his wallet. "Today is our day, after all, isn't it, my love? Would I dare disappoint you? But I have to leave now, Ayşegül and Halit are coming on the five o'clock ferry, Nil on the six o'clock. I'll have to have everything ready by then . . ." He trailed off as he made for the door.

Fehmi and Şener usually ate their anniversary dinners tête-à-tête, but sometimes they'd invite Fehmi's friend

Halit and his wife, Ayşegül, or Şener's friend Nil Erkutlar to join them. So in honor of their fortieth year together, they were going to celebrate tonight alongside their oldest, most beloved friends. "I'm ready as is," Fehmi said, watching Şener go over his list one more time, "not that I have to do anything. The task is in your hands. Can you manage?"

"Of course." Şener smiled. "But I have to hurry. Now look, Fehmi, don't eat too much and don't drink any coffee. I found the coffee you hid around the house and got rid of it, just so you know. The caffeine's going to make your heart explode one day, God forbid. I don't know why you can't overcome your caffeine addiction. If you must, though, just have *one* cup of decaf, okay? See you soon!"

Şener blew a kiss and was almost out the door when Fehmi said, "Just a second." Şener turned around, finding himself face to face with Fehmi.

"Happy anniversary, my love," Fehmi said, leaning in and placing a gentle kiss on Şener's lips. Şener was taken aback, and glanced instinctively out the window. Seeing nobody there, he turned back to Fehmi and smiled. Their eyes, which had met a million times, now met for the million-and-first time, and Şener saw himself reflected in his husband's eyes.

The same man. That man for whom his heart beat madly.

"Oh, Fehmi, my darling. You're just as you were the day we met, you haven't changed a bit. We've spent forty years together. Easier said than done! Happy anniversary to you, too, my love." Şener smiled as he opened the door.

Once the door opened, the sun, until now hidden behind

curtains, tulle, and walls, surged into the house with all its strength, and with it the dizzying smells of the newly blooming flowers across their garden, overpowering the scent of their dying, vase-bound kin throughout the house. When Şener closed the door, the house returned to its same state of sumptuous calm. His symphony of order continued playing silently behind closed doors.

Once Şener was gone, Fehmi went to the living room and knelt to the bottom shelf of their library, shoving his hand behind the books and pulling out a packet of coffee. He returned to the kitchen and put three spoonfuls in the coffeemaker. He felt like having a strong cup of coffee that morning. What he did for coffee was perhaps his one and only betrayal in their forty-year relationship. But, after all, decaf was a betrayal of coffee.

He pulled a cigarette from the pack in the pocket of his robe and lit it on the stove. As the coffeemaker began gurgling, he took a drag of the cigarette and blew the smoke out the half-open window. Fehmi watched Şener, having left his flouncing behind at home, descend the slope with decisive, upright steps, before disappearing from sight.

A smile spread across his face.

Ragout? What ragout?

Fehmi knew as sure as his name was Fehmi that they'd be having fish for dinner tonight.

BÜYÜKADA

Out of breath, Şener descended the slope from his white mansion atop the hills overlooking Nizam Beach. Even though he was in excellent health for his age, even though he never strayed from his morning stretches and careful diet, the slope always knocked the wind out of him. It was an unfortunate truth but impossible to forget. He was no longer young, no longer suited to slopes and stairs.

Nizam, where the wealthiest of Büyükada lived, was known for its mansions, each an architectural masterpiece. Fehmi and Şener's home was one such mansion. Overlooking the sea, the bay, and the distant lights of Istanbul, it was isolated from all the other houses, like a port jutting out to sea. As with every beautiful thing, their idyllic privacy came at a cost, a cost made manifest in the form of the steep slope that made life a little more difficult for the two of them.

Sometimes he wondered if they might sell their mansion

and move somewhere more central, perhaps to Maden on the other end of Büyükada, but he always put the thought out of mind immediately. But now, as he made his descent to the market, he found himself fantasizing once again about moving from the old mansion to a new home. Yet once he arrived at the asphalt road, the peace of mind he'd earned after many long years—the song of the morning birds, the rustle of the trees, the kisses from the man he was in love with—was replaced by meaningless chaos. The crowds, the tourists insisting on taking pictures of everything with their cell phones, the piles of shit left by the horses pulling buggies: they all made him renounce, once again, the very notion of moving.

He wanted to finish his shopping quickly and return to his darling Fehmi, to his darling kitchen. His peace of mind remained up there, in the white mansion on the hill. He cursed himself for even entertaining the thought of leaving the mansion where they had spent thirty of their forty years together, the mansion whose every room he had meticulously, lovingly decorated, the mansion whose every millimeter they had filled with kisses, with song, with amorous indulgence. He felt the thought of moving was a betrayal to the home they had built together, and he considered betrayal, no matter the culprit, even him, to be unbecoming.

Their sumptuous two-story wooden home, the spotlessly polished piano taking pride of place in the corner, filled with photographs of Fehmi and himself, had become to him the most beautiful palace of happinesses the world had ever seen. Only the Taj Mahal itself could compete with their home. Şener knew, though, that if he had access to enough white marble he'd surely be able to surpass the Taj Mahal as well. He put the Taj Mahal out of mind; for goodness' sake, he had never, and would never, set eyes upon it. Their mansion, with its bird's-eye view of the whole mortal world, where his one and only Fehmi waited for him, sipping his drink, reading the papers, studying his notes, was more valuable to him than even the most beautiful of palaces. What, after all, would be the price for all the memories they shared there? They were like two retired freight ships moored to their wooden pier, their mansion, which served as one of the only third parties to witness the private moments of their twilight years. Their only other witness was, of course, the yard that generously surrounded all four sides of the mansion, considered by all the islanders to be most beautiful garden on the whole island.

Like everyone who comes to realize their "situation" at a young age, Şener had agonized long and hard over what his future would hold. In his twenties, the future didn't look very positive; it extended endlessly before him as a dark unknown. He had only one dream that he wished to fulfill. *Aging comfortably* was what he called it. "We're all going to get old," he'd say whenever anyone broached the subject, "and we'll need someone to take care of us. It's inevitable. Nobody remains young and beautiful forever. The curse that afflicts people like us only appears when you get old. When you get the flu, for instance, when you don't have the strength to get up and fill a glass with water, and you realize there's nobody there to bring it to you, a shiver will run up your spine. That's when your worst nightmare begins to come true. You realize that the angel of death, whom you've spent your whole life trying to forget about, is breathing down your neck. Dying alone, entirely alone . . . That's the fate ordained for people like us. Hardly possible to imagine a more sordid death. It makes you suffer, it's an incurable cancer, metastasizing for years and discovered too late. That's why aging comfortably is so important."

God had mercifully heard his prayers and afforded him the chance to age comfortably. Old age in the lap of luxury, every minute God had given him and his husband to be spent in comfort. If he wanted, for instance, he could take a ninety-minute walk around Büyükada every single day, or he could work in his garden morning to evening; he could afford the finest of organic fruits and vegetables, and devote all his time to composing fabulous new songs. Or else he could do nothing at all, spending the whole day reclined, his feet resting on an ottoman; he could listen to the Berlin Philharmonic Orchestra's record of *The Nutcracker Suite* at full volume.

Above all else he had the right to choose how he wanted to spend his time. This right hadn't been seized from him by a caretaker in a retirement home, or by a nurse force-feeding him slop in a hospice bed; it was his to do with as he wished. He didn't squander the opportunity, and considered that right to be a gift. That was why he was still healthy, still flourishing, still in love, and that was why, in all likelihood, he had the most beautiful garden on the island.

With the first sun of summer warming his face, his heart filled with gratitude that he was aging comfortably.

He loved life.

The acacias that had heralded the spring on Büyükada now covered the streets in their golden pollen. Tourist season was already underway. It irked him that the season had started so early. He loved the summer season, but he hated that the tourists occupied the island and that he, along with the rest of the Büyükada Beautification Association, would have to spend yet another winter painstakingly cleaning up their trash and cigarette butts. The tourists would pluck the acacia blossoms only to sentence them to a sagging, crude death in ugly vases back home. He wished they'd leave the blossoms on their branches for everyone to enjoy. But the tourists didn't appreciate their beauty the way he did.

By now the cafes, teahouses, and bakeries had cast off the destitution of winter. Unfamiliar figures sitting round the tables turned their faces to the sun, soaking in the vitamin D. He greeted some of the people he recognized, pretended not to see those he knew would take more time than he had, and made his way down the slope to the Dolci Café, across from the pier.

All the islanders gathered year-round at this café, as had

been tradition for many, many years now. The ladies who lived on the island would, after their husbands left for work in the city, throw a scarf around their shoulders and come to the café for tea and coffee and gossip. Young people, too, would congregate in front of the café on sweaty summer nights, drinking alcohol and chatting noisily, goofing around as they ate ice cream.

On some days, when Fehmi had to travel to the mainland to deal with real estate or bank business, Şener would come to Dolci Café after sending him off, in order to meet up with his lady friends. He and Fehmi would part ways without even kissing each other on the cheek. Standing on the pier, they would shake hands with an unaccustomed clumsiness, and then Fehmi would get on the ferry; no sooner had the ferry begun chugging away than Şener would start to miss him.

It irked Şener that they had to shake hands to say goodbye, like they'd made some business deal or bartered a lamb for slaughter.

Were they not a couple as well, just like the island's other women and their husbands? Because in fact, they were perhaps even more closely bound to each other than the other couples were. If they were to enter a contest of love they'd have the highest chance of winning. So why couldn't he embrace his man or kiss him on the cheeks when other people were around, like all the other women could?

Their union could only play out between four walls. That was why only their mansion, their piano, and the honeysuckles in their garden knew that they belonged to each other. To everyone else, these two lovers were no more than two old friends who lived together.

Şener knew, of course, that they were talked about behind their backs. People can always sense the rhythms of a relationship between two people. They knew about Fehmi and Şener's "situation," perhaps even talked about it privately, but they would never say anything in front of the two of them.

Thank God the islanders who became their friends and neighbors had learned, over the course of many years of interactions and aside from a few unfortunate incidents, to be polite enough to never bring it up. These rules of engagement had been hard-won, had taken a lot of teaching, but the Büyükada locals had successfully passed the test. As with their superlative garden, Şener and Fehmi's particular social efforts had played a huge role in teaching the islanders those rules of engagement.

Fehmi was a member of the bridge club while Şener was a member of the Büyükada Beautification Association. Each of them gladly fulfilled the duties that fell on their shoulders, whether with events, with charitable works, with decisions concerning the island, or with anything at all that had to do with changing or improving the island. They were good friends, good neighbors, and they were as colorful as their chosen topics of conversation.

Fehmi was popular among the men for his skill in bridge; Şener among the women for his exceeding affability and talents in the kitchen. By now, they were close with all the well-to-do people of Büyükada, from the mayor's wife to the police chief, from the commander of the gendarme to its head captain. The wise people of Büyükada realized that losing such polite and warm Istanbul gentlemen would do the two of them no harm, that blacklisting these two men would only lead to their own loss of status and class. It was clear that Şener and Fehmi had won out when it came to the business of island neighborliness.

What went on between the two of them had been accepted almost like an old family secret, known but never spoken of. They were a couple who did no harm to anyone, who to the contrary were beloved by everyone for their experiences and their lust for life. No, not a couple, but two retired friends . . . Fehmi Bey and Şener Bey.

They had made so much progress over time, but the first years they'd lived here were quite difficult.

Şener had seen that expression for the first time in the eyes of the girl at the cash register of the market where he shopped, an expression that asked, *What kind of thing are you?*, a way of looking that Şener referred to as "that" look. It was always children and young people who looked at him like "that," shameless in their curiosity. Maybe that was why he didn't like children? The impudence of children almost always pierced through his heart like a spear.

That curiosity and "that" look spread in waves to other people.

But anyone who expected some kind of explanation or confession from Fehmi or Şener about their "situation" would never get it. Remaining silent, demonstrating through their actions that they considered it to be a private matter, Fehmi and Şener committed fiercely to the story that they were two old friends who had spent the thirty years and counting of their retirement on Büyükada. Their commitment to this story had afforded them the space to live as they so desired.

Every now and then, though, they would still be met by "that" look once more, almost always when meeting new people.

Şener encountered that curious look again now, making his way to Dolci Café, where he was meeting Nilgün Hanım, the pharmacist, with whom he was going shopping for groceries. Nilgün Hanım was sitting with Figen Hanım, the wife of the former ambassador to Paris, whose exaggerated gossip bothered Şener, and with another young woman whom he didn't recognize. She was wearing a linen suit ironed neat as a pin, and her eyes skimmed over the crowds thronging the island until they landed "that" look upon the wayward man walking towards them.

Şener chose not to meet her eyes as he approached the table.

"Ah, Nilgün Hanım. Pardon me for making you wait so long. Something urgent came up, that's why I'm late. I am so very sorry, please forgive me."

Nilgün Hanım got to her feet and kissed Şener on each cheek. "Worry not, Şener Bey. We were just catching our breath here. Would you like a coffee?"

"No, Nilgün Hanım, not today. We're running a bit late,

I think we should be off right away. I have so much to do today, you wouldn't believe," he said, surveying the table. "Oh! Figen Hanım . . . What a nice surprise. We never see each other anymore," he continued, shaking the dry hand Figen Hanım extended with a poise unique to the wives of ambassadors.

"Hello, Şener Bey," she said. "I don't leave the house much anymore, unfortunately. Such is aging . . . But look at you, maşallah, you're spry as a spring chicken. You could run rings round those young men." She giggled.

Şener let out a gracious laugh and turned to Nilgün Hanım, who was waiting to introduce him to the other woman.

"Şener Bey, this young lady is my cousin İlayda. She's studying journalism in England. She's in Istanbul for her summer holiday and is writing an article about our very own Büyükada. She leaves tonight. I recommended you to her. 'If you're going to learn about our island from one of us,' I told her, 'it must be from none other than the illustrious figure of Şener Bey. He's like a monument to the island, an archive of our very own.'"

My goodness! Şener thought. *Are you calling me old?* But the genial smile he played across his face masterfully concealed his resentment from the women. He preferred to keep today focused on his singular credo, that of his fortieth anniversary. He simply couldn't spend such an important day as preceptor to a woman he didn't know and who gawked at him with "that" look. If only he'd had warning of this unpleasant surprise . . . Perhaps he wouldn't have chosen to meet a stranger today.

As the three women paid their bill and made their way with Şener to the market, Nilgün Hanım earned herself a place, if temporarily, on Şener's blacklist. She had lost her good standing all on her own, even if she didn't yet realize it.

She would have to learn her lesson.

While they went about their shopping, İlayda the student journalist took the opportunity to speak to him. She quickly shed "that" look she gave him when they first met, revealing herself to be a respectful, spritely young woman with a sing-song voice. Şener came to quite like the girl as she wrote his impressions of the island in her notebook. İlayda was returning to London that night and wouldn't have another opportunity to visit Büyükada for her assignment, so Şener decided to be of assistance to her, listing off all the things he had come to love about the island over many years of living there, describing each of his favorite places one by one:

He told her, for instance, about the delicatessen in the market. The delicatessen only sold meat-and-rice köfte and potato croquettes, and only at exactly six in the evening. Wrapped in paper fresh from the oven, these piping-hot morsels were one of the islanders' steadfast pleasures.

He told her, for instance, about the Greek landlady of the Büyükada Bakery, and her famous börekitas.

He told her, for instance, that Büyükada blooms with acacias in the early spring, peonies between spring and summer, and bougainvilleas all summer long.

He told her, for instance, that all the islanders of Büyükada gather once a year at Aya Yorgi Church or Kalpazankaya on the next island over to feast together. There was a small restaurant at the end of Kalpazankaya famous for its pit-roasted lamb.

He told her, for instance, that if she wanted to swim she absolutely must go to Değirmen Beach over in Nizam. Or else she could suntan on Naki Bey Beach, surrounded by century-old pine trees. That was the beach that he and Fehmi Bey loved most. Fehmi Bey, his companion in retirement, was an excellent swimmer, could swim for hours on end.

He told her, for instance, that she absolutely had to have a cocktail in the garden at Splendid Hotel. Yes, the Splendid Hotel was the large building with red windows right on the shore.

He told her, for instance, about the significance of the Anatolia Club. Even Atatürk himself, Mustafa Kemal Paşa, loved the Club when he lived on the island, and would go often. In fact, he had been photographed waltzing with the erstwhile women of Büyükada in the old marble ballroom, and those photographs now decorated the walls of the club. Once every year the Büyükada Beautification Association organized a special event exclusively for the islanders, the Moonlight Ball, to raise money to preserve the island's orphanage. And though Şener himself had long since given up performing, he would take the stage that night every year, for the sake of the orphans. No, unfortunately, İlayda couldn't visit the Anatolia Club. Non-members were only permitted to enter alongside current members. He would of course have loved to help her, but he had important business to attend to for the evening.

Having now finished their shopping, they walked along the old cobblestone streets, in turns laughing and silent. İlayda was scribbling in her notebook, the smile on her face spirited as ever. She eyed every single mansion with admiration, imagining, like everyone seeing them for the first time, what it might be like to live in one someday.

Şener felt the need to intervene in İlayda's excitement. "Although it's beautiful here, my dear, there are many hardships as well. It's only really beautiful for us old people, retirees."

"Why do you say that, Şener Bey? What kinds of hardships?" she asked.

In response, Şener gestured at the rippling sea that extended before them. "Because, dear İlayda, we're on an island, after all. Sure, it's close to Istanbul, but it's not *that* close. During the winter or whenever there's bad weather they often have to cancel the ferries. For young people like you, this place can become something of a prison. Here you can only move about so long as the sea allows you to. It's hard, so hard . . ."

Figen, Nilgün, and Şener continued reminiscing about their hardships. Remember the lodos winds that one winter, when nobody could leave Büyükada for three days?

"So, one more thing," Şener continued. "Let me tell you why these islands are called the Princes' Islands. In truth, it's a tragic tale. In the Byzantine era, these islands were used as a place of exile and punishment because they're so hard to get to. Many members of noble families were exiled here due to conflicts over succession and family intrigue. Princes especially." Şener paused a moment and looked at the island's streets. "As soon as the princes arrived here, they would be blinded with a hot iron brand. Can you imagine? That these very streets we've spent all day walking happily, surrounded by mansions and manors each more beautiful than the last, were once populated by blind kids, left all on their own? That's why the islands are called Prinkopos, the Princes' Islands."

Şener fell silent, the melancholy legible on his face. He didn't like children, sure, but the story of the exiled princes always left a sour taste in his mouth.

Alas, though, it was now time for him to leave İlayda, Nilgün, and Figen, and to return home to his darling. He kissed them each on the cheeks, promising to see them again as soon as possible, and made for the slope that led up to his home, which sat alone in its splendor at the top of the hill.

He stopped a moment before beginning the climb and turned around. The women had disappeared from sight, and the streets of Büyükada were silent in the first sun of summer. Just the songs of the birds, the rustling of the trees, and the buzzing of the early bees.

And perhaps . . .

Perhaps, if he listened closer, he might have heard the voice of a ghost, the ghost of a young man that wandered here many years ago, his eyes gouged out by a hot iron brand.

THE GAZEBO

The porcelain dishes sat dirty on the dinner table, which rang with laughter. There was no need that night to gather up the dirty dishes and wash them right away. Domestic life could wait a little bit longer.

At a dinner among friends, if only one person at the table is laughing, the night should be considered a failure. If the whole table joins in the joking and the banter, then that dinner is an assembly of true friends and lovers. At the dining room in the mansion that night, the laughs erupted one after the other.

Şener nimbly gathered the dirty dishes into a stack in front of him and stood up. "How lucky we are that the weather is so magnificent tonight. We can all sit out on the veranda for the first time of the season. I made raspberry parfait for dessert. Would you like it now, or shall I serve it to you on the veranda, with the cognac?"

Ayşegül moved to help him but he gestured at her with a

graceful flourish of his hand as if to say *Don't worry, dear,* and winked at her. She did not insist. Among the other three people at the table, at any rate, she had been the only one to make such a move. Fehmi and Halit had fallen into an impenetrable conversation about soccer, or perhaps each was advocating for Galatasaray or Fenerbahçe that season. To Şener, there may as well have been no difference between the two teams. The other guest at the table, Nil Erkutlar, had left the very notion of clearing tables herself at the same time that she left her father's house at the age of fourteen, never to return.

Ayşegül hadn't participated in much of the conversation that night, but now, her voice full of admiration, she proclaimed, "Dearest Şener, everything was wonderful. You've outdone yourself. Just how you managed to find fresh raspberries this season, I have no idea."

Şener smiled. "I have a lady with a garden on the island of Heybeliada. She comes once in a while to help out here. They're just in season now, and I knew I wanted the first harvest. She brought them over for me, bless her."

"Bravo. Please let me help you clear the table."

"Don't be silly, Ayşegül. You're our guest and I won't have it. Believe me, it's a pleasure."

Nil Erkutlar, who until that very moment had never cared about topics of conversation like food, women with raspberries, or the work of clearing the table, cast one of her scurrilous looks at Şener. "Sweetie, I can help if you like. Ayşegül is right. You must be worn out. It's only natural when you get old, of course."

Şener turned around where he stood, plates still in hand. "I'm tearing up, truly. Renowned chanteuse Nil Erkutlar, offering to help me clear the table. I'll have a story to tell your grandchildren one day. I'll boast to them: 'Your grandmother helped me clear the table on my fortieth anniversary, can you believe it?'"

They had made a million of these jabs at one another over their friendship, and Nil replied to this million-and-first with the same smile.

The two of them had met when Şener was just starting to take the jazz piano scene by storm. Once upon a time—that's how long ago it was—Şener had performed in the lobby of the Hilton, and he rocketed to fame in the blink of an eye. For the first time in Istanbul, a hotel lobby became itself a destination for people to go on a night out, solely to listen to the pianist. His reputation began to spread by word of mouth, and the era's biggest vocalists began wondering, *Who is he?*

Indeed, who was he? Who was this handsome young man taking the genteel world of western classical music by fabulous storm? At his white piano in the lobby of the Hilton, that man, Şener, was like a prince out of a fairy tale, ready to revolt against the king.

Nil Erkutlar, on the other hand, with her stunning physique and dulcet voice, had been a beautiful young woman, graceful, delicate as a dewdrop, wanting to try her luck in the world of music. A natural blonde and brand-new to the scene, she had a mad desire to rise, to rise quickly, to become a headliner, a star. And she took every risk necessary in order to succeed at that.

One night, a handsome businessman from central Anatolia brought her to the Hilton, and after deciding she was so tired she needed to "repose there for the night," she listened to Şener play. She knew he was the right person to help her on her way to stardom and she did what she had to in order to meet him at intermission.

Thus began a fickle friendship that spanned many years, a friendship of fits and starts, of breakups and makeups, of many fights and many more tears.

In the beginning it was simple—Nil Erkutlar singing, accompanied by Şener on the piano. With Şener's musical abilities newly stoked by her blond, womanly fire, they became unstoppable, and when Bananarama Bar made them an offer they couldn't refuse, they put together an orchestra and ascended the stage of the club.

Both of their names were written side by side on posters plastered on every corner and wall in Istanbul. Slowly, their fame rocked the city. The tables at Bananarama Bar were full every night; many customers of high repute had to be turned away at the doors; there weren't enough drinking glasses for the guests; the bouquets they received, some shining with little diamonds, piled so high they poured out into the hallway; and the waiters were tasked with delivering love letters to the handsome pianist and the blond diva all night. They became so famous, in fact, that gossip began to swirl that Ajda herself, already a superstar, had panic attacks out of jealousy, wanted to transfer Şener to her own orchestra, and offered up a blank check to make it happen. But rather than being one of the daisies in Ajda's bouquet, Şener had opted to be a single red rose on his own. That rose's thorns and petals both were to be Nil Erkutlar.

Everything was going swimmingly, and just when the two of them were going to renew their contracts at Bananarama Bar for another season, during the intermission of a show one night, Şener met a university student who'd moved to Istanbul to study machine engineering, a man named Fehmi.

And a bolt of lightning shot straight through his heart! He no longer had eyes for anyone or anything but the young engineer. He didn't give a damn about fame anymore; his world began to turn on the axis of Fehmi, his "special friend."

Nil Erkutlar clocked their relationship right away. She suffered a fit of jealousy, not wanting to share Şener with anyone. The fights that broke out backstage echoed decibels louder in the main hall. But no matter what she did, Nil couldn't manage to tear Şener from Fehmi's orbit.

So fate wove its web, and Nil finally received the offer she had dreamed about for years: to headline at Istanbul Gazino, the largest cabaret in the city. Şener didn't want to start at the gazino, but Nil believed it would be idiotic to turn down the offer, so she signed on her own. She swore that she would never again speak to Şener, would never forgive him.

Her grudge, of course, didn't last long at all.

The fame that swaddled Nil Erkutlar like a soft fur was far sweeter to her than trying to keep up a grudge against her pianist and friend. Şener faded into the background, seeking every opportunity for the one thing he wanted: to dote on the young engineer. Nil Erkutlar and Şener forgave each other with a gravity befitting their relationship, and they returned to being friends again right where they left off.

Şener suggested that his dear friend, the blond bombshell, simply *had* to sing the song "Weeping like a Willow, Smiling at Love." Nil Erkutlar ran with Şener's astute suggestion and became an instant star at the Istanbul Gazino, strong enough now to forge ahead on her own with no need for anyone else.

But after a while, she succumbed to the troubling allure of fame, grew too headstrong to pay any heed to Şener's suggestions. Instead of taking the right steps for her career, she busied herself with scandals, tragic romances, and marriages; she managed to assemble a fabulous collection of jewels, but in the end she fell out of sight and became a washed-up star.

Until just a few years ago . . .

When the fervor for nostalgic music exploded, a producer discovered one of Nil Erkutlar's old songs. The song was then used in a blockbuster movie and Nil Erkutlar reemerged from the dusty pages of history and into the headlines of newspapers. She savored her renewed fame, gave interviews to newspapers one after another. She found herself a young stud of a lover, too, according to the gossip magazines. Things were truly, finally, good for her. She relished in the experience of this second spring.

Nil Erkutlar occupied a special place in Şener's life, his closest female friend for many years now. Some women and some men, no matter how old they are, be they fourteen or seventy-four, no matter where their careers might be, no matter whether they're new classmates or old divas, can't escape the orbit of one another's lives. And in this relationship which marched on and on in its endless journey, Şener and Nil Erkutlar had always proceeded hand in hand.

Nil Erkutlar produced a menthol cigarette from her purse, knowing full well that Şener hated them, and lit the cigarette from the candelabra while staring him in the eyes.

"If we can smoke," Halit interjected, "then I'll light one as well—with your permission."

Şener grabbed the crystal ashtray from the side table and placed it in the middle of the dinner table, saying, "Of course, by all means! *Some* don't even bother asking first."

Nil downed the white wine in her glass and shouted in agitation. "God, what kind of celebration is this? When's the champagne? You've been making us drink wine for hours, Şener, you tightfisted bitch. I can't believe how stingy you're being on your forticth anniversary of all days."

Şener shook his head, smiling. "Don't be silly, Nil. I was going to serve cognac with the dessert, but if you want we can open a bottle of champagne."

"Oh, pretty please," Nil said, standing up to smooth her very mini minidress. In her high heels, her tight bun, and her diamonds, she looked exceedingly garish.

Fehmi turned to Nil, with whom he got along well and

whose star power he adored, and said, "Maşallah. Would you just look at her? If Ajda was here she'd simply die of envy."

Nil blew him a kiss in response. "Thanks, baby," she said. "Of course she would. Ajda's got nothing on these legs." She smiled, entering the foyer and producing from the bag she'd left inside a bottle of champagne with an enormous bow. "Here you go, Şener, darling, open this. I don't want to spend your money. It's my anniversary gift. I had it brought from France. A special bottle, vintage Dom Pérignon . . . The best year, too."

Şener looked at the bottle and took it with a grin. "Thank you so much, Nil darling, you didn't have to go to such trouble. Bringing champagne to parties was last in fashion in the seventies, as I recall. Just like you." He laughed. "Whereas cognac is more like me. Timeless, classic, luxurious."

Nil replied in a bratty voice, "Oh cognac, of course, cognac . . . Sure, let's drink that crap. Uncle Fehmi, this cheapskate boyfriend of yours won't open my champagne."

Fehmi nodded at Şener and said, "The diva will have champagne tonight. I'm going to join her. We'll have our cognac on the veranda later."

Şener smiled, and as he pulled champagne flutes from the bar, Ayşegül brought over the ice bucket. When Şener made to pop the cork, Halit interjected. "One second," he said, grabbing the bottle. "Don't trouble yourself with that!"

Şener handed Halit the bottle and sat down next to Fehmi, taking his hand. Halit opened it with a dilatory kind of clumsiness, and the bottle let out its *pop*, the universal sound of decadence. He filled the glasses, handing one first to Nil then Ayşegül then to Şener. Fehmi and himself each took the last two glasses.

Halit raised his glass and turned to Şener. "If you'll permit me," he said, "I'd like to make a little speech."

Şener was surprised. He raised his glass and replied, "By all means."

Halit cleared his throat. "You know I'm no good at speeches like this. But I'm so happy, and I think I'm also a little bit drunk. Plus we're not as thoughtful as the esteemed Nil Hanım. We didn't have a bottle of champagne brought from France."

Though Şener knew Halit and Ayşegül were nowhere near as well off as Nil or they were, he was still ashamed at the possibility that they might be embarrassed. "My goodness, no, what nonsense! It's such an honor for us that you even came."

Halit continued. "Of course, I know. It's just a figure of speech. Like I said I'm a bit intoxicated. Both off the drink and off the food you made. But with your permission I want to raise my glass to the two of you." He raised his glass, and the other four at the table did too. "I raise my glass in honor of my dear, dear friend Fehmi and his partner, Şener Bey, who is just as precious a friend to me. The forty years you've spent so bound to one another have been a source of inspiration to all of us, have allowed us to look at life differently. And so, my dears, I wish you a happy forty years."

Cheers!

Fehmi stood to his feet, eyes welled up with tears, and embraced his friend. "Thank you so much, Halit. It means so much to me, what you said."

Two men, having chosen to overcome a boundary between them that towered as high as the Great Wall of China, having chosen to remain friends ...

Halit and Fehmi, both children of poor families, had come from different provinces to study in Istanbul. The two of them had gotten through university despite their difficult circumstances, putting their hearts and souls into their work to ensure their efforts would pay off. Having both won places in the faculty of engineering at Istanbul Technical University, they were seated next to one another in the first lecture of their first course, Construction 101, which is how their yearslong friendship began.

The dreams they'd had for the Istanbul they'd just met were as fresh and bright as their young bodies. They wondered endlessly about everything in this beguiling city. After the cold, dull world of the countryside, Istanbul's nightlife extended before them like a glimmering sea, beckoning to them with its thousand and one charms. They might not have had much money, but they were handsome, sexy, and sweet. That was already more than enough to open so many doors for them.

Neither of them had any intention of locking their lives away in the university's cold and mildewy dorms. The warmth of other beds, of lips and drinking glasses and the backstreets of Aksaray in Beyoğlu, were all crucial components of the lives of these two young machine engineers. The strange atmosphere in Istanbul, which had taken these two newly arrived country bumpkins into its palms, conquered Fehmi and Halit alike.

They knew all of each other's secrets—all, that is, except one. Halit didn't know that his closest friend had discovered other things about his life, that Fehmi had feelings he'd always known but never been able to name. The wall of manhood between them was so high it couldn't be surmounted. Hesitant to even admit to himself the secret he kept, Fehmi could surely have not admitted it to his closest friend. It was cliché: he loved Halit deeply and for that very reason he feared losing him. Because he himself still didn't know what he was, how he could define himself.

One thing. It was just one thing . . .

Halit was there the day Fehmi and Şener met.

After work one day, Halit and Fehmi had drunk liters of beer with two literature students at the meyhane under the bridge, and after dropping the girls off at their dorms, Fehmi offered up a suggestion. "A new club opened up in Beyoğlu. It's supposed to be really good. Let's go." And so they went to Bananarama Bar. Halit got so drunk that night and danced with everyone, but it didn't go unnoticed that every time he sought out Fehmi, he'd find him in a corner with the young man who played the piano, chattering away all night. He couldn't make sense of it, and so he didn't think much of it. Fehmi seemed to be having a good time.

But the good time wouldn't end that night.

Fehmi began seeing Şener the pianist more frequently.

Halit understood what was happening, and was shocked, but he never broached the subject with Fehmi. He didn't want to hear the answer he'd receive, supposing it'd damage their friendship. Fehmi likewise preferred to act like nothing at all had happened. In short, they treated each other like the people of Büyükada did, which is to say, like all ordinary people do. They knew but pretended not to know.

As soon as Halit finished school, he married Ayşegül, a young academic, and began working at a mining company. Fehmi and Şener moved into the same home, and Fehmi eventually started his own business. Around the time Halit and Ayşegül's first daughter was born, Fehmi and Şener bought the mansion on Büyükada and moved there, where they would live till death do them part.

Three years after that, Ayşegül and Halit had their second daughter, Şener was elected to the board of the Büyükada Beautification Association, Fehmi became president of the bridge club, and the two couples continued seeing each other. Though they no longer lived as close as they had before the island, they took care not to let their bond wither away.

And so, when Halit used the word "partner" for the first time that night, the night of their fortieth anniversary, it overcame Fehmi with emotion. That wall of fear had finally been surmounted. Understanding that his "private situation" didn't have to be so private, that his closest friend understood without their having ever spoken openly about it, that it didn't matter to him and that he wouldn't lose him over this "situation," Fehmi felt a deep relief. The relief of emerging from a dark closet that had been shut tight for many years.

Şener, whom Halit still always addressed formally as Şener Bey, looked at him with gratitude. He grabbed his champagne, stood up, and grabbed a sumptuous gift box from a drawer. He kissed Fehmi on the cheek and handed him the box. "Seeing as it's such an emotional moment, here you go, Fehmi, darling. I know we've long since left behind buying each other gifts on our special days, but I couldn't help myself this year. Here you go, a little gift from me in honor of our fortieth anniversary."

Fehmi looked at him in astonishment. "Wait, but this doesn't mean . . . does it? 'I got you a gift but you didn't get me one, how dare you not get me a gift on our fortieth anniversary, how could you forget that night, you never buy me gifts . . .' That's not what this means, is it?"

Şener laughed. "No, dear. Don't be silly. I wasn't expecting you to get anything, I just felt like getting this for you."

Inside the gift box was a smaller velvet box that contained a fountain pen, its navy-blue barrel inlaid with gold and painstakingly etched with Fehmi's first and last name. After the two of them had moved to the island, Fehmi had begun translating fragments of plays, old poetry, and tragedies; Şener had, accordingly, offered his dearest a thoughtful, comely gift he could use for that very purpose.

Fehmi examined the pen and looked gratefully at his forty-year life partner. "You've put me to shame again, Şener.

Well done." He pulled the card from inside the fountain pen's box. A note, written in Şener's elegant handwriting, that read:

To my darling Fehmi, my one and only,
For signing your name on my heart forty years ago. So
glad I have you, so glad you have me. I am, till death,
simply, solely, and always yours.

Your Şener . . .

After raising their glasses once again in celebration, they each refilled their drinks. Nil, who by now was quite drunk, interjected: "Ummm, Şener, do you only have something for our uncle Fehmi? We're all expecting a gift too. Come onnnn, sing us a song. Seeing as we only ever get to hear your voice at parties."

Şener shrugged. "Ah, no. Please don't! My voice is out of practice, I'm not prepared. Please don't make me embarrass myself," he replied.

Fehmi took the hand of his beloved and looked into his eyes. "Dear, I want to hear you sing too. It's *our* night. Come on, sing our song."

"Fine, then, if you insist. Who am I to disappoint you, darling?" Şener stood up and went to his piano. He lifted the lid from the keyboard, pulled the stool from underneath, and sat before his oldest friend of all. His fingers drifted gently across the keys. The notes filled the air, wafting through the mansion's walls, its upholstery, its curtains, through the ears of friends and lovers like a gentle breeze.

As Şener vamped a short, freestyle overture, it was like he was no longer in his home on Büyükada at all but onstage in a concert hall. He closed his eyes in pleasure and began addressing his audience as if in prayer.

"The two of us ... Fehmi and I, for many years we never had a favorite song together, never found our song. Because we both loved so many different songs. Somehow nothing ever quite captured the two of us. That is, until we moved to Büyükada ..."

He began playing a slightly faster rhythm as he continued.

"After we moved to the island, we finally decided on a song that was our favorite. An old Elvis Presley tune, 'Surrender,' the lyrics rewritten by İlham Gencer and famous to us as *Deniz Ne Kadar Güzel*—*How Beautiful the Sea*. It became our song. Nil, if you'll accompany me on vocals, sweetheart, I can't sing so high anymore."

He passed from his freestyle overture to the song's first notes.

"I'm playing this for my darling Fehmi. For him alone, for love alone ..."

He had lost nothing of his form, the keys of the piano practically an extension of his hands.

> "*How beautiful the sea, how*
> *I run through its waves now*
> *In its loving arms I'll be,*
> *My love, the beautiful sea ...*"

Applause rose from the table, applause for the both of them. Fehmi walked over to Şener; he wrapped his arms around his beloved, who continued playing the piano. He turned to the rest. "Since we've already heard 'how beautiful the sea' is, I want to bring you all to the place on this island with the most beautiful view of the sea. Take your drinks now, and follow me," he said, and made for the back door.

Şener agreed: "Yes. Fabulous idea." He took his flute of champagne from atop the piano and followed after Fehmi.

The old friends and lovers filed into the yard, which was encircled by a pale darkness.

"This way," Fehmi said, walking toward the back of their yard. They emerged onto a little path, hidden from sight behind a copse of bushes and little trees. The summer hadn't yet warmed the world enough, so the crickets were still in their homes; they could hear but the sound of a single cricket, the earliest of the season. They began hiking up the path through the darkness. Halit and Ayşegül had their arms around each other; Şener led Nil, holding her hand. They turned at the end of the path at a gap in the bushes, arriving at an open area above their house, surrounded by trees, from which only the pointy rooftops of the island's houses were visible. "We're here," said Fehmi.

A few steps ahead, a small cliff descended, and beyond that, the endlessly open, uninterrupted, darkening blue sea extended. It was breathtaking. Istanbul's lights glimmered like a cluster of stars in the distance. The darkness was swallowing everything, and the sea stretching toward infinity only made itself known by the murmur of its waves.

"Magnificent," Nil said, spreading her arms and walking forward. Ayşegül and Halit held each other even closer.

Şener wrapped his arm around Fehmi's and took a sip of his champagne. "Yes, it really is magnificent. We wanted to buy this land but the owner was very clear that it wasn't for sale." He pointed at a spot on the ground. "If it were ours we would have built a gazebo right there, to sit and watch the sunsets. But it wasn't meant to be, I suppose. We come up here nonetheless sometimes, to look out at the sea." Şener pulled himself closer to Fehmi.

Fehmi smiled and pulled a piece of paper from his pocket.

"Şener, darling, this is my anniversary gift to you." He slipped the paper into Şener's hands. "I know we weren't supposed to get each other gifts, but I also wanted to give you something special for our fortieth year together."

Bewildered, Şener glanced quickly between Fehmi and the paper it was too dark to read.

"This place is yours now," Fehmi said. "I finally managed to persuade the owner last weekend and bought it. This is the deed." He smiled, proud that he had managed to surprise Şener, a truly rare occurrence. "Happy anniversary, my love."

Şener couldn't say anything; perhaps for the first time in his life he was left speechless. He stepped slowly back to Fehmi, wrapped his arms around him, and kissed him on the lips.

The two men stood there, eyes closed, lip to lip, for several moments. The taste they got from each other's lips had remained the same for the past forty years: the gentle aroma of blackberry . . .

Suddenly embarrassed at the presence of the others, Fehmi pulled away from the kiss. He turned to the friends watching them and lifted his glass. "So let's all drink, let's raise our glasses to friendship. And once we build the gazebo here, you'll be the first we invite to enjoy it. You're invited in advance. Promise you'll come?"

"Promise!" they said in unison, and clinked their glasses together. Their laughter echoed across the dark waters of the sea, disappearing on its way to the stellar constellation of Istanbul, which blinked madly in the night, harboring thousands of arguments, happinesses, and sorrows.

This would be the last night they all spent together.

The five of them, there where the sea looked most beautiful from Büyükada, would never gather together again.

NEW NEIGHBORS

These early summer days on the island tended to be restless as wild horses, but today, it was a peaceful afternoon, the silence and solitude on the hills of Büyükada interrupted only by the sounds of birds. The June sun, which the residents of Istanbul were already regarding as an omen of the impossibly hot summer to come, had put its face on full garish display, setting the islanders into the rush of summer as genial as it was tiresome.

Wearing his broad-brimmed panama hat, loose linen pants, and a muslin shirt that extended to his knees, Şener busied himself planting his rose seedlings in the garden. So intensely concentrated was he on his work that a few hours had passed unnoticed as he took the new rose seedlings from their wooden crate, pruned them, and placed them in holes he'd meticulously dug with his hands.

Fehmi had made himself scarce today. He'd woken up earlier than usual the past few days, ensconcing himself in his office before noon. He told Şener that he'd found a wonderful new piece to work on. A murder mystery, a stage play, written by a young writer and not yet translated into Turkish. Şener knew by the tightly drawn curtains in the window that Fehmi was in his office.

For his entire life, Fehmi had suffered from a complex common among rural folk about being unable to speak a foreign language flawlessly. He hadn't been well-off enough as a young man to take language courses; when he did eventually come into some money, he attended a good English school and then continued teaching himself on his own. He could read and write quite well, but because he was so bashful, he could never bring himself to speak it.

That very same bashfulness had kept him from publishing any of the plays he had spent the past ten years translating in secret, viewing his work as nothing more than an embarrassing pastime. "What if they don't like it?" "My English isn't good enough for that, dear. Far from it!" "I'm just passing the time. Like solving puzzles." "It's just a hobby."

Şener, on the other hand, spoke perfect English and French and could get by in Italian because of the opera and in German because of the Turkish diaspora there. He tried to persuade Fehmi that his translations were good, that he ought to show them to a publisher, but no matter how hard he pushed, he couldn't get Fehmi to overcome his strange stubbornness.

But Fehmi said he was really enjoying the play he was currently working on, and for the first time, he had floated the possibility of publishing under a pseudonym. After breakfast that particular morning, he retreated to his office, drew the curtains tight, turned on the metronome that helped him concentrate, and toyed with the text, playing his little word games to the anxious ticking and tocking of the metronome. He was old now, and he wore himself out quickly. Which was why, after his morning work session, he went to the island clubhouse to clear his head. He needed to bury his attention in the mindlessness of a deck of cards.

Şener did not object to Fehmi's working all day and then going to play bridge. For him, it was a perfect afternoon worth spending in silence. With leftovers in the fridge, he could at last devote an entire day to his garden. Amid their anniversary frenzy, his many chores, testing new recipes, and now the new gazebo project which had blown up like a bomb in their daily routines, the garden had been rather neglected. He could sense, even from the kitchen, that the quince saplings were pissed at him.

The silence, filled with nothing but the wind rustling through the leaves, was suddenly interrupted by the clacking wheels of a horse-drawn carriage coming up the slope. When he raised his head, Şener realized that the sun, high in the sky, was beginning to give him a sunburn. He pulled the brim of his hat over his eyes, trying to see the carriage more clearly.

The weary horses passed in front of their mansion and stopped in front of the neighboring house where nobody lived.

Again? Şener thought in a momentary flash of annoyance. New occupants were arriving.

The home beside Şener and Fehmi's mansion used to belong to Servet Hanım, but after she died, her children shuttered the place, aiming to sell it. Unable to get a buyer at the price they wanted, they all but abandoned the house.

Short-term vacationers would come and stay some summers, but usually nobody came by. Servet Hanım's money-grubbing children would rent it out at exorbitant prices, and the guests would only ever stay a few days. The tourists who became their intermittent neighbors opted to spend their short time on the island not taking any interest in the two old men next door, but going to the beach, hiking, and eating ice cream. On a few occasions the occupiers had been loud young people who spent all night getting drunk on beer and whose music thumped *untzz untzz* so hard Şener was sure it meant the fabled tsunami of Büyükada was finally coming. They had called Servet Hanım's daughter Dilara to complain at length, expressing in no uncertain terms that they didn't want to deal with anything of the sort ever again.

Şener preferred an island neighbor more like Orhan Pamuk. Alone, aging, and antisocial . . .

He hid behind the jasmine bushes, trying to see who had arrived without being seen himself. His curiosity was replaced by surprise when the people who climbed out of the carriage were not strangers but the islanders Nusret and his wife Hanife. Hanife held a veritable monopoly over housekeeping services on the island, looking after most of the houses and mansions. In this way she had made herself a vital node in the island's gossip network. Whatever happened behind closed doors in one house she would share in other houses, and Şener would himself always eventually hear about it all from one or another of the ladies on the island. That was why he kept his door, which concealed so many secrets, completely closed to Hanife.

Nusret and Hanife unloaded their cleaning supplies and toolbox from the carriage, which then turned around, quickly descending the slope and vanishing from sight.

Şener was surprised. The people who rented the neighboring house seldom took care to have it cleaned beforehand; they'd simply air it out for the first few days and then settle in. He crossed to the fence separating the two properties, concealed by bushes and vines, and called out to the couple in the yard. "Good day to you, Nusret Efendi. What's all this, then? Are we going to have guests next door?"

Nusret walked toward him with genuine mirth. "Oh, hello, Şener Bey! I didn't see you there. Good day to you, too. How are you?"

Hanife stood behind Nusret, looking at Şener with the tremendous excitement and insatiable curiosity of being so close to the owner of the only house on the island she hadn't managed to enter, pulling her headscarf further over her face and giggling. Şener, made uncomfortable by the fact that Hanife was laughing at him, chose to ignore her.

"All good, the usual, Nusret Efendi. I've been neglecting

my yardwork, so I decided to take care of it today. Just the season for it, you know. If I don't put in the roses now, they'll wither on the branch."

Nusret glanced at the yard over the fence, delight in his eyes. "Well, God as my witness, Şener Bey, there's no garden like yours on the island. Paradise, it is, the garden of paradise." Şener was impatient for Nusret to move on from his garden, and Nusret wasted no time in gratifying him: "We're bringing you a neighbor, Şener Bey, soon. We came to clean and do repairs."

Şener's curiosity was piqued even further. "Oh my, a neighbor? Is someone coming in permanently?" he asked with a nervousness he couldn't hide but which, in Nusret's mind, might easily have been interpreted as eagerness to have a new neighbor at last.

Nusret pulled off his cap and rubbed his head. "No, no. Not permanent, Şener Bey. Dilara Hanım called yesterday, someone's renting the house all summer. They'll be here in a day or two, so she said to come before them and air out the house, clean it, there's a broken window in the kitchen, et cetera, go fix it up."

Şener was thoroughly astonished by the news, which would cast a pall over the rest of his day. Ever since the half-senile Servet Hanım had gone fully off her rocker, nobody had spent an entire summer in the house next door.

For Şener, summer always meant he had to exercise more discretion, be more private. Knowing that he might be watched if he wanted to spend more time outside the house or have all the windows and curtains open—it was enough to spoil an entire day Şener had otherwise wanted to fill with pink roses. He took off his gardening gloves with a peevishness he tried to conceal.

"So who are they?"

"By God, I have no idea. But they have to be rich, since they're renting it all summer ... Dilara Hanım doesn't rent it out on the cheap. Not to mention they're having it cleaned. She clearly hit the jackpot this time."

Şener's mood soured even more. "Well, then. Good for them. All right, good day to you, take it easy," he said, making his way to the wooden stairs that led up to the veranda.

Hanife, who had been standing behind Nusret and listening to their whole conversation, suddenly realized she was losing her chance to talk to the old man who always ignored her, an old man about whom she was more curious than anyone else on the island. She interjected impudently, "How's Brother Fehmi? Is he good, Brother Şeneeeer?"

Şener spun around on the stairs. Sparks of fury flashed in his eyes over her disrespect. He understood all too well what Hanife meant by this simple question. Right when he needed to worry over his own privacy, he found her tone to be full of invasive implications, and he responded with a hostility he couldn't suppress. "Surely you mean Fehmi *Bey*, I think! Yes, Fehmi Bey! Fehmi Bey is well, Hanife. Why do you ask?"

Unable to hide her smile, Hanife was surprised at the

accusatory tone in the old man's voice. She realized that her impertinence had rubbed him the wrong way. "Well . . . no reason. I was just asking, brother."

Şener took his glass of lemonade from the railing on the veranda. "I see! So you were just asking. All right, then." He took a sip and went inside.

Nusret, who wasn't as stupid as he looked and who understood the implication underlying the exchange, shoved Hanife. "Well done! What's it to you? Is it your job to ask how everyone in the world is doing?"

In one house, the windows were thrown open as the people inside began working and cleaning; in the other, the curtains were already being drawn shut. Şener watched the feverish work in the house next door from behind the newly closed curtains. He took the leftovers from the fridge, set the table, and as he sipped his drink and waited to share the news with Fehmi, his mind spun with worry about who would be moving in next door.

Fehmi returned from bridge, and though he was surprised to learn someone would be spending the whole summer in the neighboring house, it didn't seem as big of a deal to him as it did to Şener. "Why are you so hung up on it, Şener? So we won't kiss in the garden, what else is there to worry about?" he said. "Forget them. Maybe you'll like them. If they're good people, maybe you'll even make some new friends."

"I have enough friends, my love," Şener protested. "I don't want anyone lurking around our house in the middle of summer. Don't get me wrong: I'll be a wonderful neighbor, of course, I'll help them if they need anything, but if they're in the least bit curious, if they're always watching us, if they get nosy, I won't have any peace. Plus Hanife got on my nerves today. Her tone, full of insinuation . . ."

Fehmi took his troubled lover's hand. "Never mind Hanife. She's shameless. They're the ones who'll lose out; Nusret won't get the gazebo job like that. The contractors are going to come take a look in the next few days. Looks like they'll have their work cut out for them."

"Yes, definitely. That hole where the leaves have piled up will have to be thoroughly cleaned out, sweetheart. It stinks. They might even have to pour concrete. Right in the perfect spot, too. We'll have them fill it up and that's where the gazebo will go. The master carpenter's in Istanbul, I'll talk to him."

"All right. We'll take a look tomorrow and decide. I'll come to an agreement with the men accordingly. We'll have them start as soon as possible."

While Fehmi read his book in bed that night, Şener massaged his cold cream into his face and looked out the window at the house next door. *This might be the last quiet night like this. The cleaning's done, they'll move in soon,* he thought, drawing the curtain on the window that overlooked the house next door, a curtain that would not be opened again that summer, and got into bed.

He wouldn't have to wait long to find out who was moving in next door.

The following day, after surveying the area for the gazebo and deciding what needed to be done, Fehmi was getting ready to go to the suppliers in Istanbul when Şener called out. "Wait a second, Fehmi, darling," he said. "I collected a few samples from magazines, let me give them to you. So you have an idea for the materials."

Fehmi stood by the gate to the garden for a while, drawing in the morning's fresh air. The scent of the newly blossoming flowers filled his nose: strange, misty, spicy. He knelt down and touched the velvety buds of the rose seedlings Şener had just planted, caressed them gently. Removing his sunglasses, he turned his face toward the sun and let it dazzle his eyes. Just then, he heard the sound of a carriage creaking up the street. Fehmi turned his head, watching a wagon piled high with suitcases and bags slowly pass in front of the house. He tried not to look with too much curiosity, thinking it'd be rude, and lowered his head, pretending to busy himself with the plants. As the carriage passed, though, he cast the briefest of glances at it, and met eyes with someone inside.

The briefest of moments, less than a second.

Fehmi felt his heart beat hard. A feeling like the first heartbeat of a fetus in a womb. A feeling of the kind that, like a scent etched deep in your memory that surprises you, takes you back to a moment, to that exact moment in the past. A pair of eyes. An exchange of looks.

A moment of sublime contact that changes the course of a person's fate forever.

The carriage stopped at the gate to the yard of the house next door. Fehmi tried to see who got out of the wagon. From the side of the carriage closest to him, the first to descend from the carriage was an athletic-looking man with graying hair in his forties, followed by a blonde woman of a similar age.

The eyes he'd met belonged to neither of them.

The man helped the coachman with the bags while the woman leaned on the iron fence separating the yard from the road and looked at the house. Someone else got out of the carriage on the other side, the side Fehmi couldn't see, and walked to the front of the carriage, standing beside the aged horses. Fehmi could only see this third person's white sneakers; their face was obscured by the horses. The horses stomped their feet, stirring up the dust along the dirt road, just as the white sneakers dragged themselves too through the dust. Fehmi scooted to his right and was about to see the person standing by the horses when . . .

"Fehmi, darling, I found them. They were in the drawer."

When Şener emerged from the front door with clippings from the home décor magazines, he saw Fehmi standing there, and then saw their new neighbors standing around the carriage, surrounded by their belongings. The suddenness of it all bewildered him and he coughed, clearing his throat, before descending the stairs with a serious expression on his face.

Şener didn't have much time to contemplate the neighbors because the horses drawing the carriage suddenly became uneasy, rearing up on their hind legs. "Look out!" Şener yelled.

The man and the woman panicked and ran around to the young boy standing in front of the horses. Afraid, the woman wrapped her arms around the boy and turned to the coachman. "Be careful! What do you think you're doing?" she shouted.

The man, carrying a suitcase under either arm, replied: "It's fine. Nothing to worry about."

The young boy pulled himself away from the woman's arms and grumpily shouldered his backpack.

Şener walked over to Fehmi, whose gaze was fixed there, and called out to the newcomers. "The horses do that sometimes. It's the heat. Don't worry, no harm, they're just poor old animals."

The woman turned to them, seemingly comforted. "You're right. We're not used to them, so they scared us," she said, walking toward him. "Greetings, by the way. A shame our first meeting was like this, but my name is Berna. This is my husband, Cem." She gestured at the man collecting the bags unloaded from the carriage. The man greeted them from afar.

Shaking her hand, Şener said, "Pleased to meet you, ma'am. I'm Şener. Welcome. This is my friend, Fehmi Bey."

Fehmi slowly extended his hand to shake hers. It was like he wasn't there; he was still preoccupied by the eyes he'd met a few minutes before, though nobody noticed.

Berna called out to the boy behind her. "This is our son, Deniz. Deniz, dear, come say hello."

And out came the person who had caused Fehmi to freeze, the person whose eyes caught his from the carriage, the person whose face he saw when the horses reared up, the saddest, most beautiful boy in the world.

Deniz glanced ever so briefly at Fehmi and Şener, letting out an almost inaudible "hello" from his lips, and turned his back. And that saddest, most beautiful boy in the world marched toward the neighboring house, every gesture expressing his pure and seething discontent.

Awash in the scent of pink roses, Büyükada was now in the full swing of summer.

DENIZ

Alphan Preparatory Academy was housed in an Ottoman-era villa preserved by some miracle among the office buildings of Levent. One particular day that spring, its students were confronted with an unexpected scene of lurid violence.

"It was horrible, just horrible . . ." said Merve, hiccupping as she sobbed into her phone to her mom.

Güntan, a sophomore, sent a text to her father, the CEO of a gas company, that said, *There's an emergency.*

All of the juniors, dealing with acne flareups over their imminent university entrance exams, added a few more pimples to their faces from the stress of that day.

Spoiled rotten and well-bred, the precious sons and daughters of the rich families came face to face that day, for perhaps the first time in their lives, with true terror, with silent evil in their midst.

At lunchtime that particular day, the school's cafeteria was awash in a sea of blood.

Those who saw it said the floor was covered with blood, teeth, and spit. And the scent of liquor, wafting thick and heavy in the air.

The incident had come to pass through the secret phone calls, direct messages on Twitter, pointed comments on Instagram, and private WhatsApp conversations that the seniors had with one another night after night all year, after they squirreled themselves away into their bedrooms under the guise of studying. In these innocent virtual exchanges, they had imagined a much calmer duel. A great battle of words, swearing, maybe a few fists thrown at anyone who tried to cut in, shirts torn while wrestling on the ground, a busted eyebrow if the teachers on duty took their time to intervene . . . but that was it.

Nobody had predicted that teeth would come into the equation. Not even the two instigators of the incident. It had been a sweet, innocent romance, young love; that it had reached this point confronted them with the most difficult test either of them had ever experienced, but this time, the questions were about something they hadn't studied.

After the incident, as Deniz rode in the car with his mother and father back to their home in Suadiye, he thought about how deliriously his mother had wept in the principal's office. Eyes filled with tears, she tried to explain to the principal that Deniz was "not that kind of kid."

"He was probably under too much stress over his exams, and the excitement of first love made him do it." "He couldn't control himself, because he's young." "Weren't we all young once, didn't we all make mistakes?" "No, sir, no. Deniz is not that kind of kid."

Yes, that's exactly how Berna sounded, weeping in the principal's office.

And so, as they drove home in their car, Deniz recalled the whole conversation and thought about the image of his mother, crying and begging the school principal for leniency. Her makeup had run; she had embodied the role she knew best, the role of victim, this time to save her darling son, as she attempted to persuade everyone in the room to mind their own business. She had been both pitiful and profoundly hilarious. Deniz, recollecting how amusing his mom was as she wept, tried to contain his smile. He had to keep his thoughts to himself because he knew he was guilty. Because no matter how much his mother repeated her line that "he's not that kind of kid," he was, in fact, exactly that kind of kid.

But even though he tried to blow it off, Deniz was actually quite disturbed by the terror he had wrought.

He had come to school drunk out of his mind. A feeling he'd been keeping to himself, that he didn't even realize until that moment, took hold of him. His fingers latched onto Berk's hair, and he slammed Berk's mouth into the cafeteria's wooden bench with such speed and force that all of Berk's front teeth fell to the floor into a widening puddle of blood pouring from his mouth.

Everything transpired in the span of a second.

Only after he saw the blood and teeth on the ground did Deniz realize what he'd done.

Berk's teeth had gone flying, and when Deniz heard him howling in pain, he looked at his clenched hand. It held a fistful of Berk's brown hair. The Alphan Preparatory Academy uniform he wore, his cream-colored pants, white shirt, blue sweater, and his white Adidas sneakers, were spattered red. And Berk there, writhing on the ground in a pool of his own blood. The cafeteria suddenly filled with the sounds of wailing and weeping. The girls began letting out shrill shrieks one after the other like bottles of champagne popping, and their bawling coalesced with Berk's pained moaning as he covered his mouth with his hand. "My teeth, my teeth . . ." Berk probably wanted to say, but since that handsome boy's beautiful, once-symmetrical mouth no longer had any teeth in it, all it released was a fluid mixture of blood and spit, which splattered on the hems of Deniz's pants.

After looking at the brown fistful of hair in his hand, each strand with a shining point of blood at the root, Deniz knelt down and vomited everywhere. He assumed the liter of whiskey he drank earlier that day, half of it in almost a single gulp, had already worked its way out of his body, but it burned his throat as it came up and spread over the stone tiles of the cafeteria floor.

By the time the teachers on duty had run to the scene, the two most handsome boys in the school were rolling in a slurry of blood, teeth, spit, snot, vomit, whiskey, and tears.

This spectacular finale, this duel of two Romeos in the cafeteria, was really the moment the story began.

Berk, one of the incident's two protagonists, was loaded onto a gurney and carried out to an ambulance, its sharp sirens amplified by the screaming and crying throughout the school, and taken to the hospital. The teachers on duty dragged Deniz, vomit still dribbling from his mouth, to the principal's office.

A third protagonist, Melisa, fainted in the girl's restroom when she heard the news; her two best friends roused her and brought her back to her home in Etiler. Deep in the heat of adolescence, these uppity teenagers had made a series of decisions to feel like adults, all of which had culminated in the losing of teeth. And at the end of the day, they all sought refuge under the wings of their families. They had all, in short, failed the test big-time.

That was what most bothered Deniz out of the whole incident. In the end what his mother had said came to pass, and Berna turned out to be right.

"I'm fucked," Deniz muttered. But nobody in the car heard him. The family's car was in the middle of the Bosphorus Bridge, its colored lights shining. The bridge was empty, and the light bled into the passing car at a regular tempo. Lounge FM was playing in Cem's car as usual, and though Deniz normally couldn't stand the shrill whining of the music and would have long since turned it off, fiddling with the radio was the last thing on his mind right now.

Berna's makeup was by now completely ruined; she stared out the window with a weary yet strangely innocent expression—but the depressive music of Lounge FM that filled the car didn't stop her from talking to herself. "I said so. I said you shouldn't see that girl," Berna said in quiet rebellion, heard loud and clear by both Cem and Deniz.

Yes, Berna had indeed said so. "You shouldn't see her," she had said, and Deniz had of course not listened to her. Because his hormones always incited him to disobedience. How else could it have gone? He had something very powerful and very important and he knew it. Thanks to the perfect genetic code Berna and Cem had gifted him, he knew he was beautiful enough to conquer whomsoever he desired.

Youth. Beauty. Self-confidence. Deniz had enough of the three to detonate a bomb.

As Deniz's peers suffered through the ugly trials and awkward tribulations of late boyhood, the ugliest age known to humankind, Deniz remained unafflicted, managing to bypass the unsightliest phase of adolescence. He had always been a beautiful boy; now, as his androgenic hormones spread through his body, they gave his beauty another dimension and turned him day by day into an incontrovertible object of desire. His dark blue eyes had inspired Berna to give him his name, "Deniz," which meant "sea;" at this age, their once-soft gaze had begun to harden. Those sea-dark eyes now pulled everyone, young and old, to him as if caught in a rip current. The awareness, even at his young age, that he could acquire anyone he wanted had afforded him the kind of ego only those who are beautiful at that age can know.

He was determined, of course, to use all his beauty and

allure for sexual conquest. Never mind the fact that it was his last year at school; even if it were the last year of his life he wanted to sate his desires to his heart's content. He didn't give a shit about the exams. As the only son of rich parents, he knew that no matter what happened, he'd have no trouble paying his way into a good private university.

And yet, he might never have the chance to get with all those beautiful girls for the rest of his life. He might never again have the chance to get his hands on all those girls after high school ended, because they'd surely end up in America or Canada or at one of the expensive fashion schools in Italy or the most renowned business schools in London.

Night upon night he thought about those girls, each like a drop of dew. He would think about their misty rosebuds. Those buds, those flowers ready to give up their nectar to the spring, those trembling petals, those magnetic eucalyptuses, those bodies, those sticky bon-bons . . . All Deniz wanted at that age was not to study trigonometry and go to Boğaziçi University, but to get his hands on those buds, even just once.

The desire grew and grew inside him and eventually began to erupt. Over those spring months, all the desire that had accumulated in Deniz's body was practically frothing out of him.

And so, equipped with his tremendous beauty, he became unbearably cocky. Whenever he passed girls his age he imagined himself sending their skirts aflutter, like a red Ferrari racing by. He skipped class frequently to play basketball, and when the private bus service would arrive to pick him up, he'd make his way to school with a sweaty shirt, covered in dust and dirt.

Deniz and Justin Bieber were the main topics of the girls' depraved afternoon conversations, which revolved around what they would do if they had one night with them. Some of the girls, gushing like waterfalls, even imagined being with Deniz and Justin Bieber at the same time. All the twin beds of the teenage girls across Istanbul were soaking wet that spring.

As Deniz ascended the ranks of adolescent desire at his school, he eventually chose the girl that suited him most. That girl, of course, could have been none other than Melisa, the most popular girl in school. Melisa was the "most" everything at the school. Most beautiful, most popular, most blond, and most ambitious: she'd cry when she got a 90 on her tests.

She had also been in the most tempestuous relationship the Alphan Preparatory Academy had ever seen; it had been legendary. Berk, the captain of the basketball team, and Melisa, the choir's soloist.

Berk and Melisa. They began dating freshman year, and after the first breakup and eventual reconciliation their sophomore year, these two great lovers promised to be faithful to each other. But after their sixty-sixth and final breakup over the course of their relationship, Melisa was resolute. Her business with Berk was over. She was getting ready to join the Department of English Language and Literature at Istanbul University. She wasn't going to let anyone get in her way, at least until she started at the university; she wasn't going to think about anything except meeting the goals set for her by her academic advisor.

If not for the red Ferrari.

Waiting in line in the cafeteria one day, Deniz ended up standing behind Melisa. He blew a warm breath down her neck, and she didn't recoil. His breath had barely moved the tips of her hair, but his message to her had been loud and clear. They began chatting during breaks between class. They began having lunch together, but they insisted that there was nothing going on between them, that they were just friends.

In the WhatsApp conversations among the students of the Alphan Preparatory Academy, though, a real-life soap opera was unfurling.

Deniz. Melisa. Berk. What will happen? Who's dating whom? Where will this love triangle end up?

"Deniz doesn't actually love Melisa, he's just playing with her heart."

"Man, Berk struck out with Melisa, now Deniz is after her . . ."

"I think they're definitely dating, Özge. Don't you dare tell anyone I have a crush on Deniz."

"Berk's so spineless, right, bro? They made a promise, man, and now she's with that asswipe?"

"I don't think Melisa's pretty in the least, Özge, plus she dyes her hair."

While the telephone lines and internet connections of Istanbul seethed with these conversations, Deniz and Melisa had long since passed first base. Sitting on a bench along the seaside in Sarıyer on a day they skipped school together, the salty winds of the Bosphorus blowing through their hair, they made out for the first time. Their lips were locked together with the subtle taste of her strawberry lip gloss.

They learned for the first time that day that making out means mashing your wet tongues in each other's mouths. The both of them were sure in that moment that life could not be more beautiful. And that they'd never forget that kiss for the rest of their lives.

In the end, though, despite all the heat he seemed to exude, and even though he considered himself a breeding bull, he was ready in theory but absolutely lacking in practice. Yes, he knew precisely and definitively what he wanted, but he'd never been able to get his hands on a real live girl. So it was a relief that his first attempt at making out had gone off without a hitch. He wanted to speed things along from there, but Melisa was being stubbornly frigid. She had made out with Deniz and she had enjoyed it, but in truth, almost secretly, she missed Berk.

Her hopeless romantic . . . The handsome captain of the basketball team . . . The boy with auburn hair who had spraypainted "I Love You" on the wall opposite her house . . .

Late one night Melisa received a picture on her phone. The picture was of a tattoo, a small heart containing the letter M, which Berk had just gotten on his wrist. As a gesture, the tattoo was enough to drive Melisa crazy. Her attention immediately returned to Berk. Deniz's realization that

Melisa had turned her affections away from him and back to Berk made him only want Melisa more. The loss of her affection made him jealous, and the more jealous he became, the more she meant to him, the more necessary and indispensable she became. Because jealousy is a poisonous feeling . . .

Things grew only more complicated, until one day, Deniz's best friend Alper's parents left town for their vacation home, and Deniz invited Melisa to Alper's house.

In her reply to him, Melisa accepted the invitation and said they could hang out for a few hours. Deniz was ready to take their relationship to the next level. The night before the big day, he spent hours watching porn, studying up as best he could. The next morning he got himself a bottle of whiskey and went to Alper's house. He began drinking at the house at eleven in the morning, but the hard punch of the whiskey riled him up well before noon.

Afternoon came and Melisa still hadn't come.

Deniz waited another hour. There was still no sign of Melisa, and she wasn't answering her phone.

Waiting impatiently at the house, he received a message from Alper that said Melisa had left school with Berk. Nearly blackout drunk at this point, Deniz called Melisa. The phone rang and rang and finally, she answered. "Where are you?" he asked, slurring his words, and Melisa apologized, sitting hand in hand with Berk at the Kanyon Mall on their lunch break.

"I'm sorry, Deniz. I won't be able to make it. Berk and I have decided to get back together."

Melisa supposed that this exchange would take care of everything, but she was mistaken. After hanging up, Deniz chugged the second half of the bottle of whiskey, his libido and his hormones raging with the drink's effects. Then he left Alper's house and took a taxi to the Alphan Preparatory Academy.

Melisa and Berk returned to school holding hands. Melisa went to get her notes from the classroom while Berk made his way to the cafeteria to join his basketball team-mates, swaggering assuredly after having won a match that week that qualified them for the championship. Having now won back his girlfriend as well, the captain was going to bring home the championship with his high spirits and his determination.

When Berk arrived at their table, they all put their hands in a huddle and yelled, "PI-RATES!" It was right after the basketball team chanted their famous cheer for the Pirates that Berk's head was smashed into the bench.

PI-RATES!!!

And then a grave, momentary silence, before the chaos erupted.

Cem turned the car onto the private driveway that led to the garage of their apartment building and parked in their spot. The headlights went out. Lounge FM fell silent. Deniz stirred from his deep contemplation, Berna picked up the Bottega Veneta purse at her feet, and they got out of the car. In the darkness the car doors locked with a mechanical click. They began walking.

At the end of it all, they had returned to their own personal hell.

The most tragic day in the family's history was officially coming to an end. Taken in broad strokes, though, their family hadn't actually lost anything. All the terror, the blood, the noise, the tears, the yelling—yet still every member of the family was perfectly fine; all their teeth were where they belonged. And now they were safe and sound at home. Berna, Cem, and Deniz, together again, forming a perfect whole. That's what matters most to a family, after all.

They got in the elevator without speaking. Each of them looked in a different direction. They got off on the fifth floor, opened the door, and walked in. The three of them now stood silent, waiting in the foyer. Berna, Cem, and Deniz . . . The heterosexual nuclear family, all together under the same roof. All the buffoonery, all the tricks played on others, on those outside their family, had come to an end. Now they were to put on a performance whose intricacies they knew well, a performance all their own.

Cem stood in the darkened foyer; his jaw ached from clenching it all day and trying to be patient. He was under a huge amount of stress from the urban transformation project at the architecture firm he ran, and now, unable to restrain himself any longer, he struck Deniz, struck the boy with a smack whose sound was so sharp it almost lit up the room. It was the first time that the father had hit his son, and the *SLAP* sound shocked all three of them. Cem gritted his teeth as he yelled, "You punk! You're an embarrassment!"

Setting aside her shock at the slap, Berna stepped between them and, like any mother trying to protect her child, moved Deniz gently behind her back to shield her son with her body. Her eyes locked onto Cem. "Don't be ridiculous. What do you think you're doing?" She spoke decisively, clearly. Cem, who'd regretted the slap even before his hand met Deniz's face, went to the bedroom without saying a word.

Berna turned to Deniz, who held his cheek, and said in a tone that was angry but more disappointed, defeated even, "Go to your room. We're going to have a talk with you tomorrow." She entered the living room, poured herself a large glass of whiskey, took off her shoes, and threw herself into a chair. She had probably never in her life felt so weary, so depleted. It was the kind of tiredness that, as a dentist, she wouldn't feel even if she gave millions of fillings, pulled thousands of rotten teeth.

The strange weariness of being a mother . . .

Cem entered the living room, having changed into shorts and an Abercrombie T-shirt. He sat next to Berna, rubbing his head with one hand. "I couldn't control myself, god dammit." The regret emanated from his whole body. "I don't know where or how we made a mistake raising that boy. I know I haven't been able to give him much attention because of work. Is that why he's doing this? Is he trying to get our attention? I truly don't understand."

Berna replied in a quiet whisper, "I don't know, Cem. I'm so confused, it feels like it's all my fault."

"Why would it be your fault? You're a wonderful mother.

We should count ourselves lucky, we could've been in the other kid's parents' shoes."

Berna thought about the other parents in the principal's office. The threatening looks from the father, the rage of the mother . . . She got up silently, drink in hand, walked to the floor-to-ceiling window and opened the curtains. There was no sound in the night but for the dark waters beating against the Suadiye shoreline. The cars passing sporadically along the avenue flooded by in an unctuous stream of light. It felt to her like nobody else but the two of them was awake in the entire city of Istanbul. Perhaps it was only other families, living in other houses, dealing with other problem children, who were awake now.

Berna downed the rest of her drink. "So what do we do now?" she said as she made for the bar.

Cem shook his head. "Believe me, I have no idea. I truly don't know. Of course Deniz will have to be punished. If he thinks he'll get out of this easy he's wrong."

"I'm not talking about that, Cem. What we do to Deniz is the next step, but for now, what are we going to do *for* Deniz? We have to get him away from here. Berk's family could do something to Deniz. Didn't you see how angry they were? Their kid's teeth were knocked out, in case you forgot." Berna was worrying herself into a frenzy the more she thought about the possibilities. She thought about what she would do if it were Deniz whose teeth were knocked out. She'd probably go and choke Berk with her own two hands, get rid of him then and there. What if Berk's mother was thinking the same thing? Imagining Deniz's face turning blue, choked to death by Berk's mother, Berna realized she couldn't breathe. She opened the door to the balcony and went outside. There was a sweet chill to the air. The scattered lights out on the islands quivered in the distance.

Berna came back in and stood before Cem. "We need to take him away from here. There's less than a month till school's out. We'll get a report together for Deniz and take him out of school."

"Where to, Berna? I'm in the middle of a project right now, I can't just leave my work behind and go somewhere else."

Berna knew that Cem wouldn't be able to leave the city. They needed to take Deniz somewhere not too far but not too easy to get to, either. She walked back to the balcony door and looked out at the opposite shore.

As she looked out at the faint lights of Büyükada in the distance, it seemed to her in that instant that from somewhere over there, somewhere up in the island's hills, among its pine trees, a gentle laugh crossed the sea and resounded in her ears. Like a reassuring voice from a peaceful port where there were no problems at all. She knew it was impossible, but that little piece of land, surrounded by water on all sides, seemed to be calling her, to be saying, "Come, come here, the solution to all your problems is here."

Berna turned to Cem. "We'll rent a house out on the island. That way you can go to work during the day. I'll cut back on my number of patients and stay with Deniz. If anybody asks, we'll say he went to stay with his grandmother in Amasya."

Cem stood up and crossed to Berna. He kissed his wife's shoulders, and they looked out at the opposite shore together. Cem took the glass from Berna's hand and finished the drink. "So how will we convince Deniz?" Cem asked. "He'll never agree to it. He'll never go." His eyes were fixed on the distant island.

Berna turned to Cem, stern. "We have no need for his input. Seeing as he got himself into this mess, acted out with no thought of the consequences . . . It all proves he's not yet an adult and we can still make decisions on his behalf. This summer, Deniz won't take a single step without us knowing. We have no other option. We have to go to the island." She took her purse and looked at Cem again. "I'm going to bed. First order of business tomorrow will be to look at houses on the island. We'll leave in a few days at the latest. We've only got a little bit of time to get everything organized."

Cem moved to close the balcony door. But a wind stirring off the dark waters moved faster, blowing inside, caressing Berna's bare shoulders, left open by her dress, scattering goosebumps across them. The wind moved through the living room, swerved around the open door, licked into the dark hallway, and entered Deniz's room, where it washed over his face. He had listened to the whole conversation and thought to himself, *I'm not a kid.*

A strange tremor shot through Deniz for a moment. The first thing he felt, before he truly reckoned with the shock that he'd be spending the whole summer on the island, was this tremor, thrown in his face by the wind.

As though a strange shadow from somewhere far away had flown in, catching his bedroom door open in that house in Suadiye, and blown his fate into his face.

For the young boy, it was a fate that would be exceedingly cold, lonesome, and harrowing.

BEHIND THE
CURTAINS

Tick! Tock! Tick! Tock!

The rhythmic melody of the metronome interrupted the orderly silence in his office.

Tick! Tock! Tick! Tock!

It was already getting dark out. The searing heat that had baked the city all day, all the way from Pendik to Sarıyer, was slowly breaking; the sun was now setting in its golden hour, preparing to retreat to its other abode on distant continents until the following day.

Soon, perhaps in half an hour, everyone would be welcomed into the peace of darkness and would sit down at their tables for dinner. Mothers would take the green beans they'd chilled all day out of their refrigerators and lift the newspapers they'd placed over the tomato rice to keep in the flavors. The core of the watermelon would be set aside for the favorite person of the house.

Fehmi had been in his office for a while, and although the

sound of the metronome always helped him concentrate on his work, right now he was pacing in time with it.

Tick! Tock! Tick! Tock!

The metronome had done him no good today. He was supposed to be working. But what he'd done for the past few hours was a heaping pile of nothing. Sometimes he sat at his desk, trying to focus on the notes in front of him; sometimes he forgot what he was doing and look at the dictionary, wondering whether there was another word meaning "freedom" that he could use; or else he rummaged through his drawers and lost himself amongst old trinkets and knickknacks. He'd looked at so many things, from his university yearbook to the photographs he stashed away in boxes, and had been overcome by old memories that now seemed to weigh on him.

He was still distracted, even now, after hours wasted on distractions.

Sitting at his desk, he caught himself staring at the portrait of İbrahim Çallı on the wall and, full of malaise, got up and poured himself another whiskey. The evening was giving way to night, but still he felt like drinking. He took the glass and stood before the large window at the front of the room, contemplative, and looked out on the sea so reddened by the setting sun it appeared to be bleeding, like the leaf of an old plane tree. *It's just so beautiful*, he thought to himself. In the past, the thought of the sea would've called to mind only Şener, would fill his ears with the sound of an imaginary piano, but in that moment, it reminded him of something else that went by the name of the sea, something else that was just so beautiful. He was embarrassed when he realized it; his face reddened, and though he knew it wasn't the case, he felt like there was another set of eyes in the room, watching him.

He surveyed his surroundings. He was alone. He could easily, comfortably dwell on how beautiful Deniz was, how beautiful the sea was. Just as he had done at every opportunity over the past two weeks ...

Since that first moment, he had started catching himself thinking constantly about the boy. At first, these weren't silent thoughts in his head; it seemed to him like they had a voice. It had been so long since he'd felt something like it that he concluded desire must be a noisy thing.

His thoughts about Deniz were just like the ones he'd once had in the high school gymnasium, at soccer matches, at porno theatres, thoughts to which he would cling tight but which also ashamed him. Even in those days, he knew all too well what he felt, but he couldn't admit it to himself.

Now, years later, he was trying once again to force himself not to have these thoughts, and his efforts were once again in vain. No matter how much he tried to make them disappear, he never could. Whatever he did, the thoughts would claw their way out of hiding in the moments of the day he thought he was most alone. Sometimes it was while having a drink on the front veranda in the evening; sometimes after lunch, when he'd lie down to take a nap; sometimes making himself a snack in the kitchen; sometimes while scrubbing his sagging legs in the bath. The thoughts would find their way out of the depths of his brain no matter what.

He had given up trying by now. He had reconciled himself to the shame of thinking about him.

He was at peace.

He was most at peace when he was thinking about Deniz.

Fehmi had never in his life struggled to concentrate on a task, but since the moment he'd laid eyes on the boy, he couldn't focus, couldn't make any progress on his translation. There was always a monotony, always something missing, in every paragraph he wrote. His head was entirely elsewhere but even he didn't know where. He couldn't sit still, couldn't keep moving; even sleep brought him no relief. A strange malaise had welled up in him, disquieting, irresolvable, like a mathematical proof with no solution.

God, what's happening to me? he wondered, taking a sip of his whiskey. He gathered up the papers scattered across his desk and read over his notes from the previous day, which had also been profoundly unproductive. They were awful; he crumpled them up and threw them in the trash, taking off his glasses and casting his eyes out the small window beside his desk.

And there it was. The secret window of his desire that had seared itself onto the summer.

The window always kept shut tight, covered with green linen curtains edged with French embroidery, the window that protected him from foreign eyes but also hid him from perfect beauty.

This window in his office looked out at the top floor of the next house, at a room in the back with a window facing the cliff. The enormous trees, thoroughly greened by now with the bounty of summer, stood like a secret barrier between the two rooms, and so long as nobody looked too closely, they wouldn't know he stood behind it, watching . . .

So long as nobody looked too closely.

Perhaps the only attentive thing Fehmi had done for days on end was to look out his window and slyly watch this room in the next house.

This room, which had been given to Deniz by the house's new inhabitants.

As best he could tell from his office, Deniz's room was small. The bed was covered in a white duvet, and extended straight out below the window; the pillow where he laid his head every night sat directly beneath the window. Which meant that was the bed where he slept, that was the pillow where he rested his head with its gorgeous curls, that was the open window through which the island winds swept in and gently caressed him in his slumber.

Opposite the bed stood a small wardrobe. He seemed like a messy kid. In that wardrobe sat the adolescent clothes that touched his young body every day: shorts, T-shirts, caps, and white tennis shoes piled on top of one another. Sometimes his mother would come in, gather up the scattered clothes, and place them tidily into the wardrobe, but the next day, those clothes would be strewn across the room again. On occasion a faint light would come from a part of the room he couldn't see. Fehmi imagined a desk there. The desk wouldn't be getting much use. Deniz would usually lie in bed with the laptop on his lap.

Every once in a while, as he watched Deniz from behind the curtains, he saw him surreptitiously smoking cigarettes. In those moments he became impossibly anxious that Deniz could see him, and would slowly, carefully let go of the curtain that he had parted, would lean on the wall beside his window of desire and wait with a racing heart and bated breath. When he once again parted the curtain there would be nobody standing at the window; just maybe, he'd see a wisp of smoke, slithering like a ghost into the sky.

He would see Deniz returning from the beach, coming home from the market with bread, kicking the soccer ball around the backyard, listening to music with his white earbuds on the veranda of their home, and even, some nights, eating ice cream with his mother.

Sometimes when Deniz was talking to his friends on the phone in his backyard, his voice would creep into their garden as a murmur. That raucous, half-breaking voice of his. The testosterone that pulsed through his body, busy producing hair, sweat, and sperm, had saturated his vocal cords, turning him into a man with a gravelly snarl of a voice.

There in the summer heat of his desire, Fehmi didn't stop at merely observing the room in the next house, but also adopted brand-new habits. He took to watering the garden regularly every evening. Watering the garden had once been a pastime accompanied by a glass of rakı that he did on the rare occasions he remembered to; now, it became as important and routine as going to collect his Social Security on the twenty-first of every month. Because, at the appointed hour when he now watered the garden, Deniz would sometimes water the garden next door too. It wasn't something Deniz did with devotion, like Fehmi. It was a chore, an imposition more than a pleasure. Berna's imposition. Were it up to Deniz he wouldn't have gotten up from his computer at that hour, would have preferred to spend it continuing to flirt with three different girls. But Berna had given him this chore and stubbornly insisted on this incontrovertible law of the family. Taking out the trash was Cem's chore, and watering the garden was Deniz's. They were a family well-trained in home economics, a family that believed strongly in the division of labor.

As Deniz watered the garden, Fehmi would cast furtive glances at the boy. Sometimes they'd exchange a distant greeting, a slight nod of the head.

Sometimes the water spraying from the garden hose in Deniz's hands would shimmer in the sunlight, casting a rainbow in the air. Fehmi would stare at him, the boy's body practically translucent under the rainbow. And though it only happened on occasion, Deniz walking barefoot on the wet grass underneath the rainbow, naked but for his shorts as he watered the garden, it was the most beautiful thing that Fehmi had seen in his entire life. He had seen so many beautiful things, had drank of the finest wines, had sat at the fanciest of dining tables, had gone on trips to the most magnificent cities in the world, but he had never seen anything more beautiful than him, than half-naked Deniz under the rainbow.

At this point in the summer the only moments etched in his memory were these.

It was as though the empty places left behind by the memories his aging mind had lost were replaced now solely by Deniz and what he did.

Fehmi slowly got up from where he sat and double-checked the door to his office. He didn't want Şener to show up out of nowhere: bringing him a bowl of fruit, showing him yet another picture of garden furniture in a home décor magazine, or having him taste a new recipe. To have privacy in their world for two remained impossibly difficult.

He turned and walked silently, stopping in front of the window. Stepping aside, he pulled back the curtain with his fingertips and looked at the house next door. Through the open window of the room opposite him he could see the bed, and right away the bare feet near its edge. He withdrew even further, afraid of getting caught, and parted the curtain windows again, almost without moving them at all.

Tick! Tock! Tick! Tock!

The curtain of Deniz's room was fluttering in the evening wind. Fehmi could see all the way up to Deniz's calves on the bed. The darkness descending on Büyükada seemed also to descend on his bronzed calves. *How far away from sagging and wrinkling that body is, and how beautiful,* Fehmi thought.

Through the window Fehmi saw one of Deniz's legs tense—and a computer screen appeared. Though his eyes had aged, Fehmi had no trouble at all seeing the penises and vaginas on the screen, in their hardest and most engorged states, plunging forcefully into and out of one another.

Deniz was also enjoying the most private moment of his evening, and he too had locked the door so as not to be bothered. Like every other young man at this special point in life, he had a passion for masturbating at every opportunity, rubbing out loads like he was wishing on a magic lamp. Deniz was overtaken by this passion many times a day. His obsession with masturbating was on par with the frequency with which his neighbors took their blood pressure pills. In the morning: right upon waking up. In the afternoon: wherever he may be at the moment. In the evening: just before dinner. And sometimes right before going to sleep: a nightcap . . .

Deniz thought he'd achieved privacy by locking his door. But he was mistaken. On this island privacy was not won by the locking of doors. Though he had no idea, a set of eyes had caught him on the verge of a pit of pleasure.

This set of eyes, eyes narrowed in sodomizing delight, watched Deniz, taking in deeply the ecstasy and the hysteria of this intensely intimate moment. Fehmi had no intention of missing a single second of the scene.

He shuddered in fear and pleasure.

Deniz sat up slightly in bed to lower his shorts even more and lay back down. The man and the woman continued fucking on the screen, pounding rhythmically as if tenderizing meat. Fehmi watched as Deniz's right hand began moving faster, accelerating just like his own heartbeat.

Tick! Tock! Tick! Tock!

Deniz kicked his shorts off from around his ankles. *Now he's totally naked*, thought Fehmi. *That firm bubble butt grinding down into the sheets.* The bare legs in the window were bouncing, drawing small arcs, their rhythm growing more violent.

Tick! Tock! Tick! Tock!

Fehmi's weary heart had quickened, his constricted breath coming out almost in grunts. The lilac color of the evening twilight fondled his face like a pair of cotton shorts. His nose practically filled with the scent of the fabric softener on those shorts, their thick elastic wrapping around his neck, the bony feet of a young man pressing against his face. And suddenly an electrifying jolt passed through his lower body; a feeling he had long ago forgotten. A strange pulsing sensation pattering to life in his loins. Did he really still have life down there?

Did he ever. He had desire, born there in the groin, the smoothest flesh on the body, spreading from the tiniest of his blood vessels through the rest of his body, squeezing him like a vise. He had breath, he had love, he had lust . . . They had suddenly unfurled within him, revealing to him what may have been their last remaining vestiges.

He once again turned his eyes to the opposite window behind the curtains.

Deniz was tracing little circles with his knees, slowly tensing his legs and pushing his feet toward the edge of the bed. The hushed gasps and groans that even Deniz didn't hear spill from his own lips resounded in Fehmi's ears like a rapturous orchestra. Cellos, saxophones, drums, violas, sixteen-men choir, bass baritone tenor! Deniz's rhythm quickened, quickened, quickened, and with a forceful jolt, lurched in release. Fehmi was about to become party to that magnificent moment, that crescendo of the orchestra, when . . .

"God damn it!" screamed Şener.

Fehmi spun around in terror, and found himself still alone in the darkening room. It would be impossible for Şener to come in; the door was locked. When he parted the curtain and looked back out, the lights were on and the door to Deniz's room was open.

He had left.

Şener was standing over the stove, where the milk he'd been simmering to make pudding had boiled over in a moment of absentmindedness. The whole stove was a mess, covered in the white liquid. The kitchen's pristine order, disturbed by the gentle smell of burnt milk. Şener looked with disgust and disdain at the drying film of white goo on the stove, touching the sticky fluid with his fingertips and wiping it away. He clasped his hands in front of him and shouted upstairs, "Fehmi, darling! No need to worry! The milk boiled over. You keep working up there!"

Taking a sponge from the sink, he began wiping the stove. He was annoyed with himself. "How could I be so careless? I look away for one second and it suddenly decides to boil over. Damn milk." He simply couldn't bear such domestic mishaps, especially ones like this that caused him such a commotion.

He returned the stew he'd prepared for dinner to the stove to warm. A gentle murmur could be heard from somewhere far off, like an old, familiar song ringing in his ears.

He had set the table on the veranda, prepared the salad, and left the fruit in bowls of ice to cool. As he continued stirring the stew, he drew aside the small lace curtain covering the kitchen window to peek at the next house. The new neighbors were also having their dinner on the front balcony. Cem and Berna appeared on the balcony with plates and glasses in hand. Şener withdrew from sight for a moment, then stepped back to look at them again. It'd be difficult for them to see him; the honeysuckle growing next to the window would protect him from their wandering eyes.

"They're having pasta again tonight," Şener muttered to himself, petulant. "She must not be much of a cook." Several weeks had passed since they became neighbors, and nothing had yet really given him reason to be annoyed at them. They were calm, quiet people who kept to themselves. The man always left early and came home late. The woman usually spent time at home, either reading on the veranda or napping in the hammock on the balcony. It didn't take much to grasp that she was keeping some kind of watch on the boy, though Şener had no idea why. On some mornings, as Şener made breakfast, he'd see her running to catch the ferry. Apart from a few small hellos exchanged during their chance encounters, they hadn't spoken at all. *I haven't been very welcoming at all. I suppose I've even been a little rude,* thought Şener.

He turned off the stove, took the pot, and called upstairs as he made his way onto the veranda. "Fehmi, darling, no more work. Dinner's ready. Come along!"

The magnificent summer evening had engulfed the veranda. The languid scents of the flowers, especially the honeysuckle, would accompany their dinner. The planters filled with four o'clock flowers had been carefully arrayed on the side of the veranda facing the other house, concealing their intimacy behind a curtain of flowers well past four o'clock. Şener dished out the food, and as he returned inside with the pot in hand, he was met at the door by Fehmi.

"What's wrong, Fehmi dear? Don't tell me you're sick. You're red as a beet!"

"I'm fine, it's nothing," Fehmi grumbled, sitting down. Şener returned with a bottle of cold water and glanced again at the neighboring house. The three members of the family sat in silence eating their food. Nobody talking to anybody else, their faces staring down at their plates. On other nights when he'd peeked behind the curtain he'd seen them silent as well. *They're unhappy,* Şener thought. *Families that eat their dinners in silence are always unhappy.*

"What are you looking at?" Fehmi asked dourly.

Şener collected himself at once. "Nothing, Fehmi, sweetheart. I was just lost in thought." He sat down and began eating. He tried to make sense of Fehmi's weird, admonishing tone. *He must be hung up on something,* Şener thought, consoling himself. Fehmi had been acting so strange, so preoccupied of late. Şener was terrified at the prospect that Fehmi was falling mortally ill, but he chose not to say anything. Silent, he tore a piece of bread from the loaf of whole wheat and began dipping it in his stew.

As he ate his food, Fehmi glanced at him for a brief moment and they exchanged a look: brief, indescribable, and impossibly significant. Fehmi looked at the man across from him, eating his dinner in front of a curtain of flowers, with a pity he'd never felt before.

An old man, trying with utmost care not to smack his lips, eating stew.

Fehmi felt for an instant like he was entirely alone on a deserted island, like he was a castaway coming to the realization he'd never be rescued from here. Like he was a prisoner, hopeless but for the prospect of the guard's mercy. But the guard doesn't see him; he just keeps eating his stew.

And so Fehmi began to eat his stew, too.

That night, they didn't say another word to one another until they finished dinner. Just like all the other unhappy families across the world, eating their dinners in silence.

THE WEED AND THE BLACKBERRY TART

The blackberries in the dish glimmered like purple sapphires as Şener picked them up one by one and began carefully placing them with assiduous symmetry atop his freshly-baked tart, like a bride putting her dowry in order.

He was so happy doing his little chores.

And he was so happy that his life was so big he could fill all his time with little chores.

He was happier sifting the flour for this blackberry tart, preparing the custard he would fill it with, and arranging the blackberries like a work of delicate embroidery than he had been at the height of his fame, when thousands of bottles of champagne were opened on his behalf.

His hands trembled as he swaddled most of the tart with blackberries and it was as if they swaddled his heart as well. Şener looked proudly upon his work. Another thing done exactly as it ought to be.

The blackberry tart looked marvelous. He cut it in two,

placing one half on the cake stand and leaving the other on the kitchen table for Fehmi to eat. He wrapped a cardigan around his shoulders and grabbed the cake stand, then opened the door and went into the yard.

The workmen had come an hour and a half earlier, measuring dimensions for the gazebo and attempting to dig a hole. They would have their work cut out for them. This addition to their backyard hadn't been tended for years, and the leaves the plane tree dropped every winter had rotted, effectively turning the future site of the gazebo into a bog. The hole had to be dug deep, dried out, and filled again with concrete.

Şener's nerves were already on edge over these setbacks. Worst of all, he couldn't meddle in any of it.

Fehmi didn't want him poking his nose into the work. "I want to take care of the gazebo's construction, Şener. I won't stand for your meddling with the workmen, your grumbling, your needless interference. If you'll agree to those terms then we can begin, or else I'm out," he'd said. Fehmi had made the definitive gesture he always used when he really wanted something as he spoke. He *definitively* didn't want Şener involved.

For Şener, though, it brought up an old, meaningless nightmare. Their relationship dynamic was often plagued by a gendered division of labor, and though Şener always tried to brush off jokes about it, the presence of the workmen and the issue of the construction made it no laughing matter to Fehmi.

"Meddling," "grumbling," "unnecessary interference . . ."

Şener knew all too well what these euphemisms meant, that they gestured at the reason he wouldn't be allowed up to the construction site. It wasn't himself personally that was unwanted around the gazebo, but the feminine role he'd been assigned in their relationship. *Do I really give it away?* he wondered, that old feeling returning for him to fret over once again. No, he never gave it away. Especially around third parties, he was sure he played his role masterfully.

Şener was disappointed, but he wouldn't say anything, wouldn't have those arguments again. *Fehmi ought to mind his own business,* he complained inwardly. *All his gussying up lately, wearing cologne, exercising . . . He thinks he's young, has no idea he struts when he walks.*

Şener hadn't raised any objections during his discussion about the gazebo and about gender roles with Fehmi that morning, but as he got up from his seat and went up the stairs, he could restrain himself no longer. "You know already what I'm going to say, Fehmi, darling, but I can't go without saying it. Please don't let this be a repeat of the plumbing situation, which was your project and which I had to 'meddle' in to sort out afterwards. I'll never, ever forget for the rest of my life those two days we had to spend without a toilet," he said, and went into the bedroom.

He sat at the vanity in the bathroom for a while, making himself scarce even though he knew the workmen had come; he didn't go back downstairs until the voices all fell silent and he understood that he was alone at home.

Things had been weird with Fehmi already. They were sharing less with each other, and the time they spent together was suddenly punctuated with longer pauses, awkward pauses. At first Şener thought Fehmi might be sick but hadn't told him. He asked. "No, I'm fine," Fehmi replied. "I'm just busy with my translation, it's taking a lot of my time and attention." Attributing it to Fehmi's usual crabbiness, Şener decided not to pursue it, not to get on his nerves anymore. *God almighty,* he thought to himself as he primped in the bathroom mirror. *I'll leave him to it. He's an engineer after all, surely he knows how to pour cement in a hole.* It was decided. Bravo, Şener! As always he had made the correct decision, and his bratty attitude hadn't delayed in returning to him as a reward. Yes, Fehmi had disappointed him by throwing his femininity in his face, but at the very least he hadn't failed to display the courtesy to do it in advance. They'd had a coffee after lunch as a pick-me-up and discussed the gazebo at length, and Şener had taken the opportunity to calmly elaborate his thoroughly reasonable ideas.

But he still couldn't bear the tension much longer. He needed to share the anxiety the gazebo had given him all day with a woman, as soon as possible. What he needed was the scent of estrogen wafting in the air. To sit face-to-face with a woman, to share his problems without going into too much detail, to lose himself in idle chitchat ... What he wanted was the nymphic compassion only available from a girlfriend.

The long telephone call he had with Nil Erkutlar as he waited in the bedroom, which touched on a thousand and

one idle things, hadn't been enough for him. Nil Erkutlar
had of course only been able to pay so much attention to his
gazebo problem. "Hmmph, you're just like Cahide Sonku.
Washed up and lying in a gutter, isn't that right, sweetie?"
she joked, before telling him that a journalist was coming to
interview her and hanging up. She had, in short, sent him
packing from the get-go.

For that very reason, he decided to finally make a belated
visit to his new neighbor Berna Hanım, whom he had finally
concluded was an altogether seemly woman. But he couldn't
go empty-handed. The blackberry tart was for Berna. As far
as he could tell from behind the kitchen curtain, their new
neighbors were drowning, awash in a sea of pasta for dinner
every night, and they simply had to have a taste of his tart.

There in his kitchen, his peaceful refuge, Şener had
zealously prepared his blackberry tart like a monk in ritual
meditation. Never mind Fehmi wanting to keep him away
from the workmen . . . Never mind Fehmi calling Şener a
woman, saying he wouldn't understand . . .

But in the end, as ever, his blackberry tart turned out
perfect.

Fehmi found himself a place in the shade near the hole
the workmen dug, sipping lemonade from his thermos
as he looked out over the magnificent view. In truth, he
savored Şener's absence; he relished spending time with the
workmen, joining in their conversations about soccer and

women. Fehmi loved chatting with real men, sitting at the table with real men. Whether at the coffeehouse table, or the gambling table, or the drinking table . . .

He never had any fear about whether his sexual orientation might register or not. He knew that it didn't. He had always been masculine, his movements never gave anything away. He loved soccer, he knew about women, he understood the work of construction. Knowing about these three things was already enough for him to sustain a conversation with the average man. Fehmi was sure that Şener was more womanly, and so whenever he joined him in these kinds of environments, it made Fehmi feel tense.

And so he decided to turn the gazebo project into something like a solo vacation. The two workmen, a father and son who first addressed Fehmi as "Engineer Bey" before switching to the more informal "Brother Fehmi," were working in their sweaty undershirts under the searing heat of the sun. The father was in his fifties, with bulky biceps, swollen shoulders, and a slight belly. The son was lean but agile, a tireless young man. Father and son tussled playfully in the hole, jokingly throwing the rotten leaves at each other.

Fehmi was savoring the most beautiful moments of his day there alongside them. He watched the workmen toil, watched them tease one another, abetted by the renewed, subtle electricity that had been pulsating in his groin for the past few days. That gentle tingling, that tiny murmuring in his crotch, gave way to a little smile under his mustache. He was in good spirits. Very good . . . The lemonade Şener made was delicious; he had his lunch with the workmen; then he went back home for a coffee to appease Şener; he listened to Şener's suggestions, most of which he found totally ridiculous; and then he returned to the workmen with three large slices of watermelon, and the three of them ate their cold watermelon together.

What else could he need?

"Alright, Sadi Usta, it's too hot out. That's enough for today. You can pick it back up tomorrow," he called out. Sadi Usta used his thick wrist to wipe the sweat dripping from his handlebar mustache. He smiled at Fehmi, who was sitting in the small chair off to the side, his legs crossed, the broad-brimmed hat still on his head, chewing on his mustache as he watched the men work, sure that none of his gestures gave anything away.

"Thanks, Brother Fehmi. By God, I'm old now, it knocks the life out of me. Can't take too much of it. I'm not a hotblooded young man like you anymore," Sadi Usta said, extending his hand up to Fehmi.

With a nimble movement Fehmi grabbed the workman by his thick, hot wrist, which felt to him like a piece of meat cooked by the sun and by the hard day's work, and pulled him out of the hole. "You two go on, then, I'll take care of the equipment here and take back whatever needs to go home. Don't forget to come early tomorrow, all right?" Fehmi said, stuffing his hand into his pocket, pulling out a bill, and placing it into Sadi Usta's shirt pocket. "Get something sweet for the folks at home tonight." The man smiled under his heavy handlebar mustache and left with his son, leaving Fehmi alone.

Şener stood in front of Berna's door, holding the platter. He quickly scanned his surroundings first, looked over at his home. The four o'clock flowers were in just the right place; they revealed nothing. He knocked gently on the door. He heard the sounds of footsteps inside, and then a blond silhouette appeared behind the glass door.

The door opened, revealing Berna's perplexed face, which softened once she recognized him. "Oh, hello!" she said affably.

Şener replied with the same warm smile. "Hello! I made a blackberry tart using blackberries I picked from the garden today. I wanted to bring you some. It's been some time since you moved in, and I hadn't yet gotten the chance to properly welcome you. I hope I'm not disturbing you."

"No, please. You're absolutely not disturbing, please, come in."

Şener entered the cluttered living room. It was filled with newspapers, half-read magazines, and open DVD cases, and Şener glanced around looking for where he ought to sit.

"So sorry, it's a little messy in here," Berna said, hurriedly attempting to tidy up.

"No need to apologize. It's how houses are. Ours is always a total disaster, believe me," Şener lied. He could never imagine letting his house look like this.

Berna smiled as she brought the tart closer to her nose. "It smells incredible. I'm so curious to have a taste. What can I offer you to drink?"

"No need to go to any trouble. Whatever is easiest for you to prepare is fine by me."

Berna thought for a moment. "Would you like some jasmine tea?" she asked. "In our house Deniz drinks cola and Cem drinks coffee. I'm the only one who drinks jasmine tea, but I love it."

"I love it too."

"Then let me take you into the kitchen. It's a little cooler in there, and we can chat as I get everything ready to serve."

Berna chattered as she prepared the jasmine tea. "I can't really cook, or rather, I don't have the time. So the boys will just adore the tart. Deniz will love it, it really does look something else. In fact, I don't think I'll be able to restrain myself . . ." And like a misbehaved child she tore a morsel from the tart and popped it in her mouth. The crisp crust of Şener's tart dough immediately began melting in her mouth as she closed her eyes and looked lost in rapture. "Are you kidding me? It's marvelous."

Şener smiled modestly. "Oh my, it's nothing really. I do what I can. The best an old man like me can manage these days." The delicate, sweet scent of the jasmine tea in their mugs wafted up between them. "Is your husband not here?" Şener asked, taking a small sip of his tea.

"No, he hasn't come home yet. Cem's an architect. He's working on a very important project right now, so he keeps late hours at his office on the mainland," Berna replied, taking a forkful of the blackberry tart that sat in front of her.

"And your son?"

"Deniz went for a walk, he'll be back soon, I'm sure," Berna said, swallowing another large piece of the crisp tart.

After gathering the tools and equipment, Fehmi folded up the chair, put it under his arm, and began descending the steep path. It was so hot; the ground had baked in the heat all day, and the heat it emanated was already yellowing the grasses down the hill.

When he came to the midway point, whether because of the heat or because of his age, his foot suddenly slipped. Trying to grab onto something, he well and truly lost his balance and fell on his ass. He held back a swear and stood back up, flailing his arms. When he knelt down to look for his thermos, which had flown into the bushes when he fell, he noticed a slight movement in the small space between the bushes. Fehmi parted the bushes exactly as he had parted his office curtains and saw Deniz, sitting cross-legged, his back to Fehmi.

Fehmi was bewildered to suddenly find himself so close to the boy; he didn't know what to do. He had only observed this boy from behind the curtains and the flowerpots. He only managed to squeak out a shaky "Hello."

Deniz jumped at this unexpected voice, turning with a fearful look and coming eye to eye with Fehmi. He had no time to hide the thick spliff in his hand. He had no idea what to do, and glanced nervously around himself. Coming to this boring island from Istanbul, the boy had brought not just his passion for masturbation but also a little bit of weed, and the old man before him now had caught him smoking it.

"No need to be alarmed," Fehmi said. "It's my fault, I fell. I'm sorry." He paused for a second before continuing, "Don't worry, I won't tell anyone. We'll keep this our little secret."

That made Deniz happy. He extended his half-smoked spliff to Fehmi. "Here you go, then. If it's our little secret, then you should have some too."

Fehmi took the spliff from Deniz. How could he turn away this object that had touched the lips of the most beautiful creature on earth, a creature who had arrived like a beam of sunlight into his weary, monotonous life on the island? "All right, then. I used to smoke a lot. When I was your age I never went without it," he lied, and took a deep hit from the thick spliff.

As the hazy smoke spread through Fehmi's body and unlocked the doors in his brain, he wanted to leave not just his mind and his body but also his heart there among the bushes.

Berna erupted in laughter again at one of the stories Şener told her about the old ladies on the island when suddenly, as if an old memory had come to life before her eyes, she looked keenly at Şener. "I hope it doesn't come off as rude, but I have a question for you. I could be making it up, but . . ." She narrowed her eyes even more. "Might you be the pianist Şener Hürol?"

Şener blushed, turning his eyes away from Berna, and let out an embarrassed laugh. He didn't know quite how to respond. It had been a long time since anyone had recognized him like this.

His lack of an answer was all the answer she needed. "Oh my goodness, I can't believe it, you're really him," Berna exclaimed. She sat down at the table with two fresh mugs of tea. "When I was little, I must've been maybe ten, I went with my mom and dad to listen to you. I think it was in Harbiye . . . What was it called?"

"Melodi Music Hall," Şener replied.

Berna clapped her hands. "Yes! Melodi Music Hall. It was their anniversary. I was absolutely mesmerized when I saw you onstage. You were so handsome and so affecting that I couldn't take my eyes off you, not even for a second."

"Oh, my. You're embarrassing me. Those memories are long behind me now."

"Please don't be so humble, Şener Bey. I've never forgotten the image of you on that stage. I remember your voice that night too. I was secretly sipping from my dad's drink, he and my mom danced to your songs all night. My dad envied how my mother looked at you, but my mother wasn't the only one affected by you. A little girl, half-drunk, developed a crush of her own. I was head over heels for you for days afterwards," Berna said, laughing loudly.

Şener was blushing but he also relished everything she said. This only made Berna more excited.

"I really can't believe it. Who'd have thought years later I'd be next-door neighbors with my first childhood love? Anyway, though, why didn't you keep making music?"

Flustered and not quite knowing how to reply, Şener took a sip of his tea. "After a while, I didn't want to be on the stage anymore. I was so tired of nightlife, and when my mother passed I came into a fair bit of money. I didn't have to work anymore and we bought this house here on the island."

He realized suddenly that he'd spoken in the plural, and supposed the jig was up. He took another silent sip of his tea.

Berna hadn't thought to trouble her guest by asking about Fehmi, but now that he had broached the topic, she began asking, rather cordially, "You and the other gentleman . . ." but couldn't bring herself to finish the sentence. Unlike the other women on the island, she opted not to dig into the subject—the first to leave the question unfinished.

"We're friends. We've been friends for a long time. Now we're supporting each other and living together through our twilight years," he replied, using the same evasive answer he always kept at the ready.

Fehmi was pretty high by now.

"So do you smoke much?" he asked Deniz.

"No, not really. I got some from my friend before they imprisoned me here. Sometimes I'll have a little bit."

Fehmi nodded. Deniz got up from the grass and sat on the stone next to Fehmi, offering him the spliff again. As he drew in more smoke, Fehmi felt his body thoroughly relaxing. He turned his gaze to look at Deniz sitting next to him, glimmering like a statue of gold under the burning light of the sun.

He stared at Deniz, and Deniz stared off at the distant horizon. Side by side, they were so close their legs could touch, if Fehmi wanted. *God*, Fehmi thought, *he's so beautiful. The most beautiful thing I've ever seen.*

He wouldn't be able to bear the silence and the beauty for too long.

"So then, do you like Büyükada?"

"No way. What's there to like? I'm bored out of my mind."

Fehmi looked at him with understanding in his eyes and said, "Being young is one of the most difficult things in life." Deniz turned to Fehmi, his blue eyes dark as the sea seemingly brimming with thousands of different interpretations of those words. Fehmi scratched a stick at the ground as he continued. "You don't fit in anywhere, you always want to go somewhere else—but don't you dare think things will change wherever you end up going. Everything ends up the same there, believe me. I'm telling you this as an older brother. Rest assured."

Looking back at him, Deniz replied, "I think you're high. Your eyes are bright red." He laughed and took one last drag of the spliff before stomping it out with his foot.

While the men sat on the hill overlooking the neighboring

house, sharing their little secrets and giggling as they smoked, other secrets were coming to light at the kitchen table in Berna's house. Berna explained to Şener the story of their coming to the island, telling him that Deniz got mixed up in something bad without going into the gritty details about the knocked-out teeth or the blood-soaked cafeteria.

"Such a shame, Berna Hanım. He's a young man going through puberty. The craziest age for a boy. I hope Büyükada does him well and he gets his act together."

Berna nodded sadly. "Şener Bey, I wish he would . . . But he sees our time here as a prison sentence and keeps blaming us for it."

Şener felt true pity for the woman sitting across from him. Ah, men. He wanted to tell her that they're always like this, but he restrained himself. Whether young or old, nothing ever really changes. "Try not to give him too hard a time. The more you push him, the more he'll rebel."

Berna reacted with an earnest smile. "How good that you came. I go into the city twice a week, I'm also starting to get bored here myself. I'm so glad to have met you."

Almost on cue, the kitchen door opened and Deniz came inside.

"Welcome back, Deniz, sweetie. Do you remember Şener Bey? He's our neighbor," Berna chirped.

Deniz was surprised to see one of the inhabitants of the home next door after smoking out the other man who lived there, but he kept up appearances. "Hello," he said, taking a cold bottle of water from the fridge and chugging it.

Berna and Şener both looked admonishingly at him for chugging the water, for not using a glass to drink it. "Deniz, darling, you'll catch cold like that," Berna said.

Deniz looked wearily at his mother. "Okay, Mom. I'm not a kid, you don't need to stick your nose in everything," he replied, when suddenly he saw the blackberry tart on the counter and made toward it as if hypnotized.

Smoking the spliff had given him an unbelievable craving for something sweet, and he grabbed a big slice of the tart and shoved the whole thing in his mouth. "Deniz, sweetie, a plate . . ." Berna said, but before she could finish her sentence, he'd swallowed the whole thing and begun gnawing on a second piece.

Şener had intuited by the kid's red eyes and his unsteadiness that something strange was going on, but when he saw how Deniz shoved the tart into his mouth he was certain.

The kid had smoked marijuana. Having spent his life in nightclubs and in a thousand and one different scenes, Şener would recognize the eyes of the stoned anywhere.

Poor woman. Must be so hard dealing with that good-for-nothing stoner of a son, he thought to himself. "If you'll excuse me. I've taken far too much of your time, and Fehmi Bey has probably come home by now. See you again soon," he said, standing up. He kissed Berna warmly on the cheeks. He extended a cold, pedantic "good evening" to Deniz and walked to the door.

"The tart is great, thank you very much," Deniz muttered as he swallowed the second slice.

Şener smiled and went outside. Pulling his cardigan tight around his shoulders, he crossed to the wooden fence between the two houses, opened the gate, and entered his yard. Surely Fehmi was home by now. *I hope to God there's no more problems with the gazebo,* he thought as he walked in. He heard a clatter coming from the kitchen.

Draping his cardigan on the chair, he called out, "Fehmi, are you home, dear?" When he entered the kitchen, he found Fehmi huddled at the counter, his mouth full, his eyes bright red, and the tart dish completely empty.

Just like what he'd witnessed of Deniz at the house next door . . .

He felt a strange, inscrutable shudder pass through his body. *No way, you're making things up.*

Fehmi! Marijuana! Deniz!

Mustering as much gentleness and maternal energy in his voice as possible, he asked, "What's going on, Fehmi, darling? What happened? I see you've finished the whole tart."

Fehmi shrugged listlessly. "Nothing. I was just hungry."

Şener felt in that instant almost like a key had clicked in a lock.

He watched Fehmi continue wolfing down the tart, happy as a clam, and then passed into the living room without a word. He stood in front of the window, looking outside. A strange sensation was bubbling up in his stomach. It was something he'd forgotten, something whose very existence he hardly had any awareness of anymore. But it was like riding a bicycle. After you've felt it once, no matter how many years go by, when the right conditions emerge, you realize you're feeling the exact same thing.

A feeling.

The concurrence of the weed and the blackberry tart brought Şener back into contact with that feeling he'd forgotten years ago. For the sake of their forty years together, he would try once more to forget that feeling, to set himself to the little chore of making dinner. But that feeling had leapt out from deep within him, heavy, vague, muffled, with a startling "Hello!" Now that it was there, it had started eating away at him from inside, and he knew that it wouldn't stop.

What was it? What was this thing whose name he'd forgotten, muddying up the waters? What was this feeling that had come and gone, leaving his blood pulsing with something sour, something acidic?

This feeling's name was doubt.

THE MOONLIGHT BALL

The haut monde of Büyükada had been eagerly awaiting the big night.

Gossip from the Moonlight Ball would wend its way through conversations long into the snowy winter, but for now, preparations for the ball had been underway ever since the women of Büyükada had received their invitations.

After trying on at least 184 different outfits, the women had chosen their gowns for the night from the fanciest boutiques in Nişantaşı, Şişli, Etiler, and Bağdat Avenue. Most of the invitees had chosen dresses from off the rack. But the women who were on the board of the Büyükada Beautification Association or who were members of bureaucratic circles would wear couture gowns specially made by the finest fashion houses in Istanbul like Ferda Baharzade, Mustafa Valentino, Yıldırım Tailorhouse, and Tarık el Payet. All the dresses hung in garment bags that looked more like clear body bags, awaiting the moment these women would squeeze their ungainly bodies, addled by diet pills, into their unforgiving seams.

And the day had finally arrived.

Muammer, the best hairdresser on the island, had to call for backup from the hairdressers he knew in Istanbul to fulfill all his appointments. The withering heat from the hair dryers amplified the heat outside by what felt like fifty degrees.

Against the constant clamor of blowouts, gossip, and waxing-induced shrieks, hair was teased, foreheads were graced with falling sheets of aluminum foil, peach-fuzz mustaches were threaded away, and makeup was receiving its final touches. Muammer the hairdresser spent the entire day knocking back mug after lightly sweetened mug of Turkish coffee.

Having sought every opportunity to stave off the evening, the men were now obliged to tighten the ties they hadn't worn in years like nooses around their necks. They had all long since forgotten the agony of wearing ties. Their discomfort only served to remind them of the time they'd wasted at their companies and their banks and in the highest ranks of their glorious army.

With final preparations underway in every home on the island, the women chided their husbands to no end.

"Look, Hulusi, this better not be a repeat of last year. If you're going to drink that crap, do it in moderation. You embarrass me every single time."

"I wonder if Nalan Hanım and her family are at one of

the back tables? Those tables are cheap, sweetheart, they're there so everyone gets a place to sit."

"Your tie is loose, Necdet. I shouldn't be able to see your top button."

"What do you think, how fat do I look? I lost a kilo and a half but still couldn't get rid of this belly."

Once everyone had donned their silk dresses and silk ties, horse-drawn carriages bedecked in white tulle arrived like bridal coaches to pick everyone up from their homes, to take these families and their silks to the Anatolia Club. Those who hadn't been invited watched with curiosity and admiration as the crowd of guests arrived, while the tourists on the broad terrace of the Splendid Palace Hotel photographed the men in their starched, collared shirts and the women made up in a thousand and one shades of lilac and mauve and pink as they rode by in their carriages, immortalizing their memory in archives neither they nor anyone else would ever care to look at.

The carriages dropped the guests off at the beginning of a narrow stone path illuminated by candles. As the husbands and wives entered the garden at the end of the path, they were welcomed by tables arranged under the branches of the magnolia and pine trees. Arrangements of orchid and lavender sat at the center of the white tablecloths, their aroma competing with the scent of the magnolias. Candles burned in silver candelabras, flames trembling gracefully under the moonlight, and the stars in the sky refracted off the plates, dancing points of light on the flatware and the crystal glasses.

The level of pomp and circumstance at the clubhouse could be conveyed solely by words like *silk*, like *crystal*, like any word with a French *ch* in it.

Enchanté, champagne, panache, amuse-bouche . . .

All the tables were oriented toward a small stage in the middle. Many years ago, Atatürk himself had danced with young women on that very stage. Those memories had become the photographs that adorned the walls of the clubhouse.

The pianist on the stage, a consummate professional, paused at all the right moments to allow the attendees to sing along.

"Oh, God, did you love him, did you love him, did you love him, more than me?"

The special guests of the Büyükada Beautification Association yelled the lyrics to the song like it was an anthem.

Although the Moonlight Ball meant something special to everyone assembled, it was ever more meaningful for one of the people attending that night. Having bid his farewell to performing many years ago, Şener now took to the stage but once a year to play a special set for the Ball.

Getting onstage always brought back to life those feelings he'd left behind many years ago. Numbed by the fog of alcohol, everyone looked at Şener like he was an oracle, like he was the divine himself. Onstage, he was alone with his piano. He and his piano, like god and prophet. They had descended to the earth for this moment alone, had returned to inculcate their disciples into a brand-new religion.

Come on, one more time: "Oh, God, did you love him, did you love him, did you love him, more than me?"

Şener was once again at the top of his game tonight.

Wearing a tailored, peak-lapelled tuxedo out of respect for his audience but beyond that for his art, Şener was so dashing tonight. The attendees should be repaid in kind, he thought, for their donations to the orphanage. He laughed warmly from the stage and caught the eyes of a few women in the audience without averting his gaze, coyly flirting with everyone and capturing even the most hardened of hearts.

But the spectacle of his looks and his performance was for one person alone.

For his one and only Fehmi, who sat at the frontmost table. For the only other man wearing a tuxedo that night. For the secret they had kept hidden from everyone for forty years, on a night like this when everyone came as a couple. Because the only difference between them and the other couples was that they couldn't throw their arms around each other to the music, couldn't hold hands and sing along.

Oh, God . . . nobody could love another, nobody could love another, nobody could love another, more than they loved each other.

There was something exceptional about the Moonlight Ball that particular summer. Fehmi, Şener's "friend in retirement," wasn't Şener's only guest. After many entreaties to the Association, he had managed to acquire invitations for three more people, a family he'd just met but to whom he'd taken an immediate liking. Under normal circumstances, Berna,

Cem, and Deniz wouldn't have had a chance at finding tickets to the Ball that night. But as the star of the evening, Şener found an invitation for them, paid for their tickets out of his own pocket, and sent them to Berna with a note that read, *I'd be so pleased if you'd come.* He flatly refused Berna's offer of money, stipulating that the invitation was a gift. If Berna Hanım had money she wanted to give, she should donate it to the orphanage. Performing onstage that night was a gift Şener wanted to give her.

He kept casting an occasional glance from the stage at table number one in the front. Berna, excitedly listening to her childhood crush, was wearing a black gown that exposed her shoulders; her arm was slung around Cem, who sat bolt upright, his broad chest pulling his jacket open. They were savoring the night. After Şener finished his song, the garden erupted with cheers and applause; he heard Berna's voice among the cheers, slightly louder than the rest.

Table number one, where his special guests were sitting, was the table enjoying itself the most.

At the other end of the table, Fehmi raised his icy glass of rakı at Şener, beaming a deep love at him that nobody else would have recognized.

The only person at the table who wasn't enjoying himself, as far as Şener could tell, was Deniz.

As the final notes of the first act reverberated from the piano, Şener began speaking. "With your permission, dear neighbors, we're now going to take a brief intermission. In a little while, we'll pick up where we left off and sing the most beautiful love songs for the summer. Enjoy your dinner, friends!" He stood up from his stool to a round of applause and made his way into the dressing room arranged for him inside the clubhouse.

He took a sip of whiskey and began reading the cards on the flowers that filled the room. He happily studied each and every one of the cards offering heartfelt congratulations from the mayor, the governor, the gendarme commander, and Nil Erkutlar. *I guess I've missed the stage*, he thought. *Maybe I should've kept going? What would have happened if I had?* He shook his head silently. *No, it's good I stopped when I did. I couldn't have managed the stage and Fehmi at the same time. I chose my man; he's more important to me than the stage at Olimpia. I'm glad I chose him.*

Fehmi . . . Actually, though, where was Fehmi?

Every year he came into the dressing room during intermission, presenting Şener a bouquet and spending the short break with him holding hands and kissing. The only other witness to their epic love, attained with no need for anyone else, was the photograph of Mustafa Kemal Atatürk hanging on the wall in Şener's dressing room. The great commander was the only one who watched over their relationship; he looked kindly on their love, his eyes hiding secrets of their own.

Şener waited in his dressing room for Fehmi to come.

Five minutes . . . Ten minutes . . .

Stressed, he checked his watch. Not much time before he had to take the stage again. "Hurry up, Fehmi, what's keeping you? I'm going to go on late. It's not my style, it's rude to my audience," he muttered to himself, pouring another glass of whiskey.

Five minutes more . . .

Şener finished his second whiskey and, filled with malaise, began pacing around the dressing room. That strange feeling whose name he still hadn't figured out welled up again in his chest.

He checked his watch once more and left the dressing room, passing through the clubhouse's wide corridors and entering the yard to look for Fehmi.

Şener didn't allow the main course to be served during his performance, but by now they were almost finished, and the clattering of forks and knives, together with the murmur of the rather drunk islanders, filled the garden. Some of the attendees had gotten up from their tables to chat with friends at other tables, and the measured respect they displayed during Şener's performance had vanished. He scanned his eyes over the bustling crowd in the garden and still didn't see Fehmi anywhere.

He began walking toward table number one, where his guests were seated.

It wasn't such an easy task. Everyone kept stopping him to shower him with words of praise or have their pictures taken; some of the women, finding refuge in the impudence of their drunkenness, tried to kiss him.

"Ah, Şener Bey, you are magnificent."

"Şener Bey, my darling, you get better and better with every passing year. Like a fine wine."

"Şener Bey, can we take a selfie? I'll tag you on Facebook. Thank you so much."

This is why I should never leave the dressing room at intermission, he thought to himself, accepting their congratulations and their praise with humility and posing cheek to cheek for photos.

Navigating through the veritable dam of fans blocking him from the table, he finally arrived at number one. Most of the chairs were empty, and Fehmi wasn't at the table either. Şener slowly sidled up to Berna and Cem, who sat arm in arm. "So, how are we doing? Are we having fun?"

Berna lifted her head from the crook in her husband's neck and turned to look at Şener. "Şener Bey, you are unbelievable!"

Cem excitedly extended his hand to shake Şener's. "Şener Bey, thank you so much for this perfect evening. Unlike my wife, I've never gotten to listen to you before today. And boy, have I missed out."

"Oh, you're embarrassing me. It's nothing more than a washed-up old singer trying in vain to relive his glory days," Şener replied, his hand still in Cem's. He looked at the table from the corner of his eyes, seeing the empty space where Fehmi sat and the untouched plate of food sitting in his place. He leaned in to Berna. "Please forgive me, Berna Hanım. Do you know where Fehmi Bey is? Have you seen him?"

Berna glanced about, confused. "He was here when you were performing. I didn't notice he was gone. Is something the matter?"

"No, no. I just need to tell him something. Where did he go, I wonder?"

"Perhaps he's in the restroom. If you like, Cem can go look," Berna said.

Of course! The restroom. Surely he went to the restroom, Şener thought. After so much drinking it was nearly impossible that Fehmi could be anywhere but the restroom.

"No, don't worry about it. I'll take a look. Enjoy the rest of the night," he said, leaving them at the table.

The time he'd normally return to the stage had long since passed. Şener hated breaking his routines, so he moved quickly through the garden and went to the restroom in the clubhouse.

The men's toilets were completely empty.

"Fehmi Bey. Fehmi Bey? Are you in there?"

Not a sound from the stalls.

"Ah, Fehmi, I can't believe you. Where'd you disappear to?" he said under his breath, exiting in front of the clubhouse and making his way to the area where the swimming pool, the largest and fanciest on the island, open exclusively to club members, was found.

The farther away he got from the front yard where the tables were, the more the roar of the party was replaced by the chirping of the crickets. The broad leaves of the magnolia trees blocked out the moonlight, but the Japanese garden lanterns adorning the back garden cast a gentle glow.

Fehmi wasn't in the first section beyond the main garden either. Şener ran into a few waiters shirking dinner service, joking and smoking cigarettes instead. Seeing Şener, the waiters fearfully flicked away their cigarettes. Under normal circumstances, Şener would have given such transgressions a gentle dressing down, but in his hurry he overlooked them. He offered them a smile as he passed, crossed a small bridge and continued past the pool, through the trees, and toward the area where the historic wooden elevator was.

The trees had grown quite dense by now. From the main garden rose the occasional sound of the women's perky laughter.

Şener reached the foot of the wooden bridge. The historic wooden elevator, painted green, was at the other end. It was still in use despite its age, serving to lower guests slowly down to the pool so that its well-to-do members wouldn't tire themselves out on the stairs. Peering from the copse of trees at the foot of the bridge, he saw the shadow of a human form in the middle of the bridge, clouds of smoke dissipating overhead. His old eyes couldn't help but recognize this silhouette, a silhouette he'd known for many years.

Fehmi was looking down on the pool, silently smoking his cigarette underneath the trees.

Şener was overjoyed to see Fehmi, but he was also a little miffed at the love of his life. *Ah, Fehmi, darling. I guess you came here to hide your cigarette from me,* he thought, taking a few steps onto the bridge until he reached a point from which he could see down to the pool.

He was about to call out "Fehmi!" to the silhouette, to

recite that name that he'd said like a prayer so many times for so many years, but he decided to swallow it.

In fact, he forgot every word he knew, even his own name, even where he was right now. Because he was witnessing a moment that would alter the course of his fate.

Down in the pool, illuminated only by the moonlight, someone swam and splashed, and Fehmi, cloaked in darkness, blowing his clouds of cigarette smoke, was watching this person. Şener took a few steps backward, quietly taking hold of the railing, and peered down at the person Fehmi was watching.

Şener wanted to exhale all the breath from his old lungs, to be left without air and die. In that instant he wanted to die, nothing more than to die.

For the moonlight leaves no secret in the dark.

The person swimming in the pool, splashing in the black of night, was Deniz. Watching Deniz in the darkness, Fehmi had eyes for nothing else, and so didn't notice Şener there. But Şener was painfully aware of everything now. The day with the blackberry tart, that inscrutable feeling of doubt—it had grown and grown and grown and finally, like a festering wound, it burst.

He finally understood what had made Fehmi so flat since the new neighbors moved in. But now nothing was flat anymore; to the contrary, it was choppy as the rippling waters in the pool where someone swam under the moonlight.

Şener felt a knot swell in his throat. He wanted to scream,

to shout, to howl like a wounded animal, but he couldn't. He wanted a storm to emerge, a hurricane to spin to life and swallow the whole island, that pool, all the families laughing happily together, all the wives and all the husbands, everything gone in an enormous whirlwind. He wanted balls of fire to rain from the heavens, wanted one of those wayward celestial bodies in the galaxy to fall right down on Büyükada, right down on the pool of the Anatolia Club, and he wanted the boy to be decimated into nothing more than a cloud of dust. He wanted the tables above and all the people around them to be ruined by unhappiness, wanted the rakı glasses to shatter and turn into a thousand piercing, bloody shards, and he wanted everyone to slit one another's throats with those broken glasses, to bury these razor-sharp shards in one another's chests.

The betrayal he witnessed lit flames inside him that were only just beginning to burn.

My man . . . my husband . . . The person I've devoted my life to . . .

Was this it? Was this all of it? Was this all it came to?

Was this the reason I've had to put up with weeks of grouchiness, of temper tantrums, of fights you started over things so small they wouldn't even fill the seed of a fig? Was this the reason you had your nightcaps on the veranda alone, in secret, without waiting for me? Was this the reason you went on all those walks without me? Was this the reason you barely registered a sound in response to my questions? Was this why you suddenly started combing that messy hair of yours? Was this why you changed colognes, started moisturizing too much, shaved regularly every day?

Was the reason for all of this that piece of shit in the pool that you're fucking with your eyes?

He felt the whole island lurch beneath his feet. It was like the earth was boiling, wobbling; it was like a fault line had opened up, eager to swallow all their experiences and all their memories together. The magnolia trees had lost their scent, they would never smell the same again, and the vaulted sky above began to spin. He held onto the bridge's railing hard, practically digging his nails into the wood. These eyes had witnessed the death of his mother in his arms, had witnessed the loss of his most beloved friends, and yet they saw his bitterest fate in the face of a man watching a boy swim in a pool. He, that man that could be summarized, in short, as nothing more than a man . . . That man . . . *My husband.*

My husband loves another man.

When Şener saw Fehmi take a few steps back, he also retreated, stumbling behind the trees.

Deniz had finished swimming his laps of love in the pool and emerged, soaking wet.

He was bare naked.

Under the moonlight, the lithe young man glistened like a marble statue. Deniz's wet, shining, raw form made Şener feel like every sag in his body, every line and wrinkle and blemish etched like an illness onto his flesh, down to the tiny liver spots on his hands, was the burn of a ciga-rette stubbed out on his skin. *My God, he is so beautiful,* he thought. Young enough to come out victorious in every struggle, beautiful enough that no other living thing could compete with him.

Beautiful enough to steal the person I love more than anything from my hands. Beautiful enough to make me experience every sorrow on the face of the earth in the briefest fraction of a second.

Wiping away the tears that suddenly appeared with the back of his hand, he tried not to make a sound as he rushed back along the way he came. He ran through the trees. Approaching the upper section of the garden, the laughter, the whispers, the clinking glasses pierced into him. As soon as he got to the top, he quickly stopped into his dressing room, immediately pouring himself a large glass of whiskey and swallowing it in a single gulp. His breath was quickening, and his heart pulsed with the terrifying drumbeat of a death march. He leaned in front of the mirror, and as he waited for his breath to return to normal there was a knock on the door. Someone spoke in a measured tone. "Excuse me, Şener Bey. The stage is set. Everyone's waiting for you."

He had taken the stage after so many horrible things had befallen him. He was an artist from an earlier generation, one who believed the curtain falls for nothing. But tonight . . . Tonight the curtain had closed on him like a flag draped over a coffin. He emerged from his dressing room breathless, as if caught by the thick, knotty weight of the curtain, as if the curtain were in fact a fisherman's net. The star of the night, who had only just seen his husband in love with another, walked out of the dressing room like he was ascending the gallows, and the photograph of Atatürk hanging on the wall had been his only witness.

His teeth chattered and his hands trembled. *God, please don't let me faint,* he prayed, arriving in a garden so brightened by artificial light it seemed like daytime. The spotlight was at full power and caught him at the door. It followed him everywhere, like his own shadow, and for the first time, the spotlight, which he was as accustomed to as the sun itself, dazzled his eyes with its energy and force. Squinting, he stepped into the garden, where he was surrounded by applause, whistling, and bravos from the people seated at the tables. The applause, the whistling, the bravos felt suffocating, like the hand of a murderer wrapping around his throat. Mustering all the might he could, he managed to plaster a smile on his face. The only choice he had for now was denial: *Nobody can notice. Nobody can realize. Nobody can know that my husband doesn't love me anymore, that he's in love with someone else.*

Raising his hands to quell the applause, he walked over to the piano. With practiced movements he pulled out the stool and sat down. He placed his fingers on the keys of the piano, which sat before him like a black, shining ship. *My piano, my oldest friend. The only witness to my love and my damnation.* As the applause abated, his hands began dancing across the keys, moving almost independently of him.

Without realizing it he had begun playing "How Beautiful the Sea."

This song . . . This pitiless song . . . This decree of death.

Why was he playing this song, pressing hard on the keys as if to channel his rage into the piano? Among the thousands of songs in his repertoire, why this one? He had no idea why he was playing this song, just like he didn't know why he had chosen Fehmi over all those other men who had chased after him. But he wouldn't sing the lyrics. He couldn't sit before Fehmi and sing "How beautiful the sea, how I run through its waves now." He wasn't going to praise the sea's beauty—Deniz's beauty—especially not in front of all those people sitting before him.

After finishing the song whose lyrics he couldn't sing, the audience erupted in wild applause. Listening to their applause, Şener discreetly wiped away his tears with a graceful flourish of his hands. A lifeless expression on his face, he turned to the audience and nodded at them.

His eye inevitably landed on table number one. He was there . . .

Taking heavy gulps of his rakı, Fehmi looked back at him, that poisonous smile on his lips. His gaze, which had looked back at Şener with love for so many years, was now besmirched by the filth of betrayal.

Fehmi's eyes no longer concealed the lie.

Deniz sat next to him, his hair still wet. Watching the stage, his sharp eyes full of petulance and cunning.

Fehmi raised his glass to Şener. Şener turned his head away quickly and began playing another song. He sought refuge in the lyrics in order to forget that look, forget Fehmi, forget what had happened, what he'd just seen at the pool.

He sang from memory and played from memory. As soon as he finished that song, he began playing another before the applause had died down, trying to keep the performance as short as possible. He wanted this night to end. This suffering to end. A sharp pain shot through his head. All he wanted was to fall into bed and cry, but he couldn't. He was imprisoned here, among the silks, the crystal, the silver, the magnolias.

Just then, one of the waiters approached, handing Şener a small slip of paper. Taking the note, Şener recognized the handwriting right away. Fehmi had sent it. He'd written it with the fountain pen Şener had given him for their anniversary.

My love . . . I'm sorry I didn't come to your dressing room. I got an urgent phone call and I'm sorry I had to leave you alone for the first time ever this year. I'll make it up to you when we get home. I just have one request, my dear. Tonight is sweet little Deniz's birthday. In a little while the waiters are going to bring him a cake. I know you can't stand these kinds of things, but would you sing Happy Birthday for him? Please . . . I love you more than ever. Your darling, Fehmi.

Şener thought, *This has to be a joke,* and glanced at table number one. It was, alas, no joke.

A flurry of activity surrounded Berna, Cem, Deniz, Fehmi, and the other high society seated at table number one. The crowd assembled there, of which he was no part, looked like a family having dinner, and he was nothing more than a little servant fresh from the village attending their needs. A servant peering through an open door and seeing how much merrymaking all families and lovers have together . . .

And suddenly the lights illuminating the garden faded and the waiters appeared with a cake festooned with candles. The applause swelled. Berna wrapped her arms around Deniz, an expression of joy and pride on her face, and Cem placed his hand on his handsome son's shoulder as the waiters approached table number one.

Fehmi's eyes, though, were on Şener. He gazed at him as if begging. What Şener read in his eyes was not love but a mere plea. *Please, please, don't let me down*, his eyes seemed to be saying.

Şener looked at the keys of the piano. Which note was he supposed to play? Which song was he supposed to sing?

And before the young man seated at table number one blew out the candles on his cake with a single blow from his healthy lungs, Şener's hands wandered across the keys as he leaned slowly closer to the microphone.

With a tremble to his voice that only betrayed lovers could hear, he began mumbling the words to the most well-known song in the world.

"Happy birthday to you . . . Happy birthday to you . . . Happy birthday, dear Deniz . . . Happy birthday to you . . ."

AFFLICTIONS

He simply couldn't lift his head from the cool pillow.

Over the course of the past few days he'd been sweating bullets in bed; he changed his underwear and sheets twice a day, took his vitamins regularly, consumed plenty of fluids, practically swallowed cloves whole, but he still couldn't get out of bed. A headache, a sinister and relentless headache, had plagued him for days on end. He rubbed lavender oil on his temples, but they still thumped harder than a techno club.

Boom boom boom. Silent, deep.

The words he couldn't bring himself to say made his throat swell up. His nose ran; he shivered, trembled, sweat, vomited, slept, awoke, and ached. All his symptoms came on at once. Summer schedule. "What's all this in the middle of summer, dear? You namby-pamby old princess," Fehmi laughed the night before Şener became fully bedridden.

Fehmi the traitor, the coward, the liar, the fraud.

He had no idea whatsoever that it was all his fault. All that mattered to him was shaving every day, rubbing cologne on his sagging cheeks, putting on his finest clothes, gussying himself up, going outside or else stealing into his office under the guise of working . . .

The guise of working.

When Şener thought again about what Fehmi was doing locked away in his office, he lurched from the bed, suffering yet another cold sweat. His temples were throbbing with pain.

The first thing he did the day after he witnessed the rueful scene at the Moonlight Ball was check Fehmi's office. As soon as Fehmi went to play bridge, Şener entered the office, and when he parted the curtain, he saw across the way the window of a room whose occupant it was not hard to guess. He understood with perfect clarity now what Fehmi was doing locked in his office every day, whom he was peeping on to the sound of his psychotic metronome. *Maybe it's just a coincidence, maybe I'm wrong*, he thought for a moment, seeking refuge in his devotion to Fehmi. He had to be certain.

The only way to be certain was to take complete control of the situation.

The first step was to change the curtains. The green curtains in Fehmi's office were replaced by thicker, dark blue ones. He'd draw Fehmi's attention if he only changed the curtains in the office, so he changed them all, from the living room to the kitchen, from the terrace to the cellar, replacing each with the dark blues. Fehmi glared at him with uncomprehending eyes, but because they never argued over home décor he left Şener to his own devices. He had more important things to do, of course, than argue with Şener about curtains.

In the boiling summer heat, Şener's face was dripping sweat as he went up and down the stairs, washed the curtains, ironed them, and hung them up.

He hung the blue curtains with such meticulousness that only he would be able to notice the slightest millimetric change in their position, and as soon as Fehmi left the following day he checked and found them out of place. He fixed them again, and checked them again. The curtains could not hide Fehmi's furtive perversions, for the fabric was always out of place.

Next, he started looking for other pieces of evidence. He went through Fehmi's notes. After so much "work," Fehmi's translation had gone nowhere. He was still at the very beginning, but in the notes he'd taken on the characters Şener could read the traces of youth, of secret desire, of wayward attention. Fehmi was trying to create a brand-new character. A character full of life and passion.

It was clear who the muse was in all these character sketches. Going through the trash in Fehmi's office, he found little sketches dedicated to that muse. Pencil drawings, all of a young male body, sketched almost unconsciously in the margins of his discarded notes. Tiny shorts; hair on the nape of a neck; thick ankles; young, sinewy, athletic muscles . . .

In none of them were Fehmi's two leering, lascivious eyes to be found.

If Şener went to the doctor, the doctor would explain to him that his affliction had been caused by wearing himself out, working too hard; no doctor, of course, could see into the depths of a heart. The affliction that laid him out in the middle of summer was caused by something else entirely.

The momentary hate he felt after seeing them at the Moonlight Ball had quickly passed, replaced instead by another feeling: he had loved to death.

That was the true affliction that had consigned Şener to bed rest.

The affliction appeared after that harrowing day, conspicuous as a cancerous tumor, manifesting itself with as much malignancy as possible. It began in his heart and quickly metastasized to his brain. Every fold, every lobe, every molecule was now brimming with Fehmi. It was driving him thoroughly insane—worsening at full speed at a time when Şener should have been aging comfortably—destroying his internal organs and bringing him past the point where treatment would do him any good.

For Şener's forty years of affliction by Fehmi were just as fatal, just as lacking in remedy as stage five cancer. Şener's was a case in need of palliative care, of doctor's observations, even of lethal injections that would put an end to the pain.

He was certain. Yes, absolutely certain. He had no doubt that there was something between Fehmi and the young boy. It was something sexual, though certainly not physical.

Because ultimately one was a beautiful boy and the other an old man . . . Even if Fehmi tried, Şener thought, the boy would refuse him. Whatever it was that was happening between the two of them, what hurt Şener the most was that the doors had been closed to him. Fehmi was experiencing this all on his own, didn't want anybody else involved. It was not just a betrayal after their forty years together; it was an enormous secret that had come between them.

Had Fehmi come to tell him about this passion, Şener might have been able to bear the heartache, and, if nothing else, he could have listened to Fehmi, tried to understand him, tried to persuade him that it was an impossible situation. But Fehmi went on like nothing had happened, like things were normal, like his dinners still tasted the same.

And so if Fehmi wanted to keep quiet, then Şener, who was nothing if not proud, would opt to keep quiet too. Because no matter how much he loved Fehmi, pride was his other chronic affliction, and he would never bring himself to force the issue.

In fact, he was afraid to bring it up with Fehmi.

He feared that the conversation would have other, bigger, direr consequences. Because one had to be young to argue over jealousy like that. If he were twenty-five, perhaps, if he had only just begun living, he would have chosen to confront Fehmi and face the consequences, but what now? Much to his chagrin, he was simply too old to do so.

For the first time in this phase of his life Şener felt regret that he was no longer young.

But despite everything, Şener continued to maintain his routine with almost religious fervor. Meals, gardening, cleaning: all was as it had been before. Fehmi, having always been careless and inattentive, of course had no idea that Şener knew about Deniz. If he paid the slightest attention, if he looked more carefully into Şener's eyes, he might have understood. Understood how worried Şener was, how broken, how much sorrow roiled in the depths of his eyes.

Nor did Fehmi realize that he was being watched now as well. When Şener wasn't cleaning the counters, watering the garden, ironing, and cooking, he spent all of his time thinking about Fehmi and Deniz, trying not to miss even the smallest detail of Fehmi's betrayal.

The inhabitants of these two neighboring houses spent all their time with their eyes fixed on others. Berna watched Deniz, Fehmi watched Deniz, Şener watched Fehmi and Deniz, and Deniz watched the porn on his computer . . .

As the summer heated up, so too did each of their afflictions and each of their voyeurisms.

Şener noticed that whenever Fehmi and Deniz coincidentally crossed each other's paths, they greeted each other more warmly. When Deniz was out kicking the soccer ball at the dead tree, Fehmi always managed to be on the veranda pretending to read the paper. He always drank his nightly gin and tonic in the wicker chair that looked over the other side of the fence. Şener realized Fehmi never passed up an opportunity to talk to the boy next door. Worst of all, this affliction had given Fehmi renewed vitality, a lust for life.

He was no longer like the old man he'd been. He took care of himself, never neglected his exercises, sang along to the loud music he played, laughed loudly on the phone with his closest friend Halit, and chirped about like a baby chick.

The more Şener noticed Fehmi's temperament improve, the more he collapsed. The Şener whose mettle had been the object of envy disappeared, replaced by a feeble old fart. He felt like he had aged ten years in the span of a week. He wanted to spend all day in his pajamas; he no longer ironed his linen pants before going to the market; he floated around listlessly. His head was so full of other things that he neglected his twice-a-week exercises. Never mind the exercises; he hardly had the energy to even lift a glass of water. He stopped combing his white hair, which had always kept him looking debonair, and stopped shaving as well. His face was collapsing under the weight of pain and unhappiness; dark circles appeared under his eyes for the first time. The liver spots on his hands doubled in the span of a week.

And finally, that namby-pamby old princess became bed-ridden. He had been totally conquered, knocked out cold, by his affliction, an affliction the doctors called summer flu but which was in fact the affliction of Fehmi.

Silently rubbing his temples, he dragged himself out of bed, put on his cotton robe, and exited the bedroom. Passing by Fehmi's office he impulsively turned the door handle. The door was locked. Without so much as batting an eyelash, he continued down the hall and went downstairs. Nobody was home; total silence reigned behind the closed curtains of the living room. He had last seen Fehmi a few hours ago, when he was about to leave to play bridge, and he remembered saying to him, "Darling, please draw the curtains tighter." By some miracle Fehmi hadn't forgotten, and the curtains hung drawn tight.

He stood in the darkened living room. He didn't know what to do. All he knew was that he hurt, that he felt pure agony.

Tears suddenly began falling from his eyes. Though he didn't quite understand why he was crying, his tears deepened his pain—which only multiplied his tears. He went and sat on the nearest seat, the piano stool. Crying became sobbing. He closed his eyes, not wanting to see or feel anything, and wept. The more he cried the sorrier he felt for himself; the sorrier he felt for himself, the more it hurt; and the more it hurt, the more he cried. He was alone, entirely alone. Without Fehmi the house was completely empty, silent as a grave.

What if he left him?

Şener tried to control himself, but the more he thought about such things the more he cried.

Swallowing his sobs, he opened the lid on the piano's keys. He unconsciously played a few notes. They echoed in the silent house, affording him a little bit of comfort. His piano, his most faithful friend . . .

He began freely improvising on the piano. He wanted to remember the good old days, days when he was as beautiful as Deniz, days that seemed to exist a century, a hundred million years, in the past. He thought about the handsome young engineer coming to listen to his performances when they first started dating, looking up at him from the front table with excitement in his eyes and a lion's mane of a mustache that hadn't yet gone gray. Did he gaze upon Şener in those days with the same admiration with which he now looked at Deniz?

It had been a long time since he'd played for himself alone. Since he did everything for Fehmi, Şener only played the piano when he asked. Fehmi had been his muse and he hadn't felt the need for any other. He could have been so successful if he wanted; with his talent he could have ascended to become the most acclaimed pianist in Turkey, in all of Europe even. Instead he had chosen to shut himself away in a mansion on Büyükada, had chosen to cook dumplings for the island's well-to-do. He knew how alluring fame was, knew how attractive his money would have been to so many men, especially young ones. Had he continued in his profession, he could've filled this house with so many beautiful boys like Deniz. After all, nothing was easier to procure than pleasures of the flesh.

Now, though, he would play for himself alone, here at home. He imagined himself sitting in front of hundreds of pairs of eyes on the stage of a music hall, wearing a navy-blue suit. Just like the old days . . . So many beautiful women, clad in their finest jewels and open-backed dresses, their bare legs, the high heels on their feet, jewel-encrusted hands waiting ready and eager to erupt into applause over the song that would come out of his mouth . . .

The air around him seemed to fill with the smell of whiskey and clove cigarettes. He played the first notes of a song he loved but hadn't sung in years. Even with eyes closed, he knew everyone in that imaginary auditorium was holding their breath. Everyone admired him, had fallen in love with him, and he sang his song for all the lovers, betrayed and otherwise, who watched him. He began singing at a low murmur:

"Bliss without you has no taste . . .

You, my fate, won't be erased."

The imaginary crowds roared with applause. He turned slowly, nodded his head in appreciation at the empty living room. One of the teardrops that began welling up in his eyes again fell on his hand as it played the piano. He didn't stop the music, but continued singing through the tears:

"I loved you from afar, you whom I adored

Now I know longing, and I shall come no more . . ."

The ring of the doorbell brought him back to reality. He closed the lid on the piano, wiped his tears away, and got up to open the door. Had Fehmi returned already?

He was startled to find Berna standing at the door. Berna started speaking before he could say anything: "I'm so sorry, I hope I'm not disturbing you. I wanted to bring back the cake dish, and I thought we could chat a little bit as well. But it sounded like you were busy working, so if now's not a good time I can stop by later."

It embarrassed Şener that she had heard him singing, but he kept it to himself. "No, no. Work? Goodness, no, I was just passing the time with a little ditty. Please, come in."

Berna came in hesitantly. "You were singing so beautifully. I was eavesdropping by accident," she said, handing him the dish. Şener didn't reply; he couldn't muster the energy to make his usual display of humility. "Are you okay, Şener Bey? You're not looking very well," Berna continued, worriedly.

Şener shrugged. "I'm a little out of sorts these days. I haven't been able to pull myself together."

Berna placed her hand on Şener's forehead. "You've got a fever, Şener Bey. Let me make you tea with lemon. You won't get better unless you take care of yourself," she said, taking Şener's arm and leading him into the kitchen. Şener was truly in no state to object to anything, and in fact it would probably do him well to not be alone.

The two of them entered Şener's spotless kitchen. Berna seated Şener at the table, put water in the kettle, and took two mugs from the cabinet. Şener gratefully watched his neighbor and the mother of his nemesis move around his kitchen. "So, how's everything going, Berna Hanım? Have you managed to get used to island life? Is the little one still as bored as he used to be?" he asked. He knew as he asked the question that "the little one," busy as he was debauching Fehmi with marijuana and driving him wild by playing soccer shirtless in the yard, was doing just fine for himself.

Berna replied wearily, "Things are even worse than before, Şener Bey. We've become outright enemies. He keeps talking about doing crazy things. He's gotten the notion in his head now that he's going to swim from Büyükada all the way to the shore at Bostancı."

Şener was shocked. "Oh my! Nobody could swim that far. It looks close but it's actually quite far."

"Believe me, I know. But he read on the internet that people have made the swim before. If things keep up this way, he's going to swim away." Distressed, Berna shook her head. "Deniz was on the swim team at his school in Istanbul. He competed in meets with other high schools. But that doesn't mean he can swim all the way to shore, of course." She placed the mugs on the table, then with a worried expression turned to look out the kitchen window. "I know he's doing it all to get on my nerves. That's the kind of kid he is. You tell him not to do something, he'll do it out of spite."

As he sipped his tea, Şener could read the anxiety in Berna's eyes. Her eyes were filled with that mad look that mothers have when they're too attached to their children, a look that appears when their sons go without permission to the corner market, let alone swim from Büyükada to Bostancı.

That was Berna's affliction. It had conquered her many years ago. The first symptoms lasted nine months, but it became a chronic affliction when a ball of flesh and bone weighing three kilos and six hundred grams emerged from her womb, demanding her full devotion and vigilance.

He understood Berna all too well. Every child shirks the extreme protectiveness of their mother, does things solely to get on her nerves. He thought about his own mother. When he first confessed his "special situation" to Rabia Hanım, she had lost her mind, threatened him, pulled every trick in the book to put a stop to it. The daughter of an old consul, raised by governesses and with roots that reached back to the Ottoman palaces, Rabia Hanım quite naturally considered the idea of having a flouncing, mincing man for a son to be a lethal affliction upon the honor of her family. Hulusi Şener, the twice-removed grandson of a grand vizier, likes men? How could this malady, this disgusting illness, have found its way into our family? Like Şener had been doing for the past week, Rabia Hanım had doused herself in lavender oil and stayed in bed, informing Şener in no uncertain terms that if he didn't give up on that repugnance then she would renounce him as a son.

But in the end, did Şener change, could he have given up on his nature? No, of course not. He left home the first chance he got, turning the piano lessons his mother had forced him to take with the finest instructors since he was a child into his profession and becoming a musician. Rabia Hanım would've considered even a government job to be debasing, and yet Şener replied to her threat by becoming a pianist and chanteur, by moving in with a man and having him as a life partner. To Rabia Hanım, that would have been as unthinkable as swimming from Büyükada to Bostancı.

They went years without speaking, until Rabia Hanım was on her deathbed, when they came together and forgave each other.

A bitter smile spread across Şener's lips.

"He's young, Berna Hanım. It's clear as day he's doing it all to get your attention. Not to mention you're leaving the island at the end of the summer, what would be the point now, with barely any time till summer's end?" he asked, and then repeated the question, wanting clear confirmation. "You are leaving at the end of the summer, right?"

"Yes, of course. We have to. Things have calmed down since the incident, and I need to get back to work," Berna replied.

Sparks flashed in Şener's eyes. "What incident?"

Berna could no longer keep it all to herself; she decided to tell her only true friend on the island about the "minor" scandal at the Alphan Preparatory Academy in all its gruesome detail. Şener listened in horror, his eyes wide with fear and disbelief, until Berna finished telling the story, interjecting only with the occasional heavy sigh. It wasn't clear whom he was sighing for, though. Was he concerned for Deniz? Or for Berk, who'd lost his teeth? Or for Fehmi, who might have his teeth knocked out too?

Standing at the window with the tea in her hand, Berna chirped, "Ah, they're coming!" as though the cure for the anxious affliction she suffered from had been found. She ran through the door from the kitchen to the yard and waved her hand. "Deniz, I'm here," she called out.

Şener walked on shaky feet into the garden and stood beside Berna. When he saw Deniz and Fehmi approaching together in the distance, his eyes went wide in astonishment, and then his lips let out a little scream. Fehmi, carrying a loaf of whole wheat bread under his arm, had gotten rid of the mustache he hadn't touched for twenty years, and he was now climbing the slope with a smooth face that shone like the moon.

Şener's observations were indeed true. Fehmi now thought himself a young man; he simply couldn't accept his true age. After playing bridge that day, he had gone to the island's barber on a snap decision and told the barber, who always gave him the exact same trim, "Shave my mustache." The razor slid across the roots of his mustache hairs with a scratching sensation that put him at peace, and Fehmi saw, for the first time in twenty years, the area above his lip.

"You look at least ten years younger, Brother Fehmi," the barber had said to him. Fehmi relished the compliment, leaving the barber a tip that was the same amount as the haircut and shave. He bought some bread, and as he climbed the slope he ran into Deniz, who was returning from the beach.

"Damn, dude, no more mustache. Looking good," Deniz told him. "Mine's only just coming in."

Fehmi looked at Deniz, seeing a few darker brown hairs among the blond peach fuzz that he'd clearly shaved a few times. Every time he saw Deniz he had the same thought: *My God, isn't he beautiful.* "Don't worry, yours will come in soon enough," he told Deniz.

Deniz shrugged indifferently. "Nah. The girls like it better this way. Doesn't scratch them when you're kissing."

After meeting Deniz that summer, Fehmi had developed an obsession with youth and beauty. It was as though he was trying to cast off the years lost or carelessly wasted, and if he couldn't turn back time then he could at least fight against it. He thought about all the men in Istanbul who had been his colleagues and friends. They had all gone through midlife crises, and there was nothing they didn't do to try to recapture their lost youth. Some of them began wearing earrings after they turned forty; others bought sports cars or even motorcycles. Without exception they had all gotten involved in little extramarital flings. Fehmi, on the other hand, had never had a midlife crisis, had never felt the need for one. Out on the island, he and the man he lived with were aging peacefully with every passing day.

Once Deniz arrived, his desire to be close to the boy whose room he watched from behind his curtains every single day brought that affliction belatedly to the surface. Fehmi believed he deserved his second spring.

A spring that arrives late is better than a spring that never comes at all.

Deniz and Fehmi ascended the slope and were approaching the house. While Berna looked on as her one and only affliction approached, Şener couldn't recognize the other affliction, his life partner, in the distance. The disappearance of his mustache seemed to mean the old Fehmi was gone, had been replaced by another man entirely. Şener felt like he was hosting a stranger for dinner.

Berna fluttered her hands. "Oh, Şener Bey, would you

look at that. Don't they look so sweet? Like grandfather and grandson."

Şener didn't hear her; he wasn't listening. He was certain now that he had to intervene before things went even further. He studied the approaching duo: *Yes, he's a beautiful boy. That's an incontrovertible truth. Could there actually be something going on between them? Maybe Fehmi shaved his mustache off so as not to damage the boy's beautiful skin when he kisses it.*

As Deniz and Fehmi grew closer to the old mansion, an idea came to Şener's mind, and it poured from his lips like he was talking to himself: "Perhaps you should send him to study in America?"

Berna, whose complete attention was locked on her handsome son, turned to look at him with confusion in her eyes. "Pardon, what did you say? I didn't quite hear you."

Şener repeated himself: "Perhaps, I said, you should send him to study in America? You know, so many families are sending their kids there for education. It might even do him some good."

Descending the steps of the veranda to embrace her affliction, Berna paused and turned decisively to Şener. "Absolutely not, Şener Bey. There's no way I could be so far away from my son." She smiled at Şener. "Well, we'll go now, you get some rest. We still have to eat dinner. We'd love to have you and Fehmi Bey over for dinner one night. Plus, by spending some time with Deniz, maybe Fehmi Bey can change his mind about his crazy ideas."

With that, she said her farewells to her neighbors. Fehmi

held open the gate to the yard and said goodbye to Berna as he entered. Berna put her arm through Deniz's and turned to wave to Şener on the veranda.

In that instant Şener and Deniz's eyes met. An expression full of jealousy, of unhappiness, of sheer helplessness, filled Şener's eyes. Deniz had seen that expression once before: in Berk's eyes, when they crossed paths in the hallway at school while Deniz was dating Melisa. They were the wild and helpless eyes of a person from whose hands something they loved had been taken. And just as had happened in that moment at school, on this hot Büyükada evening Deniz instantly recognized the hopeless look in those eyes.

Almost instinctively, he savored it. He became aware once again of his own beauty, and he felt in every single cell of his body the power he had to cause hurt to someone simply because he was beautiful.

Whatever there was between those two old men, the sissier of the two, the one with gray hair, was jealous of him. For weeks he hadn't noticed Fehmi's gaze, but when he saw Şener's eyes he saw that look, that look of disappointment and hopelessness.

Deniz took absolute pleasure in being the object of jealousy. He would think about that look as he jerked off to his favorite porn that night, and it would heighten his pleasure to no end. Even if he hadn't done anything himself, it got him off that someone could be so helpless simply because he was beautiful.

Thinking he could acquire anything and anyone because he was beautiful . . . That was Deniz's affliction.

And so, as his affliction manifested its symptoms, he began hatching a devilish plan in his head. Freedom from this island was in fact as close as the neighbors' house. He was surprised at himself that it had taken him so long to realize. As Şener looked down at him from the veranda, Deniz looked back, greeting him with a treacherous smile and a cunning expression in his eyes.

Şener wrapped his hands around the veranda's railing and lowered his head to the pot of hydrangeas, unable to bear watching the mother and her son going home. He could barely keep himself from crying. He pulled the weeds out of the pot, his motions filled with vengeance. When he raised his head he came eye to eye with Fehmi, standing there with no mustache and his loaf of whole wheat bread. Fehmi grinned. "Well, you haven't said anything. How do you like my new look, then?" he asked.

Şener turned around without saying anything, just going inside and slamming the kitchen door hard. He went straight to the bedroom, locking the door and throwing himself into bed, not to emerge for the rest of the night.

He had the most terrible, terrible headache.

CONFESSIONS

Despite all of Fehmi's begging, insistence, and threats to break down the door, Şener did not open the bedroom door again that night. Helpless, not even deserving of an explanation, Fehmi was forced to spend the night in the guest room.

For the first time in their forty years together, they slept not in the same bed, but in separate rooms of the same house.

Despite the hellish heat of the night, they both felt the glaring and bitterly cold absence on the other side of the bed.

When Fehmi awoke, he was stiff everywhere and the small of his back was sore. It had been a long time since his back had acted up, and he was not pleased one bit by the resurgence of the pain. It reminded him how old he was, and its culprit was the temperamental man in the other room. He was so livid that even if Şener wanted to come and talk he wouldn't have said a single word. He exited the guest room and descended the stairs. By force of habit he went straight to the table and realized it was entirely empty.

It was the first ever morning Şener hadn't woken up before him and prepared him breakfast.

Fehmi angrily filled the coffee machine, plugged it in, and sat down as he waited for the coffee to be ready.

He didn't know what he'd done to make Şener so upset. The strange thing was, he didn't care either. *He's jealous*, thought Fehmi. *Just jealous. He doesn't want me to have a life independent of him. As he likes it, then.* He went to the living room library, pulled a cigarette from the pack hidden on the bottom shelf, and lit it.

As he finished his cigarette, he noticed some movement in the yard. Despite the early hour, the workmen building the gazebo were climbing up the hill, each with a pack of cement over his shoulder. Fehmi stepped onto the veranda and called out to the workmen as they reached the turn in the path. "Good morning. You're early today," he greeted them.

"Morning, Brother Fehmi," said Sadi Usta. "Yes, brother, we thought we'd start early. Look, the sky over Istanbul is cloudy. I think it's going to rain."

Fehmi looked in the direction Sadi pointed, at Istanbul. Dark clouds had gathered over the sea, surrounding the city on all sides. There was a strange malaise in the air, a darkness to it. What a senseless day for a summer storm. "All right, you get started. I'll join you in a little while," Fehmi replied rather coldly, and went back inside. He didn't feel like working on the gazebo or listening to the workmen's banter. *I'll look over it a bit and leave them. I'm not in the mood today,* he thought, and climbed the stairs to change his clothes. He opened the door to the small laundry room and, unexpectedly finding Şener there, let out a little yelp.

Şener was at the ironing board, ironing clothes. He had clearly woken up early, and had made a lot of progress on the laundry. The basket beside him was almost completely empty and the folded laundry was stacked like a mountain on the adjacent chair. When the door lurched open and he saw Fehmi standing there, he stared back emptily, the iron like a gun in his hand. A puff of steam shot out of the iron. Like a hissing snake, shooting steam instead of venom.

Without saying a word, Şener continued with his chores. It was like a ghost had entered the laundry room, the spirit of someone who died many years ago.

His actions only served to make Fehmi even more angry. He decided to ignore Şener back, grabbing a random pair of pants and a random T-shirt and closing the door behind himself. But he underestimated the distance between the door and the frame as he closed it. The door slammed shut behind him.

The sound made Şener feel like the door had been slammed right in his face. Taking it as an affront, he opened the laundry room door only to slam it shut again, as hard as he could.

Fehmi had just put on his pants in the bedroom and was still bare from the waist up, but when he heard the second slam, he suddenly felt so much rage it might shoot out of his nose. He went to open the bedroom door and slammed it shut with an even greater force than Şener had. The glass in the door almost fell out of its frame.

Hearing the noise, Şener could no longer control himself. He went into the hallway, leaving the iron on the console, and entered the bedroom.

And finally there they were, face to face.

The two old lovers, the two great beloveds, found themselves now throwing down the gauntlet, face to face like they were at the Battle of Malazgırt, surrounded by Şener's gaudy tapestries.

Time now for the reckoning!

Fehmi stood erect, staring back into Şener's eyes which were fiery with rage. He put on his T-shirt without a word. He didn't speak but his gaze clearly asked: *What? What do you want?*

Şener stared at Fehmi, trembling with wrath at his cavalier attitude; it took all his will to keep himself from wrapping his hands around Fehmi's neck. "Get ahold of yourself and stop slamming doors," he hissed between his teeth.

Fehmi smiled a bitter grin and took a step toward Şener, leaning in close to his face; he spoke calmly, word by word, almost pausing between each syllable: "I'll do whatever I want."

Fehmi had formulated his reply solely to piss him off, and in response, Şener released the full force of rage it warranted.

"Of course, of course you will. There's no doubt about that. We know all too well that you'll do whatever you want, that to you there's no such thing as respect. Vile man. Shameless. Bastard."

Fehmi lunged at him and wrapped his hand tight around Şener's arm. "Talk straight with me. I'm not a child. What the hell are you trying to say? Why am I shameless, huh? Answer me, quit with your vague insults. Talk to me like a man, all right? Like a man!"

Şener struggled to free his arm from the vise grip of Fehmi's fingers but he couldn't. His eyes filled with tears of anger.

"Let go of my arm, you prick. I said let it go!"

Fehmi released his grip.

Şener began rubbing his aching arm. "So you want me to speak like a man, huh, is that so? Like a man . . . Because you, you're such a man in everything you do, you've got nothing to hide, have you? That's what manhood is, isn't it? Manhood: scheming behind my back, saying one thing and doing another as soon as my back is turned? You think I'm going to learn manhood from you of all people? From you? Shame on you. Shame on all the years I wasted on you."

The blackest of clouds continued to swallow Istanbul, and though Büyükada was still brightened by the daytime sun, the two old men in their old house had already begun throwing bolts of lightning at one another.

"What am I scheming behind your back, Şener? Tell me. Tell me so I know as well. Yet again you've concocted some sick and twisted thing all on your own and yet again something I don't even know I've neglected to do has pissed you off. So tell me then."

Şener took a step toward Fehmi and finally asked him the question that had laid him out for days on end. "What's going on between you and that boy, Fehmi?"

Fehmi was astonished and looked back at Şener with a vacant expression. "What boy?"

Şener sneered, his eyes fixed on Fehmi's. "Don't pretend you don't know what I'm talking about. That boy, Deniz . . . What's going on between you?"

Fehmi gulped. "There's nothing at all between us. You're making stuff up, pure fantasy. What could there be? He's just a little kid."

"Liar, you're a liiiiiiiiar," Şener erupted, lunging at Fehmi. "Liar, liar, liar," he repeated over and over, raining blows down on Fehmi. Neither of them had ever even entertained the possibility of physical violence in their relationship, and so when Fehmi got over his shock at the first blows Şener threw, he grabbed both of Şener's wrists and shoved him hard onto the bed.

"Get ahold of yourself! Are you insane?" he yelled.

Şener curled up in the bed and began crying. Straightening out his clothes, Fehmi stood and watched, perplexed and even a little afraid. Şener yelled at Fehmi between sobs: "I know everything. I saw you watching him in the pool the night of the Ball. Is that a lie too? Did I make that up too? I know you hide in your office to peep on him. I saw your drawings in the trash. And you smoked marijuana with him

too, didn't you? Did I make that up, do you think I'm stupid?"
Şener had stopped crying by now, and screamed with pure
rage: "I saw the way that kid eyed you yesterday! Even he
sees right through you! Even he knows what a pervert, what
a sicko you are! Even that immature, idiot kid gets it. You
should've seen the way he looked at me yesterday."

Fehmi stuck his hands in his pocket and walked to the
window, looking out at the darkening, surging sea. The sea
was not beautiful today, but terrifying. He turned back to
Şener. "Don't be ridiculous. So he looked at you. Don't you
feel ashamed of yourself, going into my office when I'm gone
and snooping through my stuff? Can't I have a single thing
in this house that belongs to me alone, without you having
to know about it? Do I really have to share every single thing
in my life with you?"

Şener leapt from the bed and moved closer to Fehmi.
"Don't change the subject, Fehmi. I wasn't just snooping
in your office for the fun of it, I took a look after I noticed
something weird going on between you two."

"Nothing is going on between us, Şener. What do you
think could be going on? I'm just being friendly, do I owe
you an explanation for that?" Fehmi was certain he was in the
right. "Regardless, that's not the problem here. The problem
is that you always feel the need to interfere in my life. I don't
have to live the way you want me to, by the rules you set,
spending my time only with the people you deem fit."

"You have feelings for that kid. I mean, just look at you.
You shaved your mustache, you're just a creepy, leering old

fart chasing that kid around." Şener began angrily pacing the room. "You think I'm the only one who notices how horny you've become all of a sudden? What if the other islanders take notice? Do you want everything we've kept hidden to suddenly come to light? Don't you know what they'd say to us?"

Fehmi turned and looked Şener in the eyes. "What would they say? What could they say about us that isn't already true? Because you know that we are, in fact, what they would call us. Accept it. 'That' is what we are."

Şener turned away from Fehmi. He couldn't bring himself to say "that" word. Fehmi continued: "And seeing as you're so curious, seeing as you've forced the issue, seeing as you want to hear it so badly . . . Then fine, I'll tell you: yes, I like Deniz."

A long, pregnant pause.

"I enjoy being around him, spending time together with him. But there is nothing sexual whatsoever between us. I'm telling you the God's honest truth. I don't know what I would do if there were anything sexual there. But I'm so tired of it all, Şener. I'm so tired of living in this house with you, eating your wonderful meals every night, smelling the flowers as I simply wait to die."

Şener's lips trembled as he waited for Fehmi to stop talking. His voice quavered as he spoke. "So you're bored, is that so? Tell me then, are you bored of me too?"

Fehmi didn't answer. He continued standing at the window, hands in his pockets, his back to Şener. "No answer.

So it's true. You're bored of me too. Shame on you, Fehmi. I guess everything I've done for you all this time hasn't done anything but bore you. I guess all of it was worthless enough to throw away the moment you happened to meet a beautiful young man." Fehmi couldn't bear it; he turned around and tried to approach Şener, but Şener recoiled. "Don't you dare touch me," Şener hissed. "I hate you, I loathe you. I loathe you and I loathe myself."

Fehmi cast an exasperated look at Şener. "Nothing happened between us," Fehmi barked, angry again. "Nor will it. I don't know what you're saying just because you're jealous and what you really mean. But you've become absolutely unbearable the older you've gotten."

Şener moved toward the door. "We live on an island, Fehmi, and you lost your mind over the first beautiful boy to come our way. I suppose if we lived in the city you'd have cheated on me every chance you got. Some things just shouldn't be so worthless. All this time I thought this house was a sanctuary for our happiness but in fact you've imprisoned me in a hell of a lie. Shame on you. I don't have anything else to say to you."

Şener paused for a moment, then stripped off his robe and his pajamas. He went to the closet and pulled out a pair of pants and a shirt.

Fehmi watched him vacantly. "Where are you going?"

Şener dressed, and went to the door without answering. Right before leaving, he turned to Fehmi. "I'm going to answer you in the manner you apparently want to be spoken to, Fehmi, darling. I've decided that if there's no longer anything intimate between us, then I'm going to keep living my life. I'm going to go have sex too, look at other men too. You do it, so why can't I? Seeing as having sex and getting your nasty old hands on young bodies is so important to you. Then it's going to be important to me too."

Fehmi was seething with rage and jealousy. He lunged at Şener. "I'm going to kill you. How dare you speak to me like that."

Şener grabbed the vase beside him and lifted it in the air. "Not one more step. I swear I'll throw it. Don't take another step toward me," he yelled.

Fehmi stared back at Şener, his eyes furious, his breath heaving through his nose. "Go ahead. Stop wasting time. The boys are waiting for you. See, this is exactly your problem. You can't stomach the idea that someone like Deniz would take an interest in me. You ask yourself, 'he did it, so why couldn't I?' You're jealous because Deniz is interested in me." Fehmi marched up to the door. Şener, expecting Fehmi to hit him, raised the vase again, but Fehmi didn't hit him; he opened the bedroom door.

He yelled at Şener, the resentment and disappointment clear in his voice: "Go ahead, then. Fuck off. Get the fuck out of here and go get your rocks off somewhere. Cruise the parks, turn tricks on the street, I don't care. You're an old cabaret singer, after all. You know all too well how to do it. Go. Trying to teach me lessons in honor, my God. Go ahead and fuck off."

There was nothing left to talk about, to discuss, to resolve.

Şener set the vase down silently and slipped past Fehmi like a gentle wind. Fehmi slammed the bedroom door shut. He sat on the bed where they had slept for forty years and took his head between his hands and began to cry. As his tears flowed, he heard the sound of the front door shut. He ran to the window. Şener was descending the slope on trembling legs.

The hurt and the anger settled into his throat. Watching Şener descend the slope, he saw bursts of lightning strike over the city of Istanbul, saw the darkening clouds moving toward Büyükada.

The storm was approaching.

THE STORM

Without quite knowing how the time had passed, Şener found himself in the middle of an Istanbul plunged into darkness early in the afternoon. He couldn't remember a single thing from the journey. When he got off the ferry at Kabataş, all he remembered was that the ferry, rocking like a cradle on the choppy seas, had made his stomach churn. His ears rang with the fury and the venom of the words Fehmi had yelled at him.

"Old cabaret singer."

"Get the fuck out of here."

"Go get your rocks off."

"Yes, I like him."

"I like him . . ."

"I like him . . ."

Perhaps it had been those words that churned his stomach, but he didn't want to think about the reason for things anymore. Did it matter, in the end? He was hurting, whether from the waves, the insults, or the confessions.

As soon as he disembarked from the ferry, a harsh wind blew a cloud of the city's billions of dust particles into his face. The island's bewitching scent of honeysuckle was replaced by exhaust fumes, the chirping of birds by blaring horns, his calm garden by the formidable momentum of the churning crowds.

He stood stock-still in the middle of those crowds.

The city was home to so many millions of people, and yet here he was, entirely alone. He had no friend, no mother, no father, no sibling to go to, no one whose door he could go knock on. *How strange*, he thought. Up until the moment he stood on the pier at Kabataş, he had never quite realized how gravely and profoundly orphaned he was in the world. The only person he had in his life was Fehmi, and with him gone now, he was purely and simply alone.

He hadn't yet eaten today, nor had he taken his blood pressure medication. Unsure what to do, he left the pier. His feet carried him on their own. He began moving through this most colossal of cities whose every nook and cranny he knew no matter how much he had tried to forget them.

He arrived at the slope that led up to Cihangir. So different now than the Cihangir of his youth. That was of course inevitable. Having himself grown ugly, wrinkled, decrepit, how could Cihangir have remained as it was? He had now become one of those clichéd retirees who wander Beyoğlu in a blazer and tie, men who had nothing to tell except the memories of their own vanished histories, men who always made him feel uneasy.

The force of the wind staggered him. The sky looked like it was on the verge of explosion. Though the rain hadn't yet begun, the clouds seemed to be moving as if readying for the perfect moment to release the poison they contained.

Two lovers ran past him, hand in hand, fleeing the approaching storm. An acute antipathy toward their happiness swelled inside him. In the home to which they were returning, they would take off each other's clothes, touch each other's damp skin, kiss. Everything that brought others happiness only now brought him deeper into his own misery.

He passed so many people on the slopes and side streets sitting at cafés or bars and enjoying themselves. Despite the impending summer storm, the whole city was noisily, laughingly, blusteringly partaking of the many pleasures life had to offer.

He, though, was merely a corpse. A living corpse. A walking corpse. A breathing corpse.

A lonely, abandoned corpse, not even worthy of a grave.

Deep down, he knew from the very beginning where his tired, weary feet were taking him. When he turned the corner onto that street he realized it once more. So many years later his feet had once again brought him back to that place he thought he'd put behind him for good.

History really does repeat itself. You can never flee your past; you carry the key to it with you always, and when you need it most, you can withdraw some of it from the vault of life.

And there he was, now, standing in front of his past.

Like him, the sign was weathered, its paint and its gilding worn away, and though he tried to avert his eyes, so many years later, he once again registered the word BATHHOUSE.

After Şener left, Fehmi sat in bed for a while, the malaise of the darkening sky suffocating him. He got up, opened the window. The blackening clouds were engaged in a playful, brisk dance in the skies over Büyükada, advancing toward and retreating from one another in lively movements. Fehmi took a deep breath and his eyes landed on the cityline ferry moving farther and farther away from the island's pier. The ferry was making another of its countless voyages through the rolling waves from Büyükada to Kabataş. A bitter smile spread across Fehmi's lips as he watched the ferry moving toward Istanbul. He knew Şener was on that ferry. From here, the ferry seemed to him a hearse, bearing the casket of their relationship to its final resting place. A white hearse, accompanied by a funeral procession not of vultures, but of seagulls.

Fehmi stuck his tongue out to pull his mustache into his mouth as he always did when he was annoyed or sad.

But his mustache was gone.

Şener was gone. His partner was gone. From this world he, too, was gone.

The wind blowing in through the window picked up

force. The trees that they had planted in the yard with their own hands and which were now taller than they were swayed in the wind like it was the middle of winter. He thought about the many winters he and Şener had spent in this house, all on their own. Winter months when they held each other under blankets and ate fruit together ... He remembered how much he would pressure Şener to play his favorite piano concerto, how he promised he would eat fewer sweets if Şener played it, and how Şener, in the end, would play it. Another bitter smile settled onto his lips. Was Şener really on his way to cheat on him? Was someone else going to lay on his chest, on those gray hairs that had always belonged to Fehmi alone? The very thought of Şener being touched by the ineffable ghost of another person was enough to rile up Fehmi's anger all over again. He slammed the window shut and drew the curtain over the vanishingly distant cityline ferry.

He pulled a raincoat from the closet, put it on, and went into the yard. The wind tugged at the flowers in the garden, running over the trimmed grass like a father's hand through his son's hair, washing the whole yard in dark ripples and shadows. Pulling the raincoat tighter around himself as he ascended the path behind the house, he snuck a glance at Deniz's house. All the doors and windows of the house next door were closed. For the first time in a long time that summer, he didn't want to think about where Deniz might be.

When Fehmi arrived at the site for the gazebo, he

found Sadi Usta and his son standing over the hole. The hole was full to the top with wet, sticky cement. The trees surrounding the site whispered in the wind as if trying to say something, their branches creaking as their trunks succumbed to the elements. When Sadi Usta saw Fehmi approaching, he set down the long rod he was using to stir the cement.

"We've finished for the day, Brother Fehmi. Depending on the rain, it'll take a few hours for the cement to dry. If it rains, of course, it'll take longer, but we used the highest quality cement for the foundation. Even if it gets wet, it'll still set no problem."

Fehmi looked affirmingly at Sadi Usta, the meaningless gaze in his eyes clarifying he had no interest in the matter. Sadi Usta was fond of Brother Fehmi, and though he recognized that Fehmi was in low spirits, he said nothing, nodding instead for his son to pack things up. "You all right, brother?" he asked Fehmi, stepping slowly closer.

"I'm good, Sadi Usta, thanks. Just a little out of it today. I'm going to go lie down. Leave it for now, we'll take care of the rest when the weather's improved. That's enough for today."

Sadi Usta and his son said goodbye to Fehmi and disappeared down the narrow path.

After the workmen left, Fehmi stood at the edge of the hole and stared blankly at the thick gray nothingness of it. The meaningless void of the hole looked more beautiful now than the towering trees that surrounded it;

more beautiful than the endless sea reaching toward the horizon, its dark waves almost writhing in their undulations. Looking at the hole full of cement brought him peace of mind.

A droplet of rain landed on his face, jolting him out of his reverie. The droplet landed right below his eye. If someone saw him now they might suppose by his sad expression and the droplet underneath his eye that he was crying. But Fehmi would not cry. He had no reason to.

He had nothing in this life anymore. In lives that contain nothing there is no reason to laugh nor to cry.

The droplets began falling with greater speed. Fehmi pulled the hood of his raincoat over his head. He wondered whether he ought to put a tarp over the hole but felt too tired to do anything of the sort.

Under the first rain to fall on the island that summer, Fehmi began descending the path in slow, measured steps. The rain mixed with the dry earth—roasted by the heat all summer long—to stir up its warm, fleshy aroma.

The scent of soil always reminded Fehmi of his childhood, brought him back to Erzincan, where he lived with his family when he was still a kid, to the yard of his house when it rained. He and his family would take refuge inside the hollow of a great tree, and he'd crawl into his mother's arms and breathe in that scent. The scent of the earth mixed with the scent of his mother . . . He realized that he hadn't been back to his hometown since his mother's death. What would happen if he went back now, to that city where everything had surely changed, where everyone he knew was now a grandparent, where none of his relatives remained? He had no city, no neighborhood, no home of his own. The place he was born had become as unknown now as a foreign country.

He entered the house and hung up his raincoat. Just then the rain abruptly stopped. Before closing the door Fehmi looked up at the sky, perplexed by the strangeness of the weather. The rain started suddenly and stopped just as suddenly and yet the sun would not emerge and plunge the island into the familiar heat of summer.

He quickly changed, putting on a pair of shorts and a T-shirt. He loved being at home in stormy weather like this. He put one of his favorite albums on the record player. As the soft melodies of the violin and the piano filled the wooden mansion, he poured himself a glass of whiskey. He sat down in the armchair and settled into watching the darkness descend, a false winter in the middle of summer. The first sip burned in his nose even as it soothed him. Right when he was about to put his feet up and bury himself deep into the music, a hard knock came at the door. Not expecting anyone, Fehmi was worried, then glad when he supposed that Şener might have returned.

The knock came at the door again, even harder. That wasn't Şener's knock. Şener would never pound at the door with his whole fist, but would merely rap a knuckle. "Fehmi. Are you there?" he'd say. "Would you open the door, please?"

These hurried, threatening knocks frightened him. Did something happen to Şener? He ran to open the door.

Standing in front of him, soaking wet, was Deniz.

Şener descended the steps into the entryway of the bath-house. He went straight to the counter without looking around and spoke authoritatively to the man. "A room, please," he said.

The tan, handsome young man didn't move a muscle; lifting his eyes from the sports page of his newspaper, he stated, "Rooms are full. There's lockers."

"No, I want a room. I'm sure you have one, go take a look," Şener replied, producing a hundred-lira note from his wallet and tossing it in front of the man.

The man took the money. "We have one room, but it's a little musty. You can have it if you like. If a better room opens up I'll move you there." He took one of the little keys from the wall and called to the kid sitting in the next room: "Ömer. Take the uncle to number sixteen."

The pimply, swarthy teenaged boy grabbed a peştamal towel from the closet, opened the door, and led Şener down a long, narrow, dark corridor. The air smelled of mildew mixed with the sweat, armpits, and feet of men. So intense it was almost tangible, the odor almost steaming, condensing on the ceiling and dripping on them as they passed.

The length of the corridor was lined with rooms, some doors open, some doors closed, some with men waiting outside only wearing their peştamals and leering at passersby. Peeking through the open doors, Şener saw men sprawled out on pleather massage tables, their peştamals cast aside, playing with themselves. The bathhouse was unbelievably crowded, and as they passed through the crowds they eventually arrived at room sixteen.

The service boy opened the door, set down the peştamal, and left. Şener looked gloomily at the filthy room with its moldy ceiling; there was nothing in it but the massage table, a little plastic stool, and hangers for his clothes on the wall. As soon as the service boy opened the door, room sixteen seemed to Şener like an upright coffin he'd nail himself into. *My bridal chamber,* Şener thought to himself, smiling bitterly.

Trying not to touch anything, he undressed slowly. He stood there in his snow-white undershirt and underwear. He took off his socks and put on the plastic sandals he was absolutely sure were teeming with fungus. Had he known he was coming here he'd have brought his own sandals. In fact, if his story were a novel, it would start, "Şener said he would bring the sandals himself."

After taking off his underwear and undershirt, he wrapped himself with the peştamal, which was clearly unclean and which had been used before by who knows how many men to wipe up their own sperm or the sperm of other men.

Rule number one for anyone going to a bathhouse: do not under any circumstances think about hygiene. When Şener left here, he thought, he would practically have to flay his own skin in order to feel clean again.

This was not the first time he'd come to this bathhouse. Long, long ago, before Fehmi had entered the picture, he came here quite often. This place was a refuge where men "like that," whether young, old, out, closeted, rich, poor, Kurdish, Turkish, or Circassian, would all meet in secret. Everyone knew exactly what happened in here, but outside these doors, it was simply a bathhouse.

Şener began walking down the shadowy, humid corridor. He met the greedy eyes of other men. Their looks barely registered him before turning to look elsewhere. The corridor was full of men trying to cajole, flatter, flirt, and feel one another up through their peştamals. But alas, nobody wanted to cajole, flatter, or flirt with him in any way.

Proceeding down the corridor, he crossed paths with a group of young men more flamboyant than the rest, putting on a show of their revelry to everyone else. One of the boys, the one with plucked eyebrows, flicked his hair as he passed Şener and leaned in close to his friends to giggle: "Eww! What are you doing here, grandpa? You're gonna give yourself a heart attack, girlie!" They all laughed at Şener.

He was embarrassed. He pretended not to hear. Old men, especially old men "like that," were always and everywhere the butt of the joke. When he was young he had probably said similar things about old men who were surely dust and bones in the ground now; he had laughed at them, mocked them to their faces. He had never imagined then he'd one day become one of them, but now here he was: the old man the twinks made fun of at the bathhouse. Unbeknownst to Şener, the baton had been passed to him.

When he entered the sauna he found the air sweltering: thick and sticky even as it was mentholated and dry. The unbearable odor of sweat and flesh made the air even heavier. The two rows for sitting were mostly full. The men in here sweated without end, their bodies practically melting onto the ground from the roots of their hair to the tips of their toes. He couldn't bear the heat, battling against it like his old heart might stop any second. Covered in sweat, he exited the sauna. As he continued wandering listlessly, he came upon another room where everyone was going in and coming out.

He walked to the door.

When he opened it, he found himself in his own personal Sodom, his own private Tribe of Lot in all its magnificent depravity.

Fehmi stood bewildered at the door, staring blankly at his unexpected guest. He was filled with strange excitement and bottomless fear. On a day like this when the weather was so temperamental, a midsummer day when a storm was about to erupt, a day that had witnessed his worst fight with Şener in all their forty years together, seeing the kid who was responsible for all of this startled him. He felt like a little girl, opening the door to her closet in the middle of the night, only to find a handsome prince on the other side, beckoning her into another world. "Deniz? Hello. What happened?" he said, unable to contain his perplexity.

Deniz was enraged and frustrated; he sounded like he was on the verge of crying. "I got caught in the rain. I was on the beach, my mom called. She's in Istanbul today. She went to work. She kept calling me to say, go home, there's a storm coming." Fehmi sensed something strange in the way he talked but couldn't ascertain exactly what it was. "We fought, I told her to leave me alone. She kept yelling. I got mad and kicked my bag, it fell in the water. My keys were in it. All the doors and windows are locked. I'm stuck outside." He paused and asked with as much innocence as he could muster: "Can I wait here until my mom comes home, Brother Fehmi?"

"Of course, Deniz, no problem. Please come in," Fehmi said.

Deniz came in and closed the door. He followed Fehmi in, his eyes fixed on the back of Fehmi's neck, a look on his face like that of a predator sneaking up on its prey, readying for the kill.

"Make yourself at home," Fehmi said, gesturing at the living room. "Let me bring you some dry clothes." He hustled up the stairs.

Waiting in the living room, Deniz realized this was the first time he'd seen the inside of this house since his family had moved to the island; he began looking around the living room, filled with the sound of the piano and violin concerto playing on the record player. Even to Deniz's young, inexpert eyes, the arrangement, order, and feminine details of this house where two old men lived didn't go unnoticed. It reminded him of his grandmother's summer house in Amasya. Cushions, drapery, the orderly library, the piano shining in the corner ...

He noticed the framed photographs along the shelf and began examining them. One of them contained a large portrait of Fehmi during his military service. Next to it was a similar-sized photograph of the other man—was his name Şener?—playing the piano in the living room. He picked up another picture frame. It was a photograph of Fehmi and Şener, both quite young, standing side by side on a beach. The sun shone bright on their faces; they squinted their eyes and wrinkled their noses as they looked back at the camera. It looked like the other man was almost resting his head on Fehmi's shoulder.

Deniz smiled and put the frame back. He took off his wet T-shirt, took one of Fehmi's cigarettes from the side table, and lit it. Hearing the sound of footsteps, he turned to see Fehmi entering the living room with a T-shirt and shorts.

When Fehmi saw Deniz standing in front of the pictures and smoking a cigarette, naked but for his tiny swim trunks, he didn't know where to turn his eyes, how to avert his gaze. "You'll have to get by with these until your clothes dry," he said, handing Deniz the clothes. Fehmi made for the kitchen, both so Deniz could undress privately and because he couldn't bear the raw embodiment of sex and vitality standing in his living room, but Deniz called to him.

"Hey, I don't need a T-shirt. I'll just towel off. My shorts are dry anyway so I don't need to change out of them either."

Fehmi came back into the living room and stood there shifting his weight, unsure what he should do. The piano and violin concerto which so suited the winter months made him feel nervous at the height of summer, even despite the stormy weather. "All right, then, as you like it, whatever you say," Fehmi said, about to take a seat. "Oh, pardon me. I forgot to ask, what can I offer you to drink?"

Deniz smiled, settling into the three-person love-seat, and took a pillow into his lap. "Well, I'd love some whiskey, Brother Fehmi." Fehmi wracked his brain, indecisive and uneasy over the mortal risks of giving whiskey to someone so young, but Deniz continued. "I really love whiskey. My mom of course won't let me have it. Beer, sometimes . . ."

Had Fehmi not slept in a separate room from Şener last night, they would have had the opportunity to tell each other about the inconsequential goings-on in each of their days, and Şener would have no doubt relished in telling him the whole story Berna told him about Deniz, the story of whiskey and teeth and Alphan Preparatory Academy. But, alas, such is life. Not knowing any better, and despite his own misgivings, Fehmi poured two glasses of whiskey and handed one to Deniz. "Cheers," Fehmi said.

Deniz smiled. "Cheers to you too," he said, and they raised their glasses, the ice cubes clinking menacingly.

Fehmi began speaking in an admonishing, if friendly,

tone: "It's not good that you threw your bag in the water, Deniz. Your mother will worry. We can call her if you like, just so she won't have any reason to worry."

Deniz took a large sip of his whiskey. "Man, forget it. I'll tell her when she gets back," he replied. Fehmi didn't know how to comport himself before this half-naked boy; his legs bounced restlessly. It was Deniz who broke the silence. "So, the other guy, he's not home?"

The question reminded Fehmi of Şener, who had vanished from his mind the moment Deniz showed up. A shudder ran through him as he thought about Şener. "No, he's not. He went to Istanbul."

Taking another sip from what was left of his drink, Deniz smiled. "Oh, nice. So we're alone. That guy's not very nice to me. He's not like you." He was looking at Fehmi with as much charm and as much lust as he could muster.

Under normal circumstances Fehmi would have been flabbergasted by this flirtatious if meaningless pass at him, but the argument earlier, combined with the afternoon whiskey, had slightly numbed his feelings. He stared back at the boy, somewhere between daze and reverie.

Unrelenting, Deniz nodded his head at the photographs on the shelf. "You and Şener Bey . . . What are you? Are you relatives, or what?"

Fehmi gulped quietly. "We're old friends. We're living together to support each other through our old age."

Deniz didn't insist. "Oh, that's nice. Well, in that case, let's drink to Şener Bey." They clinked their glasses together.

"Just one thing, Brother Fehmi," Deniz continued. "Can you please change the music? I mean, what the hell is this?"

"Of course, right away! Sorry, it didn't even cross my mind that this isn't your kind of music." Fehmi got up and went to the record player. He went through the records, fully aware that nothing in his collection would suit Deniz's tastes. From among those closest in age to Deniz, he chose a record by the Beatles and put it on the turntable.

As Fehmi went through the records, Deniz dug a folded-up piece of paper containing a blue pill from his pocket. He tossed the pill into his mouth. Yes, along with his weed and his passion for jerking off, Deniz had also brought with him from Istanbul two tablets of shitty ecstasy that his friend had bought in Tarlabaşı. They were his little secret, and he had swallowed the first of those little secrets on the beach that morning. Made in a basement apartment in the seediest area of Tarlabaşı, the ecstasy messed him up, which was why he'd fought with Berna and why he'd kicked his bag into the sea. He swallowed the second tablet with the last sip of his whiskey from Fehmi.

The soft rhythms of the Beatles began echoing in that old house the moment he clattered down his glass on the side table.

Pale blue light illuminated the room Şener walked into. Naked men were splayed out side by side on massage tables. Many others stood lurking and leering. The room was full to bursting with men, all touching, fondling, kissing, and fucking. Directly in front of Şener, one old man sucked off another man with a sagging gut who, in turn, rimmed a third man on the adjacent table like he was slurping down a big wet oyster; a throng of onlookers stood watching this moment of debauchery, stroking themselves and each other. The seething crowd closed in around Şener. Hungry hands ran all over sweating bodies. Şener heard a slap-slapping sound nearby. Some guy was jacking another guy off, putting on a show for everyone to watch. The stifling moisture and the stink of sweat now seemed compounded by other smells whose origins he knew but didn't want to dwell on. Bitter bile welled up from his stomach, but he swallowed it. The man began whinnying softly, letting out unsettling, muffled moans. It was clear to Şener and to the rest of the steam room that he'd just shot his load. As soon as he came, he smeared the sperm from his hand onto the other guy's leg, wrapped his peştamal around his waist, and fled. Subdued whimpers, exaggerated sighs, and pained moans, each different than the last, came from the men on the massage tables.

Şener noticed a young guy standing in the corner. Under the blue light the boy reminded him, for a split second, of Deniz. He squinted his eyes and looked again; definitely not him. He wasn't anywhere near as beautiful as Deniz, but still, he was young enough, handsome enough. The pleasures of the flesh Şener sought might be found with him.

He mustered all his courage and walked toward the boy. The boy was playing with his dick, its bulge clear through his peştamal. Şener gathered his thoughts, trying to remember the rules of engagement. So much time had passed that he'd forgotten how to comport himself in these situations. Taking a deep breath, he brought his hand to the bulge in the boy's peştamal. The boy did not recoil, but gave permission for Şener to keep stroking. He leaned into Şener's ear to whisper robotically, "It'll cost you."

Şener pulled his hand away. He made his decision. "Let's go," he told the boy. They crossed through the room together, swarming with hot and hard flesh and meat in every shape and size, and left that Tribe of Lot to their own devices.

The kid asked Şener's room number, then said, "Go ahead, I'll be right there," before disappearing.

Şener got to his room, sat down on his bridal bed, and buried his head between his hands to think, trying to forget the ritual of collective depravity he had just witnessed. Was it a beautiful dream or a homoerotic nightmare? A knock came at the door. The "masseur" had arrived. The kid walked into the room and took out the condom hidden under his towel. He dimmed the light and opened his peştamal. And finally, in this room narrow as a coffin, Şener was one-on-one, alone, with a bare-naked, beautiful boy.

He took off his own peştamal. The boy, still betraying no reaction, laid eyes on Şener's thin legs. The anticipation normally palpable between two people about to have sex was completely absent from the boy's face. His blank expression was shared by the old man, who looked like he was standing before a bank teller to pay his water bill.

They stood face-to-face in the room, barely lit by the window to the corridor above the door. Şener laid his hands on the boy's crotch. He fondled the boy's penis, as lifeless as his own and Fehmi's had been for years. All that filled his palms was its flaccid heat. "I've done three massages today. Might not get it up right away," the boy said in a practiced tone.

Disappointing. But not because the boy had had three massages in the course of a single day. In the dark of the orgy room, Şener's body and the traces of his age had been obscured, but in the desolate light of room sixteen, they were abundantly clear. Şener began kneading the boy's penis a little harder. It seemed to grow. The kid pushed Şener down, took out the condom, and unrolled it onto his penis, which was still not fully erect.

The condom was green.

This was what it all amounted to. This image before him the culmination of this whole misadventure: a young man, his soft dick in a clear green condom, waiting to fuck an old man in exchange for money.

This was what it all amounted to!

"Okay, enough already," he said, giving the boy his money and beginning to put on his clothes. He left his room and thrust himself into the narrow corridor leading to the exit. He needed to get out of here as fast as possible. Unable to breathe as he moved down the corridor, he paused for a second at a half-open door. Two middle-aged men lay in each other's arms, hanging off the massage table. He had arrived right after they came, in the heat of that briefest moment of postcoital love. As if they weren't in a bathhouse, but in the honeymoon suite of a five-star hotel, as if they were lying in an eiderdown bed. The two men held each other in loving embrace, and he watched them gloomily for a moment. Then one of the men on the table noticed him. He sat up.

"Get the fuck out of here, you old perv," he yelled, slamming the door in Şener's face.

He left the bathhouse like he was fleeing the scene of a crime. The sky was pregnant with the blackest of clouds, and the wind blew madly. Retracing his steps, he rushed back to the pier and managed to catch the island ferry just before it departed. The impending storm meant all subsequent ferries would be canceled until further notice; by sheer luck, he was on the last ferry back to Büyükada.

With a sharp whistle, the ferry departed, crossing the rolling waves to Büyükada. Shivering so hard he looked malarial, Şener ascended to the ferry's upper deck.

Awaiting him there was a vast sea of white.

The deck was full of students from the Heybeliada Naval High Command, all in their heavily starched white uniforms and white hats.

They were all so beautiful . . .

The whole deck reverberated with the laughter and the banter of the young seamen, these future marines. He looked at the cadets, each brimming with life, each more handsome than the last.

What if he were to go to one of these young soldiers and lay his head on their knees and cry his heart out . . . "I used to be young like you. Handsome like you, too, believe me . . . But look at me now. I'm old, I'm ugly . . . Nobody wants me, nobody loves me anymore . . . Even my husband, the man I've been with for forty years, doesn't love me anymore. Yes, that's right: he's not my friend, he's my husband. Even he's fallen for a boy as beautiful as you. So take off your white hat! Take off your white uniform! Take off your white shoes! Take off your white socks! Take off your virtue and your innocence. Your beauty only reminds me how old I am. You shouldn't be so beautiful. You have no right! No right!" He would cry, he would sob . . .

Would these boys console him? Stroke his white hair, lay him down in their laps?

A hard wave jolted Şener's entire body. He grabbed hold of the stairway railing so as not to fall. Just then he felt a hand on his shoulder. When he lifted his head he came face-to-face with a brown-haired marine looking at him with eyes the color of honey. In his ironed uniform and with white gloves in his pocket, he held his white hat in one hand and touched Şener with the other . . .

"Are you okay, uncle?" The boy sounded concerned. "Please, take my seat if you like."

Şener shook the boy's hand from his shoulder. "I'm fine. Leave me alone," he said, making a beeline to the open-air section of the deck. Behind him he heard the sound of the cadets laughing. They had to be laughing at him. He was certain of it. Every young man, every handsome man, whether at the bathhouse, on the ferry, even in his own garden, laughed at him; they all mocked him, mocked his age, his decrepitude.

In the open-air section of the ferry, he felt like he was in the middle of the sea. Foam roared off the waves, the wind splattering it across his face. The ferry carried him at full speed through seas the color of gray mud, taking him to Büyükada, taking him home. To his own home ... Did he have a home anymore?

He leaned on the railing and stared out over the sea, which looked now profoundly ugly and treacherous. The ferry continued, slicing through the angry sea, and as it sped on, the waves opened on either side, making way.

Like everything and everyone, the water, the waves, and the foam seemed to shy away from him, seemed to be fleeing him and his woe.

Fehmi and Deniz had been amusing themselves for the last hour.

Together they had nearly finished the entire bottle of whiskey, which had dissolved any of Fehmi's misgivings, softening him like a tenderized cut of meat. For the last hour, Deniz had been making a complete fool of himself, objecting to the songs Fehmi played by saying "What the fuck is this, Brother Fehmi, huh? What is it? Is it from a hundred years ago?" and dancing, trying to imitate the movements of the twist or the cha-cha that he had seen on television. Fehmi was surprised at how drunk the boy was, chalking it up to his youth, his inexperience with alcohol. After some time he had to stand up to Deniz's stubborn insistence and refuse him any more whiskey: "Deniz, bud, when your mom gets here she'll be even angrier seeing you like this. No more alcohol for you. Maybe you can have a beer later. That'll be our excuse for how drunk you are." The topic of Berna instantly angered Deniz once more, and he swore under his breath. Then, before long, he got up to dance again, shaking his head strangely back and forth, writhing his body and rolling his eyes back to their whites like his soul was ascending. In short, the ecstasy was working.

As Deniz moved his body, Fehmi thought to himself, yet again: *So young, so helpless. And so beautiful.* A gentle swing melody began playing from the record player and Deniz crossed to Fehmi, taking him by the hands. "Come on. Let's dance. Come on!"

Brandishing a glass of whiskey he didn't know how many times he'd refilled, Fehmi laughed loudly and refused. "No, no, nooooo. Please, Deniz, bud, I can't dance. No, definitely not."

Deniz wouldn't listen to him. He lifted Fehmi to his feet, pulled Fehmi to him, and nestled his curly brown tresses underneath Fehmi's chin.

They began dancing. The smell of salt, menthol, and hormones wafted off the kid and filled Fehmi's nose. Realizing he couldn't stop Deniz, he gave up resisting. The flame of

Deniz's body spread to Fehmi, sparking him to life as their bodies grew close.

With a split-second move, Deniz tried to twirl Fehmi. Barely able to stand already, Fehmi lost his balance and the two of them tumbled to the floor. Fehmi's drink poured all over him.

Looking up at the ceiling, they laughed at length at how drunk they were, at the state they were in, at the little games they were playing. What brought them back to life was the annoying needle scratch at the end of the record. Continuing to laugh, Fehmi slowly sat up.

"Let me go change, God, just look at me. I smell like an Irishman, drunk in a ditch of whiskey." Deniz laughed at the Irish joke and ground his teeth as he continued writhing on the floor. Before going upstairs, Fehmi went to the record player. "Hmmm, what to play now?" Suddenly, he was struck by a marvelous idea. "I know," he said, choosing one of the old records and putting it on the turntable. "Deniz, bud, this song is my gift to you. It's very special to me." He put the needle on the record and went upstairs.

Deniz sat up on the floor. His laughter had abated, but the inside of his head continued spinning in gentle harmony with the world, the universe, nature, everything. He heard the beginning of a sweet melody from the record player, and then the calm, graceful voice of a man began to sing:

"How beautiful the sea, how
I run through its waves now

In its loving arms I'll be,
My love, the beautiful sea . . ."

There in the living room of that old house, smashed on ecstasy and whiskey, Deniz listened to the song Fehmi dedicated to him as the darkness of evening began to descend. He looked around himself. He wondered how long he'd been in this clean, orderly house, which exuded tranquility from every nook and cranny. In a short while his mom would return; their fights and their unhappy dinners would resume. This island, these trees, these two houses which seemed glued to each other, vexed him to no end. He wanted to be in the city, to go out with his friends, to kiss girls. Thinking now about kissing girls, he was pulled by the ecstasy into its relentless vortex of sexual bliss.

He was ready now.

He stood up slowly. The song still played as he went upstairs. He went through the open door at the end of the hallway and into the bedroom. When he entered, Fehmi was in new clothes and swaying drunkenly. They exchanged glances. Deniz was having a hard time staying on his feet. "I'm not feeling so good, Brother Fehmi. Can I lie down for a bit?" Deniz asked, getting into the bed.

"Of course," Fehmi said. "Rest here. I'll wake you up later." He was about to leave when Deniz called softly to him.

"Stay here. Don't go. Lie down with me."

Fehmi thought for a moment, though in truth he didn't think very long at all. He turned off the lights, closed the door, and got into bed, lying next to Deniz. In this bed he had shared with Şener for forty years, he was now side by side with Deniz. He was horribly dizzy, he was exhausted, his body had gone through too much stress, shock, and pleasure for one day. As soon as Fehmi lay down, Deniz pulled himself in close, resting his head on Fehmi's chest. In place of the white head of hair that Fehmi had held for years in that bed, there was now hair of a different color. A different man altogether.

Fehmi began running his fingers affectionately through Deniz's thick hair. Being touched at the peak of his ecstasy high, having his hair stroked in this way felt impossibly good to Deniz. He buried himself in Fehmi's shoulder and closed his eyes in the old man's warm embrace. Caressing his hair, Fehmi looked down at Deniz's beautiful face. At his taut skin, his perfect lips, his grinding teeth, and his chin gurning with pleasure: this baby, this most beautiful boy Barbie, was wrapped with all his warmth in Fehmi's arms. Were these the happiest moments of his life? He wasn't certain, but the one thing he knew for sure was that in this moment, he could die happy.

They lay there motionless for a long while.

Fehmi watched as Deniz's breathing slowed and he was drawn into the sweet darkness of sleep. Fehmi's brain hummed along, though, and only one thing was on his mind. Unable to restrain himself any longer, he leaned his face into Deniz's, planting a small, impossibly naïve, hopefully harmless kiss on the boy's lips.

Their lips touched gently. A flash of lightning, the first harbinger of the coming storm, cracked across the sky, brightening the dark room.

A hand suddenly pushed Fehmi's head away, and the body in his arms leapt to its feet in an instant. Stunned, Fehmi felt a hard shove against his shoulders, and his head slammed on the wrought-iron headboard. Deniz stood in front of him, flames smoldering in his eyes: "What the fuck, man? What the fuck was that?"

Fehmi tried to sit up as Deniz began retching theatrically, rubbing his lips in a hateful show of disgust. He acted like some germ, some plague had rubbed off on his lips. Like he'd been touched by a filthy leper, like he could only cast off the microbe by showing how revolted he was.

"You're disgusting. What do you think you're doing? I can't believe you. What the fuck was that?"

Fehmi leapt out of bed and tried to grab Deniz's arm. "Deniz, bud, wait a second, please. There's been a misunderstanding. I didn't mean anything by it."

Deniz shoved Fehmi again, knocking him back onto the bed. He shouted with unquenchable rancor: "Go fuck yourself, asshole. Don't touch me. You didn't mean anything by it? What the fuck does that mean? You assaulted me. You got me drunk and tried to rape me."

Fehmi suddenly realized the dangerous gravity of the situation. Things were going downhill fast. He tried to climb out of bed, to approach Deniz, speaking slowly as if trying to hypnotize him: "Deniz . . . Please, stay calm. It's all just one big misunderstanding. I apologize if I made you uncomfortable. That wasn't my intention. You misunderstood me."

Deniz laughed wildly as he continued yelling. "I'm calm, man. I'm calm. We'll see what my mom has to say about this when she gets home. She'll see she was wrong to lock me away on an island. Just look what happened here, huh? I got felt up by an old pervert. By someone she really liked here, too, someone she really trusted, someone she called 'good people' . . . Soon as she hears about this, she'll get me off this shitty island. I won't have to stay here a second longer."

Everything was spinning way out of control. Fehmi held his head between his hands, his eyes filled with fear. On the verge of tears, he could only repeat the same refrain: "Deniz, please . . ."

Deniz came to the edge of the bed and stood right in front of Fehmi. Fehmi was cowering fearfully in the bed. When he looked up, his head tucked between his shoulders, all he could see was Deniz, still half-naked, towering over him. Fehmi felt like he had shrunk and Deniz had grown.

Deniz's presence seemed to fill the whole room.

Deniz leaned his face down to Fehmi and shouted: "You think I'm a faggot like you, asshole?" At this point Fehmi was completely slack, and Deniz shoved his shoulder again. Fehmi was still in a daze when Deniz landed a hard slap on his soft face. "I'm not a faggot, you got it? I don't fuck guys. Pussy, I fuck pussy. Besides, if I was going to fuck a guy I'd fuck a young guy. You think I'd fuck an old fart like you? You faggot."

Fehmi began sobbing. This had to be a nightmare, a nightmare he couldn't wake up from, a nightmare whose end he didn't want to see. He could barely get out a whisper: "Please, don't. It's not like that. Please, calm down."

Deniz didn't even register his words. He leaned over Fehmi again, pummeling him as he continued yelling that word, which he saw hurt the old man more than his fists. "Shut up, faggot. Shut the fuck up. You and that other guy fuck each other, huh? Aren't you ashamed? Faggot." Fehmi pulled his head toward his chest, trying to withstand both the bombardment of insults and the punches Deniz was raining down on him. "You're just a faggot. Faggot. Filthy faggot. Faggot. Faggot. Faggot. Fag—"

BAM!

The sound of one hard object hitting another hard object put a sudden end to the insults, the slaps, and the tears, plunging the room into a brief and terrifying silence that felt impossibly long to Fehmi. When he freed his head from between his arms, Fehmi was met not by the sight of Deniz raging, but by his dumbfounded eyes. Those lovely eyes, bewildered, looked down at him, begging for an answer.

A narrow stream of blood oozed down the side of Deniz's head, over the red lips that had only a moment ago been raining down insults and curses. It dripped down his beautiful face and off his diamond-cut chin.

Deniz tottered feebly where he stood before crumpling to the ground like a sack of rocks. In the empty space where Deniz had just been standing, Fehmi saw a pair of familiar eyes.

The true master of that bedroom.

An ever so brief flash of lightning illuminated Şener, brandishing a bloody iron.

And Şener, with the gently admonishing tone he used to tell Fehmi he shouldn't drink as much coffee, a tone like he was saying "take your sweater so you don't catch cold," a tone like he was whispering "I love you" into Fehmi's ear over their afternoon tea, began to speak.

"I can forgive anything, Fehmi, darling. Anything. The impertinence and brattiness of a child, betrayal, adultery . . . I can forgive anything. But there's one thing . . . one thing I won't forgive. And that's a potty mouth. Especially when it's potty-mouthing someone I value more than life itself."

He stared into Fehmi's eyes, into their darkest depths.

"Nobody can come into *my* house, into *my* bedroom, and call *my* husband a faggot. Let's have some respect!" he proclaimed, placing the bloody iron on the dresser with a terrible thud that resounded throughout the darkened mansion.

PART II

We shall have beds full of subtle perfumes,
Divans as deep as graves, and on the shelves
Will be strange flowers that blossomed for us
Under more beautiful heavens.

Some evening made of rose and of mystical blue
A single flash will pass between us
Like a long sob, charged with farewells;

And later an Angel, setting the doors ajar,
Faithful and joyous, will come to revive
The tarnished mirrors, the extinguished flames.

"The Death of Lovers," Charles Baudelaire,
trans. William Aggeler

GRAVITY

A single droplet of blood runs in a rivulet down the iron, pooling atop the dresser. Droplet after droplet follows suit.

One of the droplets spills over the edge of the dresser, finds its place as a solitary spot of red in the thick, stark-white rug below before seeping into its depths. The rug's knots drink in the blood, the stain of it spreading fast.

After any great calamity, the law of gravity that pins us, our homes, our lives, to this aging planet called Earth, reveals its power once again.

That red stain grows quickly, so quickly, like an invisible tumor, vowing death. Over the last five minutes, the only sound in the bedroom has been the calm rhythm of the droplets falling onto the rug.

Drip.

Drip.

Drip.

Drip.

Frozen sitting on the edge of the bed, Fehmi is imprisoned in a kind of deafness. As if the crash of some object—an iron, for example—against a skull has irrevocably stripped him of his sense of hearing. As the sound of the blood droplets resounds in his deaf ears, he feels something happening to his body as comforting as it is troubling.

A warmth spreads over his body from his loins, come to life again that summer after many long years. That warmth reaches from his loins to his knees, and then flows down his calves, licking over his ankles and collecting in the thick knots of the white rug. As with the blood, gravity has manifested itself in this journey from his loins to the rug.

When Fehmi brings his hand to his crotch, he realizes this warmth isn't just a feeling. It is a fluid, as real as earth and sky, as inevitable as a law of physics.

He's pissed himself.

Şener watches Fehmi's movements discerningly. The fact that Fehmi has pissed himself is of course not lost on him.

It is a milestone for them.

Their relationship has come to some kind of end, has given way to an entirely new era.

The two of them are now confronted with the fearful moment all couples in the whole world will one day face: What do you do when the person you love, the person you've spent your entire life with, the person you've had the most passionate sex with, begins to piss themselves?

Like the question from that gameshow on TV ... *Deal? Or no deal?*

Deal, Şener replies to this vital proposition, opting to continue down the path, soiled by urine, that fate has drawn for him. But for now, given the circumstances of this extraordinary situation, Şener will have to hold off on the plans he has spent years making for when such an "episode" would come to pass.

The first thing to do is to get everything under control. To think quickly, decide quickly, act quickly . . . Everything has to proceed at the rhythm of the century we live in.

With Fehmi doubled over by the realization not only that he had pissed himself but also that he had killed a child, Şener taps into every fold, every point, every forgotten corner in both the right and left lobes of his brain to set himself into action.

He gathers his thoughts, trying to focus on the moment they are in now, on this moment where he and Fehmi both live and breathe while Deniz lies there dead, on this moment and this moment alone.

He needs something as significant as all the paradigm-shifting breakthroughs in the history of the world. Like Isaac Newton finding gravity when an apple fell on his head, like Benjamin Franklin discovering electricity by the strike of lightning, like Auntie Ayşe using her blue Cırt detergent to quickly remove stains, he needs an idea.

An idea to change the course of everything.

And quick.

He has to proceed systematically, step-by-step, the way he does when he makes a tart, placing each of the blackberries carefully, one by one.

Perhaps if he thinks quickly, takes action quickly, they might have a chance.

Right?

Drip.

Drip.

Drip.

He has to be fast, has to find something, if they are to . . .

Drip. Drip. Drip.

The droplets of blood continue trickling rhythmically onto the rug.

With a split-second reflex he grabs the towel sitting on the chair beside him. He wipes the towel in circles over the dresser, getting rid of the blood with an almost unconscious, almost instinctive gesture. This puts an end to the annoying distraction of the dripping sound, and stops the deep red fluid from soaking ever deeper into his rug.

The blood no longer drips.

His first move is to rewrite the laws of nature, to stop gravity itself.

THE OLD-FASHIONED WAY

Bolts of lightning lit up the room as Şener paced back and forth. He crossed to the window, its curtains still drawn tight. He parted the fabric with the tip of his fingers and peeked outside.

As he predicted, the street was completely empty. The wind was stirring up dust along the dirt road, bending the trees, assailing the flowers in the garden as if to tear them from the earth. Despite the violence of the wind, the sea was dark and empty, he could tell even from the bedroom window. The only motion in the sea that surrounded Büyükada came from the swell and the plunge of the rolling waves. There were no signs of any light, no ships, no ferries coming in their familiar silhouettes from the mainland. The storm consigned Büyükada to its all-too-familiar fate. History had repeated itself: anyone coming to the island had already come, and everyone else was now stuck.

Şener stroked his chin as he paced the room. "What

should we do? My god, what can we do?" he murmured to himself.

He needed help, or at the very least, an idea . . . He crossed to Fehmi, who still sat clutching his head between his hands. He needed Fehmi's help. If he was ever going to lead Fehmi by the arm to the toilet when he was too sickly, or feed him when his hands became unusable, or shop for him when he could no longer leave the house, then he needed Fehmi to chime in now.

Fehmi sat on the edge of bed completely vacant of emotion, a feelingless sack of meat staring in a daze at the red stain on the rug. He could no longer restrain himself and retched, vomiting all over the rug. The rug was soaking now not just in blood and piss but also vomit, stinking foully of whiskey. Once he finished retching, he began to cry in heavy sobs once more. He trembled as he wept. As if apologizing for everything, as if rebelling against the moment he came into this world, against himself, against his own life, he wept.

Another bolt of lightning flashed, brightening the bedroom.

Şener had never seen Fehmi cry. Another first in their relationship, just like Fehmi pissing himself. Normally, he found it distasteful for men to cry, even in films, but Fehmi wasn't disagreeable at all to him in that moment. There was something affable about his trembling sobs. *My God, isn't he handsome*, Şener thought to himself, *so beautiful even when he cries*.

But like regrets and grief, admiration would have to wait. He had stemmed the dripping of the blood, but a towel would not be enough to stop the passing of time. Şener placed his hand gingerly on Fehmi's shoulder. "Fehmi. Fehmi. Are you okay?" he asked. Fehmi jolted at the touch of Şener's hand, and he pushed him away, leaping to his feet.

The blood kept oozing from the body of the boy at their feet and into the rug as Fehmi glared at Şener, sparks flickering in his irises. "Don't touch me. Don't you dare. You . . . What have you done?"

Şener stared back at him. Was he really the one who needed to be held accountable right now? "I . . . Just . . . For the two of us . . ." was all he managed to say, his voice trembling.

"You killed him."

Şener scolded Fehmi with a sharp scowl. "And what if he had killed you? What if he'd gone and told everyone?"

Fehmi began crying again. Yes, he had been the reason for all of this. There was nothing else to say about it. Nothing else to do, either. All he could do was cry.

Şener believed, to the contrary, that all they could do was anything but cry.

"Okay, Fehmi. Just try to calm down. Now's not the time to argue." He glanced at the kid's body on the ground as he continued to think aloud. Communicating with Fehmi, hearing his voice, had done Şener good. He felt his mind begin to work.

"An accident . . . It was an accident. I didn't want it to happen like this. But it did. When I heard what he was saying to you I couldn't stop myself." He turned his head to

Fehmi, who was still crying. Fehmi's sobs were starting to get on his nerves now. "Enough already. If you want, you can leave. You want to leave me alone with this mess? Then go."

Fehmi didn't reply. That was the last thing he wanted, to be alone. All on his own, helpless, pitiful, his hands soiled by the kid's blood . . .

He shook his head, his hands covering his face. He didn't want to go.

"Then please try to pull yourself together. I need you to help me. Like I said . . . It was just an accident."

The notion that it had been an accident seemed to bring Şener some peace of mind. Like they had accidentally broken a vase, rather than someone's skull, like they could solve the problem by sweeping it under the rug. That accident was now splayed motionless on the floor as Şener continued pacing back and forth in the room. The sounds of the storm filled the house, and the creaking of the tree's branches echoed in the bedroom's darkness. He looked at his watch.

"We still have a chance. We can still . . . Does anyone know he's here, did anybody see him?"

Fehmi shook his head.

"Are you sure?" Şener asked.

Fehmi was sure. He replied in a soft, ashamed voice. "He was alone today. He went to the beach, his bag fell in the water. His key was in there. He wanted to wait here until Berna came back."

Şener was beginning to piece together how Fehmi and Deniz had come together, on a day that had been completely out of his control and during the time he was being person-ally traumatized at the bathhouse. He felt the jealousy pulse through him in waves, settling like a knot in his throat. He couldn't repress the anger in his voice: "My goodness, and what a good time you had waiting! So you decided you wanted to wait in our bedroom, hmm?" He waved his hand around in front of his face to chase off his knee-jerk reaction. "Agh, never mind . . . Okay, so he was alone today. You're saying nobody saw you two . . . That's very good. That's our chance."

Şener had almost succeeded in gathering his full con-centration. In the body lying at his feet he began to sense the presence of lady luck. He wanted to ride that luck for all it was worth. This nonsense wouldn't end here, not like this.

He glanced down at Deniz, who no longer looked so beautiful with his head smashed in, and muttered, "We have to get it out of the house." He could no longer let any more of Deniz's blood stain his rugs. The body had to go.

But where?

Anywhere . . . As long as it was out of the bedroom. Den-iz's presence in the house kept him from thinking straight. Alive or dead, it didn't make a difference. It had to go.

But where? Where to?

Şener's train of thought was interrupted by a sob from Fehmi, who asked, "Why did you do it, Şener? Why? Did you really have to kill him?"

Şener was by now wholly exasperated by Fehmi's sheer

lack of composure and his stupid, inane questions. He clearly wanted to have a reckoning, when he should be helping to brainstorm how to dispose of the body instead of wasting time on the why and the wherefore. Şener's patience had worn thin.

"I'm sorry, Fehmi, darling, it wasn't on purpose. I wouldn't have chosen to kill him with an iron, but alas, I simply didn't have enough time to poison him. Had I known the iron would so offend you, I'd have slowly poisoned him to death. Please, forgive me."

From this point on he decided to restrain his anger, to ignore Fehmi's ridiculous babbling, the way he cried like a mama's boy, like a sissy. Guess he wasn't the man in their relationship after all. Instead of crying like a sissy, maybe he ought to man up.

Taking a deep breath, Şener tried to concentrate again.

What would they do with the body?

They had a few options:

Burying it might be a solution. But they didn't have the time to dig a grave. Even if they had the time, he wasn't sure he really wanted to dig a grave. No, they wouldn't bury it.

What if they went and threw it from somewhere high up? Perhaps from the cliff at the top of the island? Not that, either. It'd be found easily, plus he and Fehmi wouldn't be able to carry it so far.

All right, even if they could . . . Odds were high that someone would see them. Even if they threw the body from somewhere high up, when they eventually found it, the blow from the iron would show that the incident was no accident after all.

What if they went experimental and dismembered the body? If they carried the kid to the bathtub and chopped his body into pieces small enough to go down the drain, chunks so tiny they'd be siphoned into the sewer system that Şener and the rest of the Büyükada Beautification Association had had renovated last year? Şener knew that, given enough time, he'd have no trouble mincing Deniz up into small enough pieces to fit down the drain, but things just weren't going his way today.

What if he cut the body in two, gave half to Fehmi, and took the other half himself? And they hacked each half apart as fast as possible . . . Not an option, unfortunately! The knives in the kitchen were too dull, and given Fehmi's current state as a woman gone mad, it would take way too long. Even steaks took half an hour to be minced up small enough for his kuş başı recipe, so they'd surely need hours for Deniz.

Their options were dwindling fast. Putting one hand on his hip and the other on his chin, Şener stood over the body. "No, no . . . We have to take care of this the old-fashioned way," he said to himself, kicking the body. There had to be a way that the old wives knew, but what was it?

At Şener's kick there was a stirring on the ground. Deniz choked out a whimpering, groaning wheeze, wrapping his hand desperately around Şener's ankle.

He hadn't died. He was still alive.

Şener jolted backwards and choked back a scream. Fehmi was finally coming around, but as soon as he saw Deniz's head covered in blood on the ground, the wretched sounds spilling from the boy's mouth, he shut down again.

Deniz's shallow breathing mixed with his moaning, his wheezing, his gurgling.

Şener lunged like an arrow for one of the white socks from the floor, and stuffed it all the way into Deniz's throat in exactly the same manner that he'd stuff a chicken with chestnuts, currants, and rice. The sounds stopped. Nauseated by the blood, Şener found the carotid artery in Deniz's throat and checked for a pulse. From somewhere deep inside, he could feel a faint throb that echoed the dripping of blood off the dresser.

Thump.

Thump.

Thump.

Şener moved to Fehmi and shook him. "Come on, Fehmi. We have to get it out of the house right now. Or else we're going to miss our chance. Where should we take it? Say something."

Fehmi stared blankly back at him. Nothing was coming to mind. If Deniz was still alive . . . Could they save him? He felt too powerless to suggest so to Şener. Şener, meanwhile, continued shaking Fehmi by the shoulders. "Come on! Think!" Fehmi tried to remember what he'd done that day.

The Beatles. The whiskey. The knock at the door . . .

Recollecting the many moments throughout his day,

various scenes, some happy and some terrifying, stirred to life out of his jumble of feelings. He felt lost within his own brain.

The violin concerto. The record player. The kiss in the bedroom . . .

He buried his head between his hands again. If he could just squeeze his head hard enough, he supposed he might be able to save himself from these scenes as they assaulted him.

Şener kept pacing, riling himself into a frenzy as he talked to himself. "Come on . . . Where . . . Where to move it?"

Fehmi lifted his head from between his hands. He looked at Şener and from his mouth came a whisper: "The gazebo."

The gazebo.

Şener turned and walked over to Fehmi. "What do you mean, the gazebo?"

"The cement for the gazebo. They poured it today, it's probably still wet. We can put him in there. That's the best thing we can do now. After . . . I don't know what we do after."

Şener took Fehmi's hand as an expression of profound relief spread across his face, like he'd just had the best orgasm in the world. He brought his lips to Fehmi's. *My brilliant, wonderful husband, smart as a whip. My bewildered, forlorn, but absolutely genius husband.*

"We'll figure out the after. Leave the after to me."

Fehmi, the handsome engineer, had suggested the gazebo, and that was enough for now.

Yes, the gazebo. The entire solution concealed in this three-syllable word.

Quite like the tip of the tongue taking a trip of three steps down the palate to tap, at three, on the teeth. Lo. Lee. Ta. Ga. Zee. Bo.

They took the big blanket they used on cold winter days out of the closet. Spreading it out on the floor, they pushed and pulled Deniz's body onto it. Though the body had lost a lot of blood, it was still quite heavy.

Wrapping Deniz in the blanket, Fehmi noticed that one of the boy's eyes hung open, staring back at him. The white sock in his mouth made it hard for him to breathe, but he still continued inhaling and exhaling shallowly, laboriously, trying to cling to life. Fehmi lowered his head, avoiding the eye looking at him from under the blanket. Though Deniz attempted to struggle, they eventually shrouded him completely in the warm, heavy, thick darkness of their down blanket.

Şener looked at Fehmi. "One, two, three," he counted, and they lifted the blanket by either end.

And so began that final journey. It was, though, not an easy final journey.

Given their age, they really shouldn't have been trying to carry so much weight. "Mind your back. The last thing we need now is for you to slip a disk," Şener opined. For as much savoir faire Şener had displayed with the iron, he had none of it now carrying a body in a blanket.

Half-pulling, half-pushing, they lurched the accident out of the room and reached the top of the stairs. "We won't be able to carry it down," Şener said to Fehmi. "You pull, I'll push." Şener pushed as Fehmi pulled. The mechanical equilibrium of their forty years together was on full display as they pulled and pushed the body in sync. They managed to get the blanket to the foyer at the bottom of the stairs, the boy's head slamming against each step on the way down. Şener raised his hand to stop Fehmi, opened the door, and looked outside. There was nobody to be seen.

"Okay. Let's go."

Since they didn't turn on the backyard lights and nobody was home next door, it was pitch-black outside. The moon, which would have otherwise illuminated their way, was trapped behind the clouds, and not a single beam of its hallowed light reached the ground. The wind, the mad, forceful wind, slapped them in the face as soon as they stepped outside. They were already so tired, but there was no time to rest. At the end of such a stressful, exhausting day, they would under normal circumstances have already taken their pills and gotten in bed, but alas, duty called.

They passed through their most beautiful garden on the island, arriving to the bushes that separated the unkempt land on whose peak the gazebo would be built. They passed under the branches, which harrowed lullabies in the wind, and began climbing up the path. Fehmi was out of breath. "Fehmi, darling, be careful, for God's sake. Don't let any of the branches scratch your face or poke your eye out," Şener said, admonishing him again. The two husbands used the last of their strength to ascend to the peak of Büyükada from which the sea was most beautiful, carrying with them the most beautiful corpse in the world, under the watchful silhouette of their mansion, which had born witness not just to their love but to their murder. Reaching the peak, the mansion receded from view, an abandoned lover at a loss for words, its head hanging sadly as it watched them. There at the peak, bolts of lightning flashed one after another, and the roiling clouds tore through one another at full speed. An enormous deluge was on the verge of pouring forth from the skies, to cleanse everything, to wash away their crime and all its traces. The wind assaulted them with all its violence, as if trying to stop them.

But they would not stop.

Undaunted by the motes of dirt and sand blowing into their eyes, dodging the thrashing trees that scratched at their fragile skin, they managed at last to reach the clearing on the peak.

There, only a few steps ahead, the hole full of cement spread like a grave beneath the trees.

They dragged the blanket to the edge of the hole. They were out of breath. "I'm spent," Fehmi said, hands on his knees as he tried to catch his breath.

Picking up the rod the workmen had used to mix the cement earlier, Şener dipped it into the hole.

The cement was still wet.

Wet as lips bedewed by mortal kisses . . .

Wet as a final resting place . . .

Wet as the crotch of an old lover who pissed himself . . .

Here on this peak where a few short weeks ago they had celebrated their fortieth anniversary, drinking champagne with their closest friends, they now stood with someone else entirely. They waited there in the company of a half-dead body that struggled to breathe, to wrestle free from the blanket at their feet, someone who needed now, more than ever, the help of his mother.

But Şener knew that neither of them had the luxury of waiting any longer. He made the decision for both of their sakes, and shoved the blanket, letting it tumble into the hole full of cement.

The blanket didn't sink right away. Worse, the edges of the blanket unfurled like gift wrap. Buried from the waist down in the cement, Deniz looked directly at his murderers, the white sock by now bright red with blood.

He couldn't speak but his eyes seemed to beseech them. "Please . . . Please . . . I'm begging you, don't do this. Please, help me. I won't say a word to anyone. I'll say I fell and hit my head. I'm so sorry . . . Please don't kill me," he wanted to say.

Fehmi's eyes met Deniz's, and a feeling of mercy welled up in him. The eyes of the child now submerged in cement, the child whose every move he had tracked all summer, the child who had been the star of his lovelorn fantasies, had awakened that mercy.

As Deniz's body continued its slow descent into the cement, Fehmi turned to Şener. "We can still rescue him and take him to the hospital. It's not too late. Are we sure we want to do this?" he asked.

Were they sure?

Şener thought for a moment what might happen if they rescued Deniz from the hole. If they brought Deniz to the hospital and saved his life . . . What would they say to Berna Hanım?

"I'm so sorry, Berna Hanım. My husband, whom I've always told you was nothing more than my friend in retirement, was alone with your son today and tried to kiss him. Your son resisted and said a few objectionable things to my husband: he called him, forgive my language, a faggot. I couldn't stop myself when I heard that, so I hit him on the head with an iron and knocked him out. It was just an accident, a tiny little accident . . . Then we decided to stuff a sock in his mouth and dump him into some cement. But then our consciences got the better of us and we took him back out. We're sure you understand. We are truly sorry. Your son was paralyzed after the blow to his head, he'll never walk again. He'll probably end up completely incontinent, just like my husband. You'll probably have to take care of him for the rest of his life, feed him, try to make sense of the gibberish coming out of his mouth. Who knows? But like we said, it was just an accident. See, we didn't even kill him! We saved him. Here's your barely alive son."

The answer was clear.

Şener picked up the rod and, using all his might, guided the rest of Deniz's body into the depths of the hole.

And that beautiful face, buried in its wet grave, disappeared from the face of the earth.

SUMMER RAIN

Staring out the window from her big office on Valikonağı Avenue, Berna was once again struck by a feeling that had haunted her since she was a child: that everyone except her was enjoying themselves at a great big party.

Every time the feeling came, Berna would fully dissociate wherever and whenever she might be. Just as she did now, staring out that window.

Dissociating from the dentist's chair beside her, her closest friend in the world, resembling a baby's high chair with its strange design . . . the nauseating smell of zinc oxide eugenol filling the air . . . the strange tools on the immaculate counters surrounding her . . . periotomes and luxators, curettes and elevators, 11- and 15-blade scalpels, masks and gloves, retractors, saliva ejectors, an autoclave, a mirror, tweezers, forceps . . .

White. The most sterile color. More immaculate than the finest detergents available to housewives.

At least four days of the week, in that house where her one and only son diligently studied, Berna felt she had finally found what she'd been looking for all her life. She adored being a housewife, the extraordinary quietude of its routine and lifestyle. A son, a husband, a bright, white house: the fantasy of a modern, urbane woman.

That is, until she would arrive at her office, full of her peculiar implements . . .

Every morning she would leave a home filled with the rhythms of jazz, get on the ferry, grow tenser by the minute among the maddening crowds, enter this concrete-walled room that overlooked Valikonağı Avenue, breathe in the scent of generic chloroform instead of carnations, and ensure the oral health of all the people whose names were recorded in her appointment book.

Precise little slivers of time, hour after hour, stolen one by one from her own quality time, wasted on cavities, lesions, premolars, molars, endodontics, implants, composites, amalgams, roots, canals, and dentures . . .

She was filled with an odd malaise. From her window she saw the streets of Nişantaşı emptying, purging themselves of their human excess. She always felt the rain, especially summer rain, really suited the city. In the summer, the only people who remained in Istanbul were those who couldn't go away on holiday, the poor, and people who didn't love their families enough to visit them; whenever a sudden rain fell, the streets grew even calmer in their absence. It struck her as profoundly mystical that people lose their bearings in the face of nature, that their ordinary rhythms suddenly change, that they carry those strange canopies called umbrellas, and that men selling those umbrellas scatter like shit spilling out of the sewers the instant the first drop of rain falls from the sky.

A few hours earlier, she had fought with Deniz. It was probably the seventh time this week they'd had such a vicious fight. These days, they fought over everything: when dinnertime was, why he hadn't finished his assignments, why he drank more beer than he was allowed, so many other things, big and small. Their most recent fight had taken place over the phone.

"Go home, Deniz. You can't swim in this weather!"

"Stay out of it, Mom. There's nothing here. Just a few clouds."

"There's a storm in Istanbul."

"This prison isn't as close to Istanbul as you think."

"Ugh, not this prison business again! Summer's almost over and you're still fixated on that."

Her voice had, without intending to, once again crossed into that tone that drove Deniz insane: the whining, carping, wheedling tone of an overinvolved mother.

"Besides, don't you have assignments to take care of? You're procrastinating again, see?"

"Mom, come on, quit it already. Really. You're the same here as you were back home. Leave me alone."

"We already learned what happens when we leave you alone. You need to listen to us a little better."

A loud laugh . . .

"Ha, Mom . . . You're saying I'm still fixated, but just look in the mirror."

A brief silence.

"Deniz, sweetheart, everything I do I do because I love you. It's all for you."

"Okay, so what? Your love is getting on my nerves. All I want is for you to leave me alone. Get off my back already!"

He hung up. Those were the last words Berna heard from Deniz: "Get off my back already!"

She felt enraged the moment he hung up, thought about calling him back and putting him in his place. But some instinct stopped her. She decided to not call Deniz again for the rest of the day, to leave him alone, to sort things out when she got home.

Again filled with the feeling that everybody but her was enjoying themselves at a great big party, and fighting off that insatiable malaise, she continued watching the wind racing through the streets, the summer rain as it fell.

Quality time to watch the rain, though, was about to run out, because the singer Candan Erçetin opened the door to Berna's office and swished eagerly in. About to embark on another countrywide tour in a week, she wanted to have a routine checkup beforehand, to whiten her teeth a shade brighter out of respect for her audience. Berna shook Candan Erçetin's hand, smiling. She would spend the next hour dealing with the cheek retractors that would broaden Candan Erçetin's mouth, with buzzing and whirring and blue lights, with the bright overhead lamp that would reveal every last detail of that incredibly large, taut mouth, and last but certainly not least, with that pink tongue worshipped by millions for the beautiful songs it would sing to its adoring fans next week.

Candan Erçetin left the dentist's office an hour later.

Berna checked her appointments for the following week, gave instructions to her assistant, and, picking up her bag with an uneasiness nobody else noticed, she exited onto Valikonağı Avenue. As soon as she stepped onto the street, the force of the winds almost knocked her feet out from under her.

The weather wasn't as endearing as it looked from inside the window; it was brutal, pitiless. Much as she loved the summer rains, she was not a woman made for storms. That was a truth she'd have to face soon enough.

First she called Cem. After two rings, it gave a busy signal. She received a text message right after: *Darling, I'm in a meeting. I'll call you when I'm done. See you at dinner tonight.*

It upset Berna even more that she'd have to return home all on her own.

Once the misadventures began, they knew no end. Classic. All the taxis were full. Trying to hail a taxi, she noticed she was standing in front of Venüs Bakery. She went in and got a huge box of Deniz's favorite fig cookies, hoping to bury the hatchet. It was the only time that day luck would be on her side, and right when she left the bakery, she managed to catch a taxi and hopped in the back seat. "Kabataş, please. It's urgent," she said.

But urgency was meaningless in early evening Istanbul. In the maddening grind of rush-hour traffic, it took forty-five minutes of stopping and starting for her to travel the short distance to Kabataş. Tossing the driver a large bill without even looking at the meter, Berna got out and ran to the pier for the ferry to the islands. At the ticket machine, she noticed that the gates were closed; she looked up and saw on the electronic signboard that ALL VOYAGES TO THE ISLANDS HAVE BEEN TEMPORARILY SUSPENDED DUE TO WEATHER CONDITIONS.

Having spent her whole life between Nişantaşı and Bostancı, Berna had no idea that it wasn't easy to get to the islands on stormy days. The island had given her her jazz rhythms, family meals, Deniz's socks and assignments, more frequent and more passionate sex with Cem, the games of neighborliness, evening walks, but transportation remained a problem. Berna tried her luck, asking the men in the small boats and fishing vessels along the pier to take her. It wasn't just the cityline ferries, but seafaring altogether, that was suspended.

God would, in short, not allow Berna to return home.

The malaise inside Berna ballooned in her stomach, pressed against her lungs. The panic practically overcame her body as she dug her phone out of her purse and, reneging on her earlier pledge, tried to call Deniz.

Deep inside a pit of drying cement, Deniz's telephone began to ring. Quite naturally, he couldn't pick up. Berna kept calling and calling until the signal jammed and she heard the metallic voice of that robotic crone admonish her: "The person you are trying to reach is not available." She hung up and tried to force herself to calm down. Deniz hadn't answered the phone simply to get on her nerves. How could that be, though? How could he not answer? In weather like this, no less ...

An anxious shadow passed quickly over her face, dark as the clouds enveloping the skies of the city.

That same anxious shadow passed over the faces of Fehmi and Şener, standing at the edge of the pit when they heard the phone ring, and it did not disappear so quickly.

They had overlooked something, they had made a mistake ... A careless but lethal mistake that would change the course of everything, that would bring them to ruin.

Standing over the pit, they listened to the phone ring and ring and ring and ring and ring and then fall silent.

Fehmi, for his part, felt grateful for that sweet, familiar iPhone ringtone. It punctured the thick silence that had deafened his senses.

Şener, on the other hand, could not have been further from gratitude.

As soon as the phone stopped ringing, he whispered like there was someone else present, someone apart from him, Fehmi, and the body in the pit, someone who was listening in.

"We have to get that phone."

Fehmi didn't answer. Şener fixed his eyes on the pit, practically trying to pull the phone out with his eyes, and then nudged Fehmi.

"Come on, Fehmi. Get that phone. Hurry. You need to get it before the cement dries."

No response.

"Fehmi, Fehmi, let's go . . . If you don't get that phone, they'll be able to locate it. I said get that phone!"

Fehmi turned his head to Şener, terrified. "Me? You want me to get it? Why don't you?"

Şener became suddenly even more serious, his face looking like he couldn't believe the words Fehmi had just uttered. "Fehmi, darling, surely you don't expect me to stick my hands in that nasty slop."

Of course he wouldn't. Because when the kitchen sink clogged up, for instance, clearing the drain was Fehmi's job. It didn't matter if Fehmi was in his office, or toiling away on his translations, or napping, or sitting on the toilet . . . Şener would summon him and have him clear the clogs in every sink in the house. Şener valued his hands more than anything else on his body, so of course it was unthinkable that he'd stick his hands in anything remotely unclean. Whether it be a sink drain or a grave containing a corpse . . .

That was Şener's truth.

Coming to terms, yet again, with Şener's truth, Fehmi's head began computing like a calculator. Deniz had died. Şener had killed him . . . No, he couldn't lay the blame on Şener alone; they had both killed him. It was an accident, but Deniz had died regardless. Besides, it wasn't just Fehmi coming unhinged; Şener was too. Şener had had enough courage to slam an iron against a child's head hard enough to kill him, but now he drew the line at sticking his hands into wet cement.

Fehmi looked at Şener. Two men all by their lonesome. Two old murderers who'd killed someone so young. Two husbands who knew already, sure as they knew their Social Security numbers, which of them would stick their hands into the cement.

It was time for Fehmi to come to Şener's aid.

It was time for the man to step up to the plate.

Fehmi had always thought of himself as the man of the family, and so he, having been responsible for unclogging drains for the whole of their relationship, knelt at the edge of the thick, sticky pit of cement.

As he plunged his arms down to his wrists in the wet slurry, Fehmi thought of the men in the bathhouses of Berlin who stick their entire arms inside one another, men whom he had heard legend of but never seen himself. When the cold, slippery, lumpy cement went past Fehmi's wrists, his fingertips hit something hard. He latched on desperately and began feeling it. A taut Achilles heel. The cement had begun to dry, so it was difficult for him to move. He slid his hands up the body. Those must be Deniz's thighs. Finally, he was becoming acquainted with these thighs, which he had always expected to be warm and supple. Now, though, they were cold as ice. He had fantasized over them thousands of times, had imagined them over and over again in his private moments, had seen them agile and limber filling Deniz's cotton summer shorts, and now, he had his hands on them in the frigid depths of the cement. He grabbed hold of something which he took to be Deniz's swim trunks, pushing the boundaries of even his most degenerate dreams wherein he had never imagined himself touching anything above the boy's thighs. He began running his hands all over the shorts to find his phone.

"You still haven't found it? Hurry!" Şener's impatient voice rang out behind him.

Fehmi turned and glowered angrily over his shoulder. "That's enough from the peanut gallery. If you think it's so easy, then you come do it."

Şener laced his fingers over his chest. "No, dear, that's okay. You were always so keen to feel him up. Maybe while you're down there you can give it a tug."

Fehmi felt something hard in that instant and, absolutely enraged by Şener's bratty impertinence, pulled his hands out of the cement.

Covered in gray slurry, the phone was in his hand.

"My love, you're wonderful," Şener said, kneeling down and wrapping his arms around his man, who was dripping sweat from his forehead. Then he got up and began pacing again. "We need to rid ourselves of that phone right away. Go up the hill and throw it into the sea from the peak of the cliff. There won't be anybody out in this weather, but still, be careful. Then come right home. I'm going to go clean everything up."

Şener began gathering up the rods and shovels covered in cement and cleaning up the surrounding area as Fehmi rushed down the slope. He ran through the yard of their mansion, reaching the front gate and inspecting his surroundings. There was nobody. He sped into the street and began climbing to the highest point of Büyükada.

When he turned into the forest there was only him, the night, the darkness, the trees, the silence, and the clouds spitting down rain as they brawled in the sky.

He had walked in this darkened forest so many thousands of times, had sat at the foot of the pines and sipped white wine, had read his favorite novels, but he had never come here this late at night, much less while there was a storm. The forest was desolate, eerie, unsettling.

The trees leading up to the peak beat themselves in lamentation above him, whispering not their usual lullabies but screaming at him: "murderer, murdereeeeer." The scrappy bushes at the feet of the trees seemed to be shouting to one another like forty million thieves, announcing his arrival. "That's him ... That's him ... That's him ... That faggot. That faggot. That faggot murdered the boy ..."

All he wanted was to get rid of the fear that overwhelmed his body. He thought for a moment about running away. What if he threw the phone into the sea, ran to the pier, rented a boat and crossed to Bostancı ...

Then what?

What would he do then?

What if he called Halit ... Would his closest friend help him, even if he were a murderer? Would Halit and Ayşegül open their door to him, keep him safe, keep it secret until he came up with a plan, or at least until he calmed down a little?

Fehmi sadly knew all too well that "no" would be the answer.

No.

A definite No.

NO. NO. NO!

Even his best friend, his blood brother, wouldn't want to get his family involved once he heard what happened. Nobody, not a single soul on this earth, would want to stand with Fehmi in this outright murder, committed over nothing more than a measly little kiss.

He was either with Şener or he was against him. Either together, or on his own. Like playing backgammon—six and five: the lover's leap . . . Acey-deucey: Either together, or on his own.

Truly, why had Şener done it?

Crossing through the forest toward the the cliff, closing his ears to everything in nature calling him "murderer" and "faggot," Fehmi thought about the moment when the iron collided with Deniz's head. He thought about Şener. If he hadn't killed Deniz, wouldn't everything be so much easier? He could have pushed Deniz, shaken him up, yelled at him, tried to stop him, perhaps even beat him up . . .

But killing him? Wasn't that really just a little much?

"Alas, I didn't have the time to poison him," Şener had said as they stood over the body in their bedroom. Did that mean he would've poisoned Deniz, given the time? Those tricky tarts, those deceitful dolmas, all the goddamned mantı, the börek, the compotes . . . Could he have been putting trace amounts of poison into those foods which he said he was "making for his one and only beloved," upping the dose little by little every time?

Fehmi thought briefly about how lockets, like mirrors, have two faces. The forest had stopped crying out, the wind somehow lacerating him in silence.

Şener knew about Deniz. He had said so when they fought that morning. So did that mean he'd always planned on killing Deniz and was just looking for his chance? Didn't that chance present itself to him after he returned from Istanbul, heard the conversation in the bedroom, and bashed the kid over the head with the first thing he could grab? Even after they realized Deniz was only wounded, Şener hadn't shown the slightest bit of mercy, hadn't hesitated for a second to stuff a sock down his throat, had been entirely coolheaded about the whole affair. Şener had come up with the idea of tossing him in the cement from the very beginning, and had merely baited Fehmi into thinking it was his idea.

Could it be?

Breathing deep, heavy, and quick, Fehmi tried to gather his thoughts. This was the first time he'd been able to think it all over. Had Şener planned all this ahead of time? Was he now drawing Fehmi into his nefarious plan?

He began taking stock of the situation like a callous traitor.

Fehmi hadn't killed Deniz. But the two of them had tossed him in the pit together. "I had no choice," he could say. "I was forced."

With the dastardliness and the cunning of a viper nourished in Şener's bosom, he looked at the cement-covered phone in his hand. This phone was his last chance. Once he threw the phone off the cliff, there would be no turning back.

What if he ran away? Fled?

What if he went to the police, told them everything, might he have a chance? He might get a more lenient sentence, for confessing, for his shock and remorse.

His only chance was to sell Şener out. If that was his plan, he had to do it right away.

He arrived to the flat area where the trees cleared and where, a few steps ahead, the cliff ended in a sheer escarpment. The clouds seemed no more than a breath's distance away, and he sidled among them as he approached the cliff's edge. In the emptiness a few steps beyond his feet, he could see the wet rocks below, the fierce waves beating against the shore, the whole sea as swollen and churning as a drunkard's stomach. Wind, water, sky: everything bled into each other, each playing its role on a pitch-black stage that blotted out the moonlight. The dramaturgy of night was as palpable as the Shakespearean tragedies he so loved to translate.

He had no idea what to do.

Should he go? Stay? Toss the phone? Keep it?

The moment of decision was nigh. As soon as he threw the phone away, he would be guilty of destroying evidence.

Right then, an enormous bolt of lightning burst over the sea.

Seagulls somersaulted like vultures after carrion over the foaming sea, over its rolling torrent of waves, which was completely illuminated by that burst of lightning. From the edge of the cliff, Fehmi watched as the dark waters were scintillated ever so briefly.

It was a moment akin to the one Berna had had that day, about all the parties she hadn't been invited to.

As if God was saying to him, "I've taken your photograph. You, Fehmi, are a coward, a traitor, a scoundrel. I caught you scheming on this cliff, and I took your photograph. You can't flee from your sin no matter how hard you try, because I've got your record here. To think about selling out the single person trying to help you: you are as damned as the black of the waters."

A second bolt of lightning flashed in the sky after the first.

The waters were aglow before they plunged back into immediate darkness.

He no longer had anything to think about.

With a single, decisive motion, he threw the phone he'd been clinging so tightly to as far as he could throw it.

In the momentary brightness of a final flash, amid what some would call summer rains and what others would call a hurricane, the very last trace of Deniz vanished.

THE PLAN

Baking soda. Dish detergent. Carpet cleaner. Two caps of laundry detergent. A bar of soap, melted down. A little bit of stain remover. And the secret ingredient he shared with no one: two bay leaves, both for the fragrance and to get rid of the deepest recesses of blood.

With this concoction in hand, Şener was scrubbing hard at the rug in their bedroom.

No visible trace remained.

A forensic report would of course find scant traces of flesh and blood among the millions of knots in the rug. But Şener crafted a meticulous plan as he scrubbed, hoping things would never reach that point.

If he had more time, he'd scrub the whole house for days, even weeks; he'd clean, scrub, Cif, scrub, scour, and scrub some more . . .

If he were able to clean as deep as he wanted, even the forensics team might not find a single trace of Deniz's DNA.

Still, he felt like he had done his best in the brief time he had. Right after Fehmi left and with the help of the wind, he tidied up around the pit and erased their tracks up the path, returned home, wiped their door knocker with his shirt, and set to work in the living room. He did his best to tidy up the living room as his stomach churned, trying to keep from gagging, tasting the sour bile of the ulcers he had suffered for many years. He felt like vomiting not because he had become a murderer today, was no longer an ordinary old man. In fact, the murder was the last thing on his mind, the least nauseating thing in that moment.

As he put the cushions back, placed the whiskey tumblers in the kitchen sink, wiped away any possible fingerprints, and scrubbed the rug in the bedroom like a maniac, he simply couldn't shake the thought of Deniz and Fehmi fooling around here all day.

They must've sucked each other's nipples, nibbled each other's earlobes, licked each other's lips, and . . .

He was soaked in sweat. Taking off his glasses, he wiped away beads of it from his forehead. The rug in his bedroom looked good as new. He managed with great effort to move the bed slightly as well, just enough to cover up the place where Deniz's blood had pooled.

Lightning exploded over and over in the skies above Büyükada. He ran to the window and looked out. Like the flashbulbs for a Gucci shoot, bolt after bolt of lightning burst through the sky, illuminating the whole island; the rain fell in fits and starts, galloping like a horse before ceasing completely. For all he could fix things, wipe them up, scrub them away, stopping the rain was out of his control.

"What's keeping you, Fehmi? Hurry up already," he muttered to himself. It was normal for Fehmi to run late, but it always irked Şener nonetheless. Especially now, waiting for Fehmi to return on his own from the forest, he was losing his mind. What if his darling Fehmi's heart malfunctioned, what if in his rush he fell and hit his head, or had a brain hemorrhage, what if his blood pressure spiked, or a snake bit him, or a dragon swallowed him up . . .

If something happened to Fehmi he wouldn't be able to go on living. He knew that all too well. He would neither flee nor hide nor carry out his plan, but would simply await his fate. If they wanted, they could beat him, they could spit in his face as they lynched him, they could drag him through the street by a rope around his neck and hang him from a tree . . . He wouldn't care a bit. He couldn't think of a greater punishment than living without Fehmi. Ah, Fehmi, sweet Fehmi, his one and only Fehmi . . . A grief more chronic than diabetes, a grief that would blind him, would tear him limb from limb.

He looked at the bed, which he alone would notice was out of place.

This bed . . . Had Fehmi and Deniz lain together in this bed? Had this bed been where their hands fondled each other, where they stuck their tongues in each other's mouths and swallowed each other's spit, had one of them climbed on the other, wrapping his legs tight and . . .

He couldn't stop himself this time. His hand shot to his mouth and he opened the door to the bathroom, collapsed to his knees in front of the toilet, and vacated his stomach. He hadn't eaten anything for hours and only acid came up. Its acrid taste burned hard in his nose.

Despite the storm, the air still had the weight of the summer season. The humidity in the half-bathroom and the stress were wearing out his heart. He stood up, looked through the cabinet to find a bottle of pills, and swallowed one.

When he closed the medicine cabinet he came face-to-face with his reflection. There was something different about him. The face he had known for so many years was exhausted, but that wasn't what was different. Exhaustion was a customary thing. He would exhaust himself toiling in the garden or making dough for mantı. But now, in his reflection's eyes, there was a light that shined.

The eyes looking back at him seemed ambitious, like those of a young woman preparing for her university exams and hoping to get a perfect score in math. Or the impetuous eyes of a young man ready to flee his home ... Or the eager eyes of a girl sitting on a bench along the Bosphorus, nibbling hungrily on her lips, hoping the handsomest boy in school would kiss her ...

Eyes that shone, that burned with fire, that saw like they'd never seen before.

Surveying this unaccustomed face in the mirror, he felt the heart medicine spread through his rib cage and calm him down.

The door downstairs shut.

He ran to the top of the stairs and looked down. Fehmi was leaning against the front door, out of breath. He stood where he did every evening, usually with a loaf of whole wheat bread under his arm, where Şener would kiss him on the cheek, where Şener would say, "Welcome home, my love." It was around the same time he got home every evening. Were it not for the terror on Fehmi's face and the piss stain on the front of his pants, Şener would otherwise have characterized it as a normal evening. A normal evening when he would come out of the kitchen and welcome Fehmi in, when they would eat the same green beans, watch the same boring television shows that normal families did, a normal evening where, best case scenario, they would embrace each other in bed for a change of pace, and if the mood was right Fehmi would rub himself against Şener from behind, and if things were ideal, he'd nibble on his neck and they'd fall asleep in pure bliss.

But it would not be a normal evening, neither for Fehmi nor for Şener nor for that kid who jerked off without fail every night.

"How'd it go? Did you get rid of the phone?" Şener asked, rushing down the stairs.

Fehmi was so tired he couldn't answer. He nodded in assent.

Şener approached him, impatient. "Where'd you throw it? Did anyone see?"

Fehmi was curt. "I threw it from the cliff up there," he

said, entering the living room. Şener was slightly annoyed by the vagueness of the answer but said nothing more to Fehmi, leaving him alone to survey the living room.

Fehmi stared agog at the living room, purged of the traces of the day, brought back to normal. Almost like nothing had happened at all. Almost like a kid named Deniz had never come to life, had never come to this island, had never come into this living room, hadn't come to a grisly end in the bedroom and wasn't currently going stiff in a pit full of cement.

As if all they'd done was smush a measly little mosquito and continue on with their lives.

Fehmi used the back of his hand to wipe away the tears gathering in his eyes. All he wanted to do was to cry, to call out, to wail. From now on, this house would not just remind him of his happy days with Şener, but also of the moment when Deniz danced barefoot across the floor.

He pulled himself together when Şener called "Fehmi!" from upstairs, realizing he was alone in the living room. "Fehmi, come upstairs, darling," the voice called again.

Fehmi made for the staircase. He ascended helplessly, like a convict climbing the narrow stairs of a gallows.

The bedroom was empty.

"I'm here."

The voice came from the main bathroom. He opened the door to the steam-filled room. Şener, checking the temperature of the water filling the tub, turned to look at him. He was setting into motion a plan he'd had in mind for years, a plan for what to do if or when Fehmi became the kind of man who pisses himself. It would start, of course, with a hot bath.

"Come now, dear, let's take those clothes off. It's time for you to take a bath." The first bath after the first piss. Şener would have wanted to experience this moment under different circumstances, but no such luck. Fate had ordained that it be preceded by murder.

Şener brought the water to the right temperature for Fehmi—Fehmi liked the water closer to hot than warm—and poured lavender-scented bubble bath into the tub. He knew he could always trust the soothing power of lavender. He looked to Fehmi, his eyes full of compassion. "You had a difficult day, I know. I'm proud of you. Now we have some time to wash up and rest a bit," he said, standing up and crossing to Fehmi. He slowly began taking off his husband's clothes. Undoing the buttons on his shirt, sliding it off his shoulders. Fehmi's chest appeared, covered in white fur. Şener looked lovingly upon this body he'd known for so long. His hands once again passed through those white chest hairs he had caressed time and again. He couldn't possibly remember how many times he had kissed this chest, how many of these hairs had come off in his palms during their feverish lovemaking. Şener kissed Fehmi's Adam's apple, unbuckling his belt with one hand and beginning to unzip his pants. The urine-covered pants fell around Fehmi's ankles. Fehmi stood there doing nothing, like a virgin about to climb into bed with her forbidden lover for the first time. Şener had always made the moves the first time they made love: he did the same now, the first time they committed murder.

A single teardrop rolled down Fehmi's cheek and landed on Şener's liver-spotted hand.

Şener took off Fehmi's underwear, wet in the front, and helped this familiar, now-naked body into the bath, like Fehmi was a baby taking his first steps. Şener took the dirty clothes from the ground and threw them into the hamper, and when he turned around, Fehmi was sitting in the water watching him. *My God, he's still so handsome*, Şener thought. He undressed himself until he, too, was completely naked.

He didn't get in the tub right away. In the foggy brightness of the bathroom, Şener's pale skin looked almost transparent. Droplets of mist did not land on his gauzy skin but seemed to pass through him as they continued floating through the air. He seemed to be made of nothing but mist, breath, and air. He would meld with the man looking back at him from the tub, they would enter into each other's molecules, would turn to vapor in the air, would perhaps become a bubble of lavender essence in the tub, would perhaps condense into a droplet on the spigot and drip back into the water.

He got into the tub. Sitting in the tub of hot water, swathed in the scent of lavender, they stared at each other.

It was as if they had met a fortune-teller when they first began dating, who told them that forty years later to the day, they would sit across from each other in precisely this position on a stormy summer night in a bathtub in a house on Büyükada. It was as if the prophesied moment had finally arrived.

They looked at each other as though relishing this impossible premonition, their good fortune.

It brought them back to the time they first met. The young pianist and the handsome engineer. They sat in this tub like they were in their twenties, rediscovering each other, falling in love all over again.

Şener reached out and took Fehmi's fingers, kissing them and pulling him in close. Fehmi turned around, splashing water over the edge of the tub, and settled into the space between Şener's legs, his back to Şener.

Another bolt of lightning flashed across the sky.

The lightning scared them, but they knew there could have been no safer place or time in the world than there, now, in that embrace. The lightning could strike the sea, the island, the graves of the dead, but never that tub where the two now sat. Hot water, the scent of lavender, and the hands of a lover . . . After their mothers' wombs, this was the only true place of refuge for them in that moment.

Şener took the sponge from the edge of the tub, dipping it in the water to get it wet. Then he kissed Fehmi's wrinkled neck before beginning to wash him.

"Don't be afraid, Fehmi, darling. I'm here."

He lifted Fehmi's arms and scrubbed his armpits.

"I'm here and I'll never leave you. We'll get through this, I promise. If we carry out our plan, carefully, together . . . We can do it."

Fehmi listened to him in silence. They had spent enough time dealing with the murder on their own. Pretty soon, other players—the boy's mother, his father, and the police—would enter the picture. He still thought they could try their luck a different way.

"What if we give ourselves up, Şener? If we go and confess everything before Berna Hanım and Cem Bey get the search underway? If we say there was an accident?"

As Şener continued scrubbing Fehmi, a hidden smile Fehmi couldn't see crossed his lips.

"That's not possible, Fehmi, darling. Confessing won't get us anywhere. The first thing the police would suppose is that two old men lured a young boy into their house, had their way with him, and killed him." Şener shook his head in disbelief. "We know that wasn't the case. We alone . . . It all started with 'that' word he weaponized against you. But we alone know that, and we can't tell anyone."

He embraced Fehmi even more tightly from behind, and began scrubbing Fehmi's sagging belly and thighs in the hot water.

"To be honest, I don't want to see Berna Hanım standing in court with a handsome picture of the kid or crying and cursing us to a bunch of journalists. I want to support her through it all without thinking about what caused all this, and I certainly don't want to lose you in the end. I can't live without you, Fehmi."

He seemed to be speaking not with Fehmi but with the bubbles, the water, the steam, or else with a larger ghostly presence that enveloped everything.

"I don't want this to turn into a big drama about their

picture-perfect family, the handsome architect father, the successful dentist mother, the murdered son. I couldn't stand it. Think about it, is there any judge or prosecutor who would believe us? What idiot lawyer would take our case and defend us? Who would support us?"

Şener had worked himself into a frenzy, and Fehmi grew tense. He was stunned that Şener had been able to think things over in such detail during the short time they were apart. While he'd been busy contemplating confessing to the police and selling Şener out, Şener had been coming up with a plan. Şener squeezed the sponge underwater again and continued speaking as he gently scrubbed Fehmi's withered penis.

"Yes, who would support us? We're the only ones who can do each other any good, Fehmi, darling. In our family that's how we resolve things. Just like all other normal families . . ."

Moving his legs underwater, Fehmi pulled his knees in to allow Şener to scrub his legs.

"Not to mention, Fehmi, darling, if it gives you peace of mind, I don't think what we did was all that wrong. That kid was way out of line. I won't hear any different from anyone. He needed to be punished for saying what he did, and you can be certain his mother grounding him wouldn't have been enough."

Impassioned, he threw the sponge into the water. He took Fehmi's hand to comfort him. It had been such a long time since the two of them had sat in the tub like this. Whenever they took a bath together in the past, they'd make love before getting out. The flames of that passion may have been extinguished, but their place was now taken by the compassionate arms of love, respect, and fidelity.

Fehmi took Şener's two hands and held them; once he felt Şener calm down, he encouraged him to continue. "All right, dear. Let's not think any more about Deniz. That part's over. What do we do from here? What's your plan?"

Şener replied in a decisive tone: "My plan is this, Fehmi, darling: We don't do a thing."

Fehmi turned his face to Şener's. "What do you mean? Don't do a thing . . . ?" he asked, his voice full of hesitation.

"That's right, not a thing . . . We'll do what we've always done best. We'll stay in the closet."

Fehmi continued staring blankly at Şener. Şener ran his finger over Fehmi's chin and, bringing his face a little closer, looked deep into his eyes.

"Yes, my love, exactly that. If we don't get mixed up in it then nobody will have reason to suspect us of having anything to do with the disappearance of some disobedient problem child. Think about it, two old men . . . What would we have to do with anything, right? Of course, we can't remain completely silent, that would draw attention. We'll help Berna Hanım however we can. When they look for the kid, we'll be as worried as she is, raise as much hell as she does. But we have to do it all to just the right degree so nobody suspects us. Of course we'll give our statements to the police, tell them what we did on the day of the incident. I was in Istanbul, you were at home sick. I have a ferry full of witnesses; if you've got a witness that'd make things easier for us."

Fehmi stammered out, "The workmen building the gazebo."

"Great, they'll confirm you were at home. Ultimately they don't know when the kid left or where he went. They'll probably eventually find the backpack he threw into the sea. All we have to do is try to direct their investigations toward the possibility that he was lost at sea. I'll take care of that bit, leave that to me. All you have to do is perfectly play the role of a concerned neighbor. That's it."

Fehmi wasn't entirely convinced but he still didn't say anything. Şener got out of the tub, put on his bathrobe, and brought Fehmi his.

"Come now, we've got to hurry and rest up a bit. A long night, and many long days, await us."

They went to the bedroom. Fehmi put on freshly ironed underwear and clean pajamas. When he got in bed, Şener was standing in front of the mirror in their half-bathroom, wearing his pajamas and rubbing lotion into his hands. Looking at Fehmi through the mirror, Şener repeated himself to make sure he understood.

"Everything will be just like us. Just like our relationship. It'll all be hidden in plain sight. We'll share in that family's grief, play a key role in the search and rescue efforts. But we'll guide the whole process. The only thing we have to do is persuade people that the kid was lost at sea. Because there's no body and no trace to find." Şener turned away from the mirror, massaging in the lotion, and walked to the bed. "I want you to take extra care. It might seem easy but it'll be quite hard. There's a very fine line between not enough and too much. If we leave the slightest opening everything could come out."

Fehmi nibbled nervously on his lips. His eyes were brimming with tears again. "What if the police dogs search around the house? The dogs will smell him in no time."

"Don't be silly, Fehmi, how many times have you seen police dogs come to the island over some dumb kid lost at sea? Even if they did come . . . they wouldn't smell him through the cement."

"What'll happen when there's no body in the sea? They'll deepen the search."

"Honest to God, it's the police's problem at that point, not ours. Did he run away, or did his body get caught on a rock along the seafloor and get eaten by haddock, or did he get carried away by the currents? Let them keep trying to find him. If they can, of course."

When Şener pulled back the blanket and climbed into bed, Fehmi was trembling underneath. He turned Fehmi towards him and kissed him on the lips as if to soothe him with a soft lullaby. Fehmi was tense as a hound dog sensing the approach of danger. His trembling wouldn't end, only growing worse instead. Listening to the winds blowing madly outside, he whispered fearfully. "And the storm? If the rain gets worse, the cement won't dry. If the police come to the backyard they might want to check the wet cement."

His eyes were locked on Şener's, awaiting his reply. From where he lay, Şener looked out the window. A hopeless expression rippled across his face. "I know. That part is up to God. The only thing we can do is pray for the rain to stop."

Fehmi sobbed, sidling closer to Şener. He was afraid, he was trembling, he was cold.

Şener caressed his hair, planting a gentle kiss on the crown of his head. "Come now, try to sleep a bit."

Fehmi shook his head. "I don't think I'll be able to sleep. I'm so afraid, Şener."

Şener reached gingerly over to the side table and pulled a medicine bottle from the drawer. He broke one of the tablets in the bottle in two, giving half to Fehmi with the glass of water on the side table. "Take this. It'll calm your nerves. It'll help you sleep."

His voice seemed decisive, even commanding. Fehmi looked at the piece of white pill in his hand. After taking that pill he would awaken to something entirely unknown. He wasn't sure if he was ready for that. The thoughts he'd had alone in the forest returned. Somewhere inside himself he still didn't fully trust Şener.

What if the pill . . . was something else?

Şener looked firmly into his eyes. "Take it. You'll feel better."

Unable to muster the energy to object, Fehmi tossed the pill in his mouth and drank the water. Nestling into Şener's arms, he closed his eyes. Şener continued caressing his hair, speaking gently, slowly, to calm him down.

"Sleep now, my darling. Don't be afraid. I'm always here. I'll always be here. I'll never leave you. We'll get past this bump in the road together. We still have so many beautiful days to spend together . . ."

Fehmi felt a strange heaviness begin to descend upon him.

"Don't be afraid, my love. We will succeed. We can do it as long as we do what we've always done. Nobody will suspect a thing. Don't be afraid, Fehmi, darling. Don't be afraid . . ."

An artificial, chemical sleep emerged from its cave and pounced on Fehmi, wrapping its dark limbs around him. Even if Fehmi wanted to resist, the sleep was stronger than he was.

"Don't be afraid, my love. We'll be free of this. If the rain stops we'll be free of this."

Fehmi felt a gentle warmth swaddle his whole body. The warmth embraced and immobilized him. Descending into the inescapable, imprisoning darkness of that warmth, he could still hear the words of Şener, who continued stroking his hair.

"My love . . . My darling . . . My husband . . . All we have to do is be what we are. We'll succeed if we can be what we are. What we are . . . What our relationship is. What our family is . . . We'll be free of this because we're faggots . . ."

A deep, impossibly sweet feeling, the feeling of lying between your parents after a nightmare and closing your eyes in a bed warmed by their bodies, enveloped Fehmi. A veil of compassion light as tulle enshrouded him. The feeling buried Fehmi in a bleary darkness, not unlike that of the child plunged into eternal slumber outside, underneath the bursts of lightning.

The last thing he heard as he fell asleep, just barely, uncertain if it was real or not, was " . . . because we're faggots."

THE PRAYER

After Fehmi fell asleep, Şener continued stroking his hair for a while before he got up and went onto the balcony. Leaning on the railing, he looked at the raging clouds that kept churning above him. Rain that could spell the end of everything was still falling.

Without taking his eyes from that blackest of skies, he fell to his knees at the balcony railing.

And he began praying for some impossible mercy.

"God . . . Asking, begging of you is beyond our right as your sinful servants. I know that well. Maybe for that very reason I've asked very little of you my whole life. But now I am in need of your forgiveness and aid, endless as the deep seas.

"God . . . Everything that happened tonight happened under the watchfulness of your ninety-nine eyes. What happened in every second, you alone can know. You, after all, have written all of this as our fate. I have no right to beg forgiveness for the fate you ordain for us, neither on my behalf nor on Fehmi's nor even on poor Deniz lying in that pit. All three of us deserve every punishment you ordain for us in the end.

"You whose grandeur is indisputable; you who created the wide seas and the great mountains and the burning deserts and the thousand and one creatures of the world . . .

"You who created billions of people across this earth, who created families, mothers, fathers, children . . .

"We, too, were made in your image; we, too, bear the traces of your rainbow colors. You who created all those other people of flesh and bone created people like us from helva wafers, cotton candy, and bonbons.

"This here is my family and I must protect it. That is why I entreat you with a single prayer, my God. Please, I beg you, show your might, your endless power . . .

"And calm this storm!"

No sooner had these words come out of Şener's mouth than something miraculous happened. The impatient clouds churning in the sky were as if by a forceful blow from some invisible hand sent scattering, and the rain came to an immediate stop. The full moon waiting behind the clouds appeared in the sky in all its majesty.

And the light of the full moon obscured for hours fell upon the white hair of an old man on his knees, surrounding him in a halo, brightening him like a saint.

THE SCREAM

Bam! Bam! Bam!

BAM! BAM! BAM! BAMBAMBAMBAM!

Fehmi, sleeping like a baby, was startled awake.

It sounded like the door of the old mansion was about to break. As if the door was groaning, choking, sobbing, suffering, as if a god who hadn't heard its prayer might hear its pain.

Let the games begin. For they had arrived.

Police? Gendarme? Soldiers? Islanders brandishing torches and pitchforks, eager to burn their house down?

They'd been caught before they'd had enough time to set their plan in motion. The day that had even in the depths of their sleep seemed like a nightmare up until that very moment suddenly became real with the banging at the door.

BAM! BAM! BAM!

Soaked in sweat, Fehmi sat up in bed. He turned on

the bedside lamp by force of habit, put on his glasses, and glanced around.

The left side of the bed was completely empty.

The pillows hadn't moved a millimeter; the covers remained undrawn, the sheets unwrinkled. Şener hadn't even gone to bed. Nor was he in the room. Fehmi was all alone and the banging continued from outside.

BAM! BAM!

Fehmi was still groggy from the pill Şener gave him, but the dizziness he felt getting out of bed stemmed more from the terror of being awakened, all alone, by the noise.

He didn't know what to do.

BAM!

Everything he thought of doing when he went to throw the phone off the cliff about fleeing, calling the police, confessing, begging for mercy: Şener had done precisely that. He'd merely acted faster than Fehmi.

What else should he have expected? After all, Şener was just as much as a traitor and a coward as he was. Şener had knocked him unconscious, gathered all his belongings and fled the island; he had long since vanished, leaving Fehmi to deal with this madness alone. "They'll hold me responsible for everything! How could I have been so oblivious?" he murmured to himself as he began frantically pacing the room. The knocking and the yells continued coming from outside. He slid his soft slippers on his feet, put on his dressing gown, and left the bedroom. Walking toward the stairs he wondered what he should do. He had no idea.

Trying to gather his thoughts, he began descending the stairs. In the middle of the staircase, he noticed a shadow standing in the entryway, where the banging on the door echoed loudly.

BAM BAM BAM!

Şener was waiting for him.

Their eyes met.

Of course he hadn't abandoned Fehmi. In every relationship there is but one traitor, and in their relationship, that traitor was Fehmi. Fehmi felt ashamed once more. Cold sweat poured down his back. That his first thought was to distrust Şener, to think he'd been abandoned, to suppose betrayal, did nothing but push him deeper and deeper again into the murky realm of shame.

The noise at the door allowed him to contain that shame for now. Holding his breath, he glanced at the door that seemed like it would fall down at any moment, before he returned his gaze to Şener. This would be their last moment alone before things got out of hand. The struggle of life and death was about to begin.

Şener seemed to be silently asking, "Are you ready?" before he placed his hand on the doorknob.

Fehmi gulped. He nodded gently in acceptance of their fate. *I'm ready*.

Şener turned the knob and the door opened. And that hot and sinister summer night on Büyükada, and all of its dark humanity, poured into the house.

———

Berna no longer had any idea how long she'd been crying. She measured how much time had passed not by her tears but by the hours that had elapsed since she'd been able to reach her son. In that time, the time of Deniz, she had been crying for ages.

"Get off my back." That was the last thing she'd heard from Deniz. After that, an unknown. She had waited helplessly at the Kabataş Pier for a ferry that would not depart due to the storm; she couldn't find a way to the island and had since spent the subsequent time crying and trying to look for Deniz.

While she waited on the pier, Berna felt from deep within a sense of hopelessness and helplessness. A crowd had assembled around her, watching her condition deteriorate, and she simply couldn't explain herself to them as she wept. Her son was on the island and wasn't answering his phone? "And so what?" a woman had said to her, her lips painted blood red. "His battery's probably dead, sweetie, don't worry."

Berna, unable to reply, her eyes full of pain, stared at the woman. What was that horrible, sinking feeling she'd felt all day, then? That feeling that everyone except her was enjoying themselves at a great big party?

She was in no state to explain herself to anyone, so she opted to continue crying and begging.

"God, please, help me. Please."

It took two hours for God to decide to help Berna.

By then, night had fallen. Once the storm over Istanbul had slightly abated and began moving toward the islands,

Cem, who had canceled his meeting and come to the pier, and Berna, her face puffy from crying, found a motorboat whose captain agreed to take them to Büyükada.

It was a voyage that seemed to never end. It felt like they were moving as slow as a caravan of forty camels along the Silk Road. On the open sea, Cem and Berna held each other. The motorboat continued through the darkness, rising and falling over the churning waves.

The only noises around them were the cries of the gulls, the sputtering of the motor, and the howling wind across the clamorous sea.

Berna stared into the darkness as they approached Büyükada, waiting to catch sight of the island's first lights as they came into view. She was filled with anxiety like a weary castaway lost at sea for days, wanting nothing more than to climb on land and kiss the earth. At long last, the scattered lights on Büyükada appeared through the storm. The boatsman fixed his wide eyes on the sea, and growled: "The storm's not stopping. Shouldn't have gone to sea tonight . . . Dammit. God willing the waves won't push us out, or else I won't be able to moor the boat."

Cem replied in that reassuring voice he used to mollify things, "Thank you, Captain. But it's a matter of life and death. We can't get in touch with our son. God as my witness, please help us."

A matter of life and death . . . God as my witness . . . For the first time in twenty years of marriage Berna was hearing the word *God* come out of Cem's mouth. Cem's rural roots had slipped from his mouth in this moment of fear, as life and death, as God and prophet.

Hearing God's name, Berna felt the tears she had subdued for some time now begin to well up again. Like she was at a funeral, waiting calmly until the plaintive voice of the hoca began reciting the Qur'an, which would send her weeping almost to the point of self-flagellation.

It was the first moment she felt like she was arriving to a dead Deniz. Rising and falling over the waves, approaching the distant lights of Büyükada glimmering in the darkness, somewhere inside her, from a place so deep she didn't know its name, a bitter fear came suddenly to life.

She supposed the great big party she hadn't been invited to had long since ended.

The soft weeping of her lament dissipated like foam over the waves. *God, please help me. Please, please help* . . .

And at long last God heard her prayer, for as the lights of Büyükada became clearer in the distance, a miracle happened. In an instant the black clouds blanketing the sky vanished and the full moon appeared in all its majesty. The dark sea luminesced briefly as the boat chopped through the waves.

The sea calmed and the rage of the waves dissolved.

Berna looked around. She couldn't believe her eyes. The rain and the wind had stopped and the weather had cleared. God was helping them. Perhaps they could leave this ill-starred night behind them as nothing more than a bad joke.

Cem held Berna close and whispered, "See, everything's

turning out okay. The weather's improving. When we get home we'll find Deniz fast asleep. You'll see that you spent your whole day eating away at yourself for nothing."

Berna brought her handkerchief to her eyes again without reply.

Was Deniz really asleep in his bed? Was his hand stuffed under his pillow, a habit he'd had since he was a baby? Had he drawn the covers, was he shivering? Did he eat or did he go to bed hungry? There was chicken in the fridge, if only he'd warmed it up.

Once the motorboat reached the pier, Berna and Cem hopped onto dry land without a word of thanks to the boatsman; they jumped in the first carriage they found and began racing up the hill. The steep incline left the nickering horses panting. Just like Berna. Just like Cem.

The silence was deafening as they reached the peak. Berna glanced at the neighboring house, but the carriage's speed didn't permit her to catch sight of the figure in the window on the ground floor, looking out anxiously at the road. In her state she wouldn't have even noticed a full marching band behind that curtain, let alone a single person. She was too fixated on their own home, which waited silent in the darkness under the moonlight as much as their neighbors' home did.

Berna leapt from the carriage before it had come to a stop and ran to the door. She slammed it open and stormed in.

Silence.

Into the living room.

Silence.

Into the kitchen.

Silence.

Cem, racing upstairs.

"Berna, darling, don't be afraid. He's here sleeping."

Her ears pricked up like a hyena's. These were the words she hoped to hear.

"Berna, darling, don't be afraid. He's here sleeping."

"Berna, darling, he passed out drunk, the little jackass."

"Berna, darling, he's kicked off the covers. Do you want to come give him a kiss and tuck him back in?"

Overcome with fear, Berna ascended the stairs to the top floor, her legs trembling. Cem stood in front of Deniz's room, panicked as he dialed a number on his phone.

"Berna, darling, he must have fallen and hit his head. I'm calling an ambulance."

Clinging to the wall she passed into the doorway of her son's bedroom. That same woman's voice came from the phone against Cem's ear. "The person you are trying to reach is not available . . ."

Pushing past Cem, Berna entered Deniz's room.

The room, brightened by the moon, was entirely empty. Pale, pure light filtered through the tulle curtain that hung over the closed window. The bed was as Berna had made it that morning, untouched. The cotton shorts Deniz wore at night lay folded on the corner of the bed. A pair of white socks, probably tossed on the floor that morning, awaited her.

Berna knelt down and picked up the white socks. She began shuddering. Cem's eyes met hers.

And a sound like a snarl, like a lament, like a prayer, came from Berna's lips. An indescribable sound. A howl of fear and helplessness . . . a sound like the one that brings life into the world when a mother, with one final effort, pushes her baby out . . . or the terrified greeting of a baby, unable to understand where it is, a baby pushed out of the womb and tumbled into this void we call life. A sound only mothers and babies would know . . .

A wail! A requiem! A scream!

The storm had fully subsided; even the leaves on the trees barely moved. The air began growing palpably warmer.

Cem took Berna into his arms. There on the floor, for a fleeting few seconds, they savored a brief respite of closeness over their child whose life lay hanging in the balance.

And then the animal instinct to save the child erupted, first, of course, from Berna.

With a quick motion she loosed herself from Cem's arms. "Şener Bey and Fehmi Bey . . . perhaps they know something," she said.

"Berna, darling, it's so late. Let's not bother them, let's go straight to the police," Cem replied, but Berna wasn't listening; she was already on her way out of the house. Like a fluttering tulle curtain, like a swinging pendulum, like a drop of dew trying to fall from a leaf, she ran, she crossed the gate between the two houses, and she entered the front yard of her only true friends on the island.

She ran, she passed through the garden filled with the scent of roses, of jasmine and honeysuckle, a garden that was doubtless the most beautiful on the whole island, and she began pounding on the door of the old mansion.

BAM! BAM! BAM!

BAMBAMBAM!

After a while she heard footsteps coming from inside. The light came on in the entryway and the door opened.

Standing before her with sleepy, bewildered eyes, wrapped in his dressing gown, was Şener, trying to understand what was happening. Behind him, Fehmi waited at the foot of the stairs, looking on in fear.

Şener put on his glasses. "Berna Hanım. What's going on? Is everything okay?" he asked, his voice full of concern as he took a step toward the trembling woman on his doorstep.

Berna began sobbing; the only word that came from her lips was "Deniz . . ." Then a dizzy spell suddenly took hold of her and she fainted there on the doorstep, at Şener's feet.

THE POLICE

The subtle, sharp, cooling scent of kolonya . . .

A piquancy that shocks from within, almost like you're in a lemon grove. Like you're touching the droplets of dew on the still-ripening lemons on an early holiday morning.

The fresh scent of kolonya, which leaves its gentle burn in your nose . . .

"Berna Hanım, Berna Hanım! Are you all right?"

The blurry lights seem to be spinning in the ceiling but there are voices around her. An old man . . . That angelic face, those angelic eyes looking back at her full of so much worry. You remember, Berna, how often you were sick as a kid. You were brought to the hospital, barely conscious, in a taxi going at full speed. On that thin line between life and death, you opened your eyes for a brief moment and saw your mother looking back at you. This man, looking at you like that now.

The light coolness in the scent of the lemon kolonya.

"Berna Hanım . . . I think she's coming to. Berna Hanım . . . Are you all right?"

Berna slowly sat up in the chair. One hand in Şener's, the other in Cem's as he wept silently. Fehmi stood beside her holding a bottle of kolonya. Şener was massaging the kolonya into her wrists as he muttered almost sermonically: "Oh, my dear. Oh, my poor, unfortunate girl."

"Berna, my love, are you all right?" Cem asked, throwing his arms around her.

"I'm fine, it's nothing," she lied. Her eyes, still full of worry, met Şener's as they looked for an answer.

With an expression of pity legible on his face, he jumped right in: "I'm so sorry, Berna Hanım. Cem Bey told us everything. I'm sure there's nothing to worry about."

Berna turned to Cem. "Call the police," she said.

Cem began dialing as Fehmi asked, "Do you know the number?"

"Is it not 155?"

"Cem Bey, if you call 155, they'll connect you to Istanbul. It'll take hours for them to get here. I think you should call the Büyükada Police Station directly."

Fehmi went to the stack of cards next to the landline in the entryway, grabbed one, and handed it to Cem. The number Cem dialed rang and rang and rang and rang and nobody answered.

"No answer," Cem said angrily, and dialed again. Fehmi stood next to the worried father while Şener still clung to

Berna's hand. They had each taken their role in solidarity with the appropriate gender.

Şener slowly let go of Berna's hand and got to his feet. "They won't be at the station at this hour, Fehmi, darl . . . Fehmi Bey. They've most likely gone out on patrol since the storm just subsided."

"All on patrol at once?" Berna asked, bewildered.

Şener nodded in exasperation. "Berna Hanım, you wouldn't understand. Every police officer in the world is useless, but the island police are somehow more useless than the rest. Not much happens here apart from a broken liquor bottle or a minor argument. So all they do is loiter and loaf around."

Berna leapt from her seat. "I'm going to lose my mind. Let's go. Let's go find the police. Deniz is still missing."

"You're absolutely right, Berna Hanım. But panicking in situations like this only makes things worse, believe me. Let's try to remain calm. You're worried right now, it's normal. So just listen to us, let us come with you. Wait two minutes, I'll just change my clothes quickly."

Without waiting for Berna's assent he sped upstairs. Cem dialed the station again. Berna paced frantically back and forth until Şener came downstairs and pulled on a jacket. It had really taken him less than two minutes to get ready.

"Fehmi Bey, go on then, change your clothes as well," he said, gesturing with his head. "Cem Bey, have you looked around outside the house yet? Maybe he had an accident nearby, fell or something . . ."

Berna interjected. "No, we didn't look. Let's go."

"Berna Hanım, let's split up so we don't lose time. We're four people, let's split into groups of two."

Şener knelt at the bottom of the cabinet in the entryway and pulled out two flashlights. He gave one to Cem and handed the other to Fehmi, who was coming down the stairs. "Fehmi Bey, you look around our house. By the cellar, in the backyard, around the area above the trees, in the front yard ... Make sure your flashlights are working."

Fehmi pressed the button on his flashlight; its beam glowed in the darkness like the eye of a wildcat and faded away.

"Cem Bey, you go look around your house. Be sure to check the open lot on the other side, the yard, even the road leading up to the forest. Maybe he fell somewhere."

No sooner had these words come out of his mouth than Şener, involuntarily trying to ward off the jinx, tugged on his earlobe and knocked three times on the edge of the wooden side table.

"Berna Hanım, you and I will go to the station. It certainly won't be easy to find a policeman on the island right now." They assembled in the entryway. Şener turned to Fehmi and Cem. "If you don't find him, come directly to the station, we'll reconvene there," he said, and opened the door.

The pungent smell of the earth, warming after the heavy rain, hit them in the face like a breath of hot eucalyptus.

———

Berna and Şener practically ran down the steep slope, and by the time they arrived to the main square, the clock tower indicated that it was already past midnight. Entering the courtyard of the police station, Şener glanced around sheepishly. "Just as I thought. Normally there's a police car here, but not right now. They're probably making their rounds," he said, leading Berna into the building. The waiting room of the station opened onto three rooms. The first two were empty. In the third, behind a table covered in folders and documents, sat a policeman in his thirties. He had been dozing off, but the noise of them storming into the room startled him awake.

The officer's badge read Erkan Aray, and Berna lunged at him, almost in pure supplication.

"Officer, we have an urgent situation. My son has been missing for hours. He's not answering his phone, nor is he at home. I'm afraid something might have happened to him. Please help."

"Remain calm, ma'am, of course we'll help," Erkan said, trying to shake off his groggy daze. "Just a second," he continued, taking the walkie-talkie from the desk and broadcasting himself over the radio signal that covered the island. "Officer Erkan to the police car . . . Officer Erkan to the police car . . ."

The walkie-talkie only returned a static sound.

"Officer Erkan to Officer Hasan . . . Officer Erkan to Officer Hasan . . ."

Officer Erkan's dispatch from the station received no

response from Officer Hasan because at that moment, Officer Hasan and Officer Tarık sat at Lale Toast Shop, greedily eating their second paninis of the night as they contemplated ordering another with sausage and potatoes while they ogled the legs of a group of Swedish girls in miniskirts. Their walkie-talkies were on silent, left in the police car parked up the street. They had circled the island twice and, as the case had been for the previous thousand nights, there were no incidents worth noting.

When Officer Erkan got no response, he languidly put the walkie-talkie back down and turned to Berna. "They'll respond soon. I'll call them now on their cell phones."

Berna was overcome with trembling, though it was unclear whether she trembled out of anger or out of worry. "My God, I'm losing my mind. What kind of place is this? Are there no other police? Call them already! My son's missing, I'm telling you, my son . . ."

Erkan was annoyed by her breach of formality. Especially here, in his workplace, at the station . . . He glared at Berna as he dialed on his cell phone. "There's no other police officers. I'm trying to help you, ma'am, but I said I need you to remain calm, so . . ."

Şener, who had been standing silently behind Berna the whole time, felt the need to intervene, and interrupted the officer. "I understand, Officer . . ." He leaned in and straightened his glasses, making a show of reading the name on the badge. "Officer Erkan . . . But this is a very delicate situation. This good woman is worried to death about her son. Especially with the storm today, we're concerned, God forbid, that something might have happened to him. I live on the island, the situation really is urgent," he said, trying to mollify the tension.

"I get it, I get it. I'm already trying to help," Erkan said, dialing the number.

The phone rang twice and Officer Hasan, his mouth full of sandwich, finally answered Officer Erkan.

"Hey, Hasan . . . There's a man and a woman here at the station. The lady's son is missing. Did you see anything on your rounds? No? Okay. Go take a look again, more carefully this time, all right, hoooooooney? All right." He hung up the phone. "Do you have a picture of him?" he asked.

Of course she did. Berna opened her wallet and pulled out Deniz's last yearbook photo, wearing his Alphan Preparatory Academy uniform. After so many hours had passed she was laying eyes once again on Deniz's face. Extending the picture to Erkan with trembling hands, she began crying again, and Şener resolutely squeezed her shoulder.

After he looked at the photograph he turned to Berna. "I thought you meant a little kid, this here's practically a full-grown man . . . He's missing? Maybe he went somewhere else. Couldn't he be at a friend's? Did you call everyone?"

Berna shook her head. "I looked everywhere. No. He wouldn't go to a friend's or something. He wouldn't, he couldn't have left the island . . ." Her crying devolved into sobs as she spoke. "Look, my son is a bit of a problem child.

Anything could have happened to him. Aren't there any more police teams here?"

"Ma'am, this is Büyükada, there's no teams or anything. Just a few officers. All the units are in Istanbul and we'll only be able to reach them in the morning. They won't come as long as there isn't anything urgent."

Berna cried out in agony. "This *is* urgent!"

"No, not urgent like that. Let's first wait to hear from the other officers. I already told you, the search teams can only come in the morning, don't you understand me?"

They turned at a sound from the front door and saw Fehmi and Cem. Both of their faces bore expressions of helplessness: they didn't find what they'd been looking for. Şener, who had tried to remain silent so far, released Berna's shoulder, stepped up to the front of the desk, leaned back down to Erkan, and stared him in the eyes.

"Look here, young man. My patience is almost spent. The missing child, Deniz, suggested to his mother that he might try swimming to Bostancı, did you know that? He might have tried it today and swam into the open sea. This is a life-or-death situation we're talking about, and you're about to be responsible for the whole thing. Understand? Everything is going to be your fault if you don't start the search right now, I can promise you that."

Erkan gulped. "Are you threatening me?"

Şener leaned over the desk even more, his nose almost touching Erkan's, and continued speaking in a peremptory tone. "No, I'm not threatening you. I'm telling you exactly what will happen if you don't call for the search teams right now. And like I said, I'm an islander. I know everyone here. I know your supervisor and his wife, I know the mayor and his wife, I know every single person of any import on this island and all their wives. See those trees out there, you know, the ones planted last year? I had them planted. Remember when you all wanted a new police car? We made that happen. Please don't force me to get any more impolite," Şener said before slamming his hand with a BOOOMMM down on the desk.

BOOOMMM.

"You will bring the coast guard to the island, and you will do it now!"

IN SEARCH OF LOST CHILD

The following day was one of the hottest days that summer.

Air conditioners in cars cranked to maximum, asphalt melting and clinging to shoes, newly poured concrete for the construction blighting the city petrified by the sun, and on Büyükada, the largest of the Princes' Islands, everyone was in search of a lost child.

The expert teams had arrived from Bostancı with the first rays of morning, and though the police had already turned Büyükada upside down in their search, these teams used their own methods to investigate. They had started scanning security camera footage first thing in the morning, the experts combing through freeze-frames from the whole day. The search on land was accompanied by a coast guard boat in the sea, circling the island over and over, examining the bays, beaches, and orphaned shores where so many people would swim that day. Despite all their efforts, they had yet to find anything. The teams were deliberate, the coast guard boat was moored to the pier, and the officers scanning the camera footage zoomed in one by one on persons of interest. There was but one sure thing for now: every second that passed without results, that flowed away like the tick of a metronome, dwindled hope for the boy's survival.

"In cases of missing persons, the first twenty-four hours are crucial," said Ziya, the commissioner heading up all the teams from Istanbul. "After that first twenty-four hours, unfortunately, the chance of finding missing persons alive begins to decrease. God willing, we'll find little Deniz alive and well and deliver him to his family."

In another room of the police station, Berna's condition worsened the more time passed; sitting in wait, every lost minute felt like it knocked ten years off her life. Cem had practically lost his mind, running from one room to the other, trying to learn any information at all from the police, the results of the coast guard survey, the latest reports on the security camera footage, and his fear and anxiety were only growing. Fehmi and Şener had also been there all night; they looked at least as tired as Berna and Cem, trying to console the aggrieved parents, to listen for any new developments no matter how small, and of course, to wait for images from the security cameras. Had the cameras caught something? It was a question that afforded husband-and-wife the smallest sliver of hope, while it plunged husband-and-husband into a deep and uncertain terror that they masked as best they could.

Ziya entered the room where Berna and Cem sat, and

when he began his interrogation, Fehmi and Şener remained at their side. Ziya took the parents' information and asked them why they had moved to the island. Berna and Cem told the whole story of Deniz's scandal at the Alphan Preparatory Academy in all its grisly detail. Ziya made no comment as he took down notes.

"Was there an issue at home, a problem that arose recently?"

Swallowing her feelings, Berna told him about their phone call that day and the ongoing problems at home. She finally admitted it to herself: the problem was between her and Deniz. It was the first time she'd said so aloud.

"Did he have a place he might have gone, a relative or a friend?"

Berna and Cem listed off the possibilities.

"Did anything of note happen yesterday?"

It was a normal day filled with the same events of every other ordinary day. A day so normal one might kill out of boredom . . . The only differences were that there had been a storm and that they hadn't been able to return to the island. That was it. That was the only thing out of the ordinary on a day that completely altered the course of their lives. They hadn't been able to make it to this godforsaken island and now their son was gone. Sometimes life can be summed up so simply in a single sentence.

"Was there anyone he knew or spent time with on the island?"

No, nobody. After the incident at school Deniz had

essentially been grounded, and he was usually at home. The only person he knew beyond them, the only person they might consider his friend, was Fehmi Bey.

"Fehmi Bey? Who's Fehmi Bey?"

"I am, sir."

Ziya lifted his head from his notebook and looked for the first time at the old man who stood with the family, at the ready like a first-aid kit, the old man whose hand he had shaken upon entering but whom he hadn't really noticed. He sized up the old man, suspicion in his eyes.

"Fehmi Bey . . . What are you to the boy?"

"We're their neighbors, officer. We live in the house next door."

"We?"

Şener cleared his throat. "Yes, we, sir . . . We live together. Last night Berna Hanım came to us first when she realized Deniz wasn't at home. We're here to help them."

Ziya looked Şener up and down. Then, shifting his eyes back and forth between Fehmi and Şener, he returned to his notes. "Where were you yesterday?"

"I went to Istanbul, sir. I had some shopping to do. Then when I realized the storm was coming, I came back on the last ferry."

"And you?"

"I was at home. I wasn't feeling well, so I spent the whole day resting."

"So you were at home. Did you see Deniz at all yesterday?"

"No, officer."

"Did anything happen that stood out to you?"

"No. I hardly left my bedroom. I worked a bit on my translation, then took some medicine and slept."

"Do you remember the last time you saw Deniz?"

Fehmi scratched his forehead, thinking. "I don't quite remember ... The last time ... was probably a few days ago, in the evening. We crossed paths in our yards and chatted."

"What did you talk about?"

"Just small talk, this and that ..."

"So you're the only person on the island with whom he was friendly. Did he say anything to you that might have to do with his disappearance? Anything you noticed ... Please, tell me anything that comes to mind. Sometimes a detail that seems insignificant can make all the difference."

"Well, we didn't talk about private things like that. In the end, we didn't really share a deep friendship. He's young enough to be my grandson, after all ... He was just a lonely kid, so bored here, I can say that much. It seemed like he wasn't happy to be on the island."

Berna sighed mournfully. Fehmi continued in the silence that followed her sigh.

"The only thing is, I just thought of it. Last week ..."

"Yes?"

"Last week he asked how long we've lived on Büyükada. After I said we'd been here thirty years, he asked me if I knew anyone who had swum from here to Bostancı."

"What do you mean? What did he say exactly?"

"That he was on his school's swim team. He said he'd won

trophies, that he was a very good swimmer. He said that he could swim from here to Bostancı in an hour and a half . . ."

"What did you say?"

"What could I say? I said I'd never heard of anyone doing that. I did my best to tell him it's impossible, that Bostancı looks close to here but that it's a kind of optical illusion. I told him he shouldn't try something like that under any circumstances. I'm just realizing now that it didn't seem like he paid me much heed."

"He said the same thing to me, officer."

Everyone turned to look at Berna.

"Recently we had the same discussion at home. He'd gotten hung up on swimming back to the coast. We got in an argument over it."

Ziya continued taking notes while everyone else in the room looked down at the floor, like they'd all collectively arrived at the same conclusion.

"And you . . . Şener Bey, wasn't it? After you returned from Istanbul did you notice anything?"

"No, sir. I came straight home, made our dinner, then rested and went to bed. I didn't notice anything out of the ordinary. We were at home together all night. The weather was so bad, we couldn't do anything else even if we wanted to. Then the knock on the door woke me up."

"All right, then. Thank you. Just . . . I just have one more question."

Şener replied in a concerned, beneficent tone. "Of course, officer, by all means."

"You . . . and Fehmi Bey . . . live in the same house . . . so?"

"So . . . I'm not sure I understand what you're asking?"

Ziya pointed crudely at Fehmi and Şener. "You, I'm asking . . . You two. What is your relationship?"

Şener leaned slightly toward Ziya. "Is our relationship important enough right now to put into your notes?" There was a pregnant pause. Şener continued, his tone limned by palpable anger, "If it's crucial information that will help you find Deniz, then I'd be more than happy to tell you anything you'd like to know about our relationship."

Ziya began stammering. "No, no, you misunderstand me. That's not what I meant. I just . . ."

Şener raised his finger and cut Ziya off. "Please, officer. I understand perfectly well what you meant. We are two old people who came here today to help this family, our neighbors. Now, for whatever reason, our private life suddenly seems to be an object of interest for you, a respected officer of the law. To be frank, I am disappointed in you. Let me clear up any concern you have: Fehmi Bey and I are friends. I hope that'll be enough for your report. If not, I'd be more than happy to give you more private details."

"Şener, please . . ." Fehmi felt the need to try to intervene.

Unable to bear this unending conversation any longer, Berna jumped to her feet. "Please, officer, I am begging you. We have a much more urgent problem on our hands than rooting through people's private lives."

Recognizing his misstep, Ziya fell silent; he continued

looking over his notes until another officer entered the room, breaking the tension.

"Captain, we just got the boy's phone records. His signal was last picked up on the island last night. After that, there's nothing. And we have a clip from the camera footage. Would you like to take a look?"

Everyone in the room stood up anxiously, passing into the next room and joining the officer who sat in front of a computer screen.

The clip came from a camera on a street parallel to the main square that surveilled the road leading all the way to Nizam, at the end of the island. The trees on the empty street were swaying violently in the wind; a plastic bag flew by, and a young man with his hands in his pockets entered the frame from the lower left corner. He was wearing swim trunks and a T-shirt and carrying his backpack on his back. The kid raced to the end of the street and disappeared from sight.

"That's him," Berna whispered under her breath. For an instant she seemed strangely happy. She wasn't sure whether she'd ever see her son again, that son whose final goodbye to her was "Get off my back," but he had suddenly reappeared like a ghost, evanescent in the black-and-white footage, and reentered her life. Wordlessly, she leaned toward the computer screen and ran a finger over his black-and-white silhouette.

"There's no other images, captain," said the officer at the computer.

Şener had been staring with rapt attention at the screen, his hand on his chin. "God help us . . . That road leads to the beach facing Bostancı. Ah, son, I hope you haven't done something crazy," he muttered to himself, placing his hands with compassion on Berna's shoulders.

Ziya's gruff voice broke the silence. "All right, examine the other images. Especially those later in the day." Then he turned to the other officers in the room. "Now, colleagues . . . Let's have the coast guard circle the island again. Have them investigate not just the shores but the open waters. Preliminary evidence suggests that the boy might be at sea. Aside from that, let's do some research into the incident at school. And let's talk to Istanbul, have them survey the surface off Bostancı's shore."

Then Ziya turned to the island's local police force.

"Now, you guys, let's not skimp on our efforts here on land while the search at sea continues. Let's assemble a team of volunteer citizens to keep searching. We should also have one of our computer forensic analysts investigate the boy's computer right away."

The policemen in the room ran around to carry out their duties as Şener leaned down to Berna. "Berna Hanım, if you like, let's go home. There's no reason for us to wait here. We'll be best suited to help the officers investigating around the house." Şener took Berna by the arm while Fehmi walked over to Cem.

"Let's go try to find some volunteers, Cem Bey," Fehmi said. "Our word carries a good amount of weight here on the island, so we should be able to get anyone who's available to help with the search."

Cem shook Fehmi's hand with gratitude. "Fehmi Bey, you must be so tired. I can't thank you enough. Believe me, I'm at my wit's end," he said, beginning to cry.

Fehmi gently rubbed Cem's shoulder. "Never you mind me being tired, Cem Bey. It's your son we're talking about here. All I want is for us to find Deniz."

Şener and Berna left the station and began walking arm in arm toward their homes up the hill. "If you like, let's get a carriage," Şener suggested, to which Berna replied, "No." She wanted to walk. She wanted to walk along the street where her son had last been seen by the security cameras, wanted to touch the cobblestones which his broad, bony feet had stepped upon, wanted to breathe in the air that might still carry the slightest whiff of his babylike scent. Under the punishing sun on that first day without Deniz, they began walking home along Büyükada's streets, which seemed to have swallowed Deniz whole.

Like a mother returning home after work, her hands full with groceries; like a father standing in the yard with the tricycle he promised his daughter, the streamers on its handlebars blowing in the wind; like migratory birds reaching, by heart, the same destination year after year; like a murderer always returning to the scene of the crime, the two neighbors trudged up the slope, arriving at the top of the sleepy hill, each of the houses silent as a grave.

By the time they arrived home, Fehmi and Cem had

arrived at the clubhouse where Fehmi played bridge every day. The other men gathered around them when they entered. Everyone listened and learned what was happening. Each of the men came to Cem, quietly offering their apologies and condolences. Men, after all, support each other not by joining arm in arm, but by remaining silent, girding their pain. Fehmi collapsed down at a table and, taking a bitter sip from the Turkish coffee quickly provided to him, began to speak. "Friends, I'm sure we've all heard by now what happened. The commissioner says that the first twenty-four hours are absolutely crucial. Right now we're still in this critical window, and we as the people of Büyükada must support our neighbors as best we can. Deniz is our son and our brother as well. So we need to form a search team independent of the police. We know this place better than anyone. We have to search every single corner of this island, every last place we can get to. What I ask of you is that you'll help us."

"Of course, Brother Fehmi. You bet we'll join the search," the men of the bridge club said, taking out their phones, calling their friends, neighbors, acquaintances, and game partners.

Fehmi joined a group of fourteen people to search the cliffs around the Aya Yorgi Church. Despite the heat and the exhaustion of being up all night, he combed the area more quickly, more anxiously than everyone else. "Deniiiiz, Deniiiiz," Fehmi and the other members of the search party cried out, their hoarse screams disappearing into the depths of the otherwise-silent forest along the slope; those screams perhaps terrified the ghosts of the monks patiently enduring their ascetic suffering, or else the Byzantine princes left here by their families, their eyes burned out.

The teams of islanders found what they were looking for hours later, on a desolate beach at the far end of the island. Teenagers had been combing the beach step-by-step, and by the time they found a backpack washed ashore it was nearly evening. The blue backpack had been torn up by the sea all night, but it still contained a wallet and a set of keys. When the teenagers brought the backpack to the station, everyone looked on in silence. This bag was the one they had all seen on Deniz's back in the security camera footage.

Berna learned about the bag at home, Cem weeping into the phone when he called. The police officers who'd searched Deniz's room and found nothing of note took the computer and left. The news ushered in Berna's long-awaited and complete nervous breakdown, and she began sobbing with unstoppable violence. Şener stood over her, filled with concern. Realizing he wouldn't be able to calm her down, he left Berna buried in the pillow on Deniz's bed and went downstairs to make two phone calls.

His first call was to the wife of the mayor. Şener thanked Ayla Hanım for their aid and, his voice full of sadness, delivered the news that the poor kid's backpack had been found. He made a request of Ayla Hanım: "Ma'am, I don't want to think the worst, I keep telling Berna Hanım there's still hope, I want to keep her calm, but if you ask me, things are looking grim. What we need to ensure, from here on, is that the grief-stricken family can at least get ahold of their son's body. That he be given a grave at the very least. That's why I wanted to ask if you wouldn't mind speaking with the gentleman and having him ramp up the search efforts at sea?"

His second call was to Hanife, the woman who cleaned every other house on the island but his, to make a reservation for her to come two days later. Though Hanife's schedule was busier than ever, carrying gossip about the missing boy from one house to the next, she was shocked that Şener was lifting his embargo and said she would gladly come to clean. The mayor's wife would do what she could, but all the other women on the island also needed to tell their husbands over dinner that the kid was lost at sea. The only person who could reliably spread the rumor was Hanife.

Not wanting to leave Berna alone that night, Şener looked after her until quite late. She had fainted a few times, overcome by crying and screaming, and he stroked Berna's hair, rubbed wet muslin over her wrists, and tried to calm her with soothing words. He practically had to beg her to eat anything, preparing her some light appetizers, but she wouldn't touch any of it. Finally, when he had made her a glass of warm milk with cinnamon, he left the kitchen and found Berna on the front balcony, looking out over the lights of the ships combing the sea.

"Berna Hanım, you haven't eaten a thing. Please don't do this to yourself. At least drink some milk. It'll do you good."

Berna stared back at Şener, her eyes blank and sodden.

Not wanting to insist, Şener set the milk down on the balcony table, wrapped the shawl he held over Berna's shoulders, and began looking out at the sea alongside her. His conversation with the mayor's wife—"That he be given a grave, at the very least"—had had its intended effect, because the number of coast guard ships had tripled. This was the first time in its history that Büyükada was witnessing a search and rescue operation of this scale, the first time it had mobilized so many resources, all for the missing boy. The coast guard ships were accompanied by all the islanders with boats, who shined their flashlights into the water to assist in the search efforts. Dive teams from Istanbul had already carried out their first underwater investigations but had yet to find anything of note. From the balcony of Berna's home it all looked so tiny and insignificant, the boats shining like little pearls as they circled the island in the darkness, trying to find a clue, no matter how small, trying to find, perhaps, a limb or a body part floating up from the seafloor to the surface.

Standing silently alongside Berna and watching the islanders' efforts with profound pride, Şener glanced through the trees for a moment, at his own house. Fehmi, too, stood watching the boats move like trembling points of light. As if on cue Fehmi turned his own head, and the two of them, standing on the balconies of the neighboring houses, looked at each other. The darkness didn't quite permit them to communicate through this exchange of looks, but each knew all too well what the other was thinking.

In cases of missing persons, the first twenty-four hours are crucial. After the first twenty-four hours, the chance of finding the missing person alive is cut almost in half. The next most important timeframe is the first week, 168 hours. Because at the end of the first week, if there is a body lost at sea, it rots, it bloats, and it always finds its way to the surface.

The coast guard ships trawled the surface of the ocean for several days, but the extensive search yielded nothing. A week after Deniz's disappearance, once those 168 hours were almost up, Şener managed through his efforts to persuade the Büyükada Municipality to have an undersea oil exploration vessel called the Barbaros Hayrettin Paşa brought to the island. The ship, it was said, could map the seafloor with such delicate precision as to produce a perfect facsimile of it. It had never once not found what it was looking for.

After 168 hours, the Barbaros Hayrettin Paşa undersea oil exploration ship had scanned the seafloor dozens of times. Its facsimiles located sunken caïques, mossy rocks, lost treasure, bicycles, and love letters tossed into the sea, but it was unable to find even the tiniest trace of what it was looking for.

Not a single trace of the lost child.

Two months later...

BERNA

SEARCH INCONCLUSIVE!

HEARTBROKEN MOTHER WANTS GRAVE FOR SON

PEOPLE OF BÜYÜKADA PROTEST FOR EMERGENCY
RESPONSE

WHERE IS DENIZ?

HOPES SHATTERED

LOST BOY STILL MISSING!

The dinner table, covered in newspaper clippings, was full of headlines that all announced the same tragedy. Even through the tightly drawn curtains, it was clearly a sunny autumn day, a last warm holdout from the most painful summer in all of history. A bright and shining day in the middle of the false summer, a deceitful stage in the shifting balance of the seasons that corresponded to who knows what darkening point of autumn . . .

A false spring. A summer of death. A season of mourning.

Berna sat at the dinner table, precisely as she had done every day for the last two months, reading the clippings once again and once again and once again.

LOST CHILD STILL MISSING

BARBAROS HAYRETTIN PAŞA SEARCHES FOR DENIZ

HOPES SHATTERED

By now she had memorized the tragic headlines. She practically knew by heart what punctuation marks they used and how frequently, which ones used the wrong postpositions, where there were and were not contractions, which sentences in which articles were actually fragments.

For two months Berna spent every day combing the newspapers for everything written about Deniz, finding every single piece, cutting them out, filing them, taking them out of their files again and reading them once again and once again and once again, filing them back, taking her antidepressant, tossing back a sleeping pill, and burying herself in her bed.

Until she'd do it all over again the next day.

Unlike other families who saved up money for their sons to study abroad, Berna was saving up the newspaper clippings of her son's death. *This must be*, she thought cynically, *what they call a dead investment.*

Wearily, she set down the clipping which proclaimed her hopelessness in bold Helvetica and returned to her other new habit. Picking up the finely bound, blue-covered yearbook stamped with the logo of Alphan Preparatory Academy, she began turning the pages, her eyes vacant.

The graduation photographs, the portraits in cap and gown, the many smiling faces of the students who graduated high school that year passed before her like a funeral procession. When she got to her son's student number, 1324, she stopped and laid the open page of the yearbook in front of her. She lit a cigarette.

On that page of the yearbook, surrounded by a filigreed border of flowers, in fine calligraphic font, it said *In memoriam* . . .

The only page of that year's Alphan Preparatory Academy yearbook without a cap and gown portrait was the *In memoriam* . . . page for student number 1324.

Instead of a picture in his graduation gown, the page featured a picture of Deniz in his school uniform, a white shirt covered by a navy-blue sweater. The very same photograph plastered all over the newspapers, the very same picture she had taken from her wallet that very first day at the police station, the very same picture that had done the search no good at all. Berna looked once again at the photograph on the left side of the page. How many times had she imagined the person in that photograph wearing a graduation cap, the tassel dangling over his face, his white shirt replaced by a black robe? How many times had she fantasized that his page was no different than the rest of the pages in the yearbook?

How many times? A thousand? A million?

The *In memoriam* . . . page. In a yearbook brimming with

energy, excitement, youth, the future, it was the darkest, emptiest, most meaningless, most unfair page.

Beneath his headshot was Deniz's date of birth, a hyphen, and the infinity symbol. He didn't die. He lives on forever in our hearts . . .

Perhaps that was the only hopeful thing on that page of the yearbook. Forever. Its seemingly endless empty space, its vast nothingness in which we know not where we stand, its meaninglessness which gives us no idea where we're going. Like life itself, forever was a journey with no clear beginning or end. Forever: it meant absolute equality.

The page for student number 1324 also featured pithy notes that his classmates wrote about him. All marked by the narrow lexicon of the young. From "We'll never forget you" to "You're always in our hearts," all lies, all dishonesty, all veneer . . .

Berna's eyes scanned vacantly over all those notes, which meant nothing.

She had plenty of time and nothing to do.

Everyone wrote about how much they loved Deniz 1324, what a special kid he was, the unforgettable days they shared together, that he would always occupy a place in the corner of their hearts.

Reading these lies once again and once again and once again, she once again let out a doleful sigh. Feeling nothing, she stared down at the mannerly yet empty words, written with a skilled mendacity belied by the students' age, brimming with the pride their well-to-do families taught them.

Looking at that page of the yearbook, she thought about her own high school classmates. Who, for instance, had been the most handsome boy at her school? What had she and the smartest girl in class talked about in the cafeteria? Who had been the boyfriend of the most beautiful girl in school? What little she could recollect about her own high school classmates all these years later, so, too, would the students of Alphan Preparatory Academy hardly remember Deniz after the years passed. He had made a place for himself in quite a few people's lives by virtue of his little incident, but the details of that, too, would almost vanish as time went by. When they pulled out their yearbooks to show their own future kids their high school years, their years of joy and hope, perhaps they would only remember Deniz when they reached his page.

But that was it. They think now they won't forget him, but in the end, they will forget. All it would take for them to forget was for their hearts to fill with other memories.

Memories about anything except Deniz.

There would never again be another memory of him. All the memories, prospects, and hopes for his life had come to an end one stormy day.

Berna continued turning the pages of the yearbook, her eyes still emotionless. After all the pictures in graduation gowns, she came to pictures the students had taken of one another in the cafeteria, at picnics, and on field trips.

Childhood photographs where they played grown-ups: boys on the shore of manhood, girls on the precipice of womanhood . . .

Kids buried under one another in a playful game of dogpile, girls huddling together in front of a whiteboard, students standing over a radiator chatting, a group photo taken on a field trip somewhere historical . . . Her eyes landed yet again on Berk and Melisa, standing side by side in the field trip photo.

Berk, with his gleaming white teeth, and Melisa, beautiful as ever . . .

As with the graduation photographs, she had no idea how many times she had imagined Deniz, not Berk, standing beside Melisa on that field trip. Perhaps a hundred thousand, perhaps three million and sixty-six times.

And not just the photograph—she had conjured up in her imagination an entire fabulated field trip so many times: Deniz and Melisa falling asleep on each other's shoulders aboard an overnight bus crammed full of boisterous teenagers, perhaps even kissing, then having a group breakfast the following morning, going to the fortress in the city and taking a group photo there.

If the boy in that photograph were not Berk but Deniz, Deniz would have come home overjoyed. He would have told her everything, and they would have ordered pizza for dinner. Like all happy families, they'd laugh together, tell jokes, and eat their dinner; she would grab a napkin and reach over to wipe some sauce from the edge of Deniz's lips, and Cem would crack open a beer for their son.

Berna had to stop herself from smiling as she imagined it all. Because her son had no such field trip photo. He was in that yearbook with an ordinary, if still flattering, portrait. And of course: he would live forever in all their hearts.

Having exhausted herself, Berna set the yearbook down and began studying the photographs scattered across the table. Pictures taken at the memorial ceremony for Deniz at the Alphan Preparatory Academy. In one of them, Cem received a symbolic diploma in the school's auditorium, holding a bouquet of flowers under his arm. The pretend diploma for Deniz's graduation, bestowed almost mockingly ... In another photograph, Cem again, this time standing in Deniz's classroom, looking down at a desk covered in flowers. The portrait used in the notices about Deniz's disappearance had been sized up, placed in a frame, on top of the desk ...

Berna hadn't gone to a single one of these ceremonies, these farewells, these memorials, these gatherings for people to "come together, hold hands, and mourn Deniz." She did not want to go to that school, to stand there like a statue, made stone by her pain, like some Monument to Profound Suffering.

She did not want a single one of them to look at her. Berna couldn't even bear the thought of standing alongside them, of being surrounded by the pungent vitality of their youth. "We're your children, too, you're our mother now, Mama Berna," they'd lie, and she didn't want to have the slightest thing to do with it.

She would be nobody's Mama Berna ever again.

Not a single one of those students in that enormous school was her child. She hadn't been able to come to the aid of her poor, her downtrodden, her only son; she hadn't been able to do anything but lose her only child, and she refused to be Mama Berna to anyone else.

For just as time would heal all wounds, it would also heal the lie that anyone shared her pain.

Over the past two months, everyone eventually came to realize they had no place in Berna's world, which revolved around one single person. Her acquaintances came to visit her on the island, finding her colder than a gurney in a morgue; unable to bear her ranting and raving, her refrains of "Ah, where is he?" or "My God, my poor baby boy, what happened?" any longer, they slowly vanished themselves, like a silk scarf slipping from her shoulders. The show was now coming to its end. The stage was clearing and Lady Macbeth was preparing to deliver her final, crushing soliloquy.

Berna wasn't the only one who felt glad to be rid of those visitors. Cem would no longer have to apologize to their acquaintances, their relatives, or their faithful friends on Berna's behalf either.

Cem. There was Cem, of course.

Among all their friends, their relatives, and the human trash at the Alphan Preparatory Academy, it was Cem's grief alone that struck her as genuine. And she was endlessly grateful to him for all that he did. Bless him. If not for Cem she didn't know how she'd have faced it all.

Through the whole ordeal Cem had done everything he could: he had dealt with everyone who called or asked, had handled the police, the journalists. He did it all on his own. She was thankful for it. Because it had given her the opportunity to dedicate herself to her new lifestyle to her heart's content: the living room remade into the room of the dead, a home built on the ground of her depression. A grim little world of her own in which she'd glance over newspaper clippings and field trip photos like she was glancing through a furniture catalogue.

"SALE! SALE! SALE! Did you lose your child? This fall, we're pleased to offer you the newest, latest suffering: modern tragedies that will rip your heart out over and over again! Pay upfront or for a whole lifetime!"

There in the dark abode of her depression, festooned with her carefully selected memories, there was no room for anyone else, not even a husband. She didn't want anything to interrupt her concentration, which she felt she had to dedicate to her suffering. If what she went through was a book, it might have been called *A Room of One's Own Mourning*.

Since Berna spent all her time appointing this abode with carefully chosen pains and memories, Cem had endured the whole ordeal of hunting for Deniz alone, losing his mind, punching holes through walls, continuing to spend long nights scouring Büyükada even after the volunteer search and rescue operations had ended, all in the hopes of finding even the tiniest trace of their son.

Sometimes Berna would stand at the bedroom window at some late hour, looking out over the streets of Büyükada, illuminated only by streetlamps, awaiting some imaginary being, and she'd see Cem returning home. Cem, returning once again and once again and once again from defeat . . .

When she saw Cem at the gate, Berna would get in bed at once, turn her back, and close her eyes, waiting for Cem to get into his own ice-cold side of the bed. Each of them knew the other was not sleeping, but they opted not to speak, opted to deepen the rift between them, to lie in bed eyes wide open, staring meaninglessly at points on opposite walls. Until the exhaustion and the hopelessness knocked them out cold.

Night after night they slept with a gap between them in bed because they filled the empty space in that bed with dreams of their lost child. Every night at some late hour, the corpse of a boy would clamber up between them, would lie in state all night between his mother and father still as stone.

Cem and Berna began fighting, too, throwing whatever they got their hands on at each other. They cried, they flung accusations, they did and said every abominable thing a couple can possibly do and say to each other. These fights never found any resolution, and they were as meaningless to Berna as the visits from friends offering condolences. No matter how much they raised their voices, no matter who screamed that they hurt more, in the end every fight became habituated, as routine as saying, "Don't forget to buy bread on your way home." And so rather than eating each other alive, they opted to eat their own hearts out instead. Or at least, that's what Berna started doing, for she planned to spend a very long time wallowing in her grief.

But one night, and one night alone, as they screamed and shouted, as they practically wailed at one another, they made love. It was the middle of another fight . . . Suddenly, without saying anything, they pounced on each other. They dug their nails into each other's skin, spit in each other's faces; when Cem was on top he choked Berna; he watched her face get red and her veins bulge as he went in and out of her. Berna beat against Cem's strong body with her fists, her teeth, her nails. They moaned, they sobbed, they said the most hateful things to each other . . . After their painful sex ended and they had exchanged bodily fluids with animalistic fury, they lay there breathless. For the rest of the night, they didn't exchange a single word.

The following morning as Berna had her breakfast (or, more accurately, a cup of coffee and a cigarette), Cem said to Berna that he wanted to go back to the house in Suadiye. He didn't want to spend any more time here.

He couldn't bear it that this hell of an island was eating away at him day after day.

He wanted Berna to come too.

Starting over . . . Maybe where they left off . . . Continuing on with their lives . . .

Berna merely pretended to listen to Cem's plans for returning to Istanbul. She wouldn't go, of course. Her bereavement had taught her, like an actor, to use her blank eyes to express meaning and substance. That had been perhaps the only benefit of all her visitors. She had developed the skill to pretend like she was listening, to wear a mask of attention that disguised her lack of interest.

In the end they decided that it would be best for the two of them to take some distance from each other. They kissed each other farewell at the door, Cem disappeared down the slope with a small duffle bag, and she had no idea now how long it had been since he left.

And so, in the end, Berna was alone on Büyükada. It was another afternoon of reading newspaper clippings, smoking cigarettes, and ruminating. She just loved living in her depression like this. It was quite comfortable here, her lease was long, and she would not be leaving for quite some time.

She returned the clippings scattered across the table back to their files, closed the yearbook, and meticulously stacked the photographs like a deck of cards.

The sun was about to set. Another summery autumn day was coming to an end. The island was already painted in the sun's lewd shades of orange and red. It was the hour of the day Berna loved most. It used to be that she loved the sunrise, but now, it was the sunset. After her son was gone, she had become a woman who turned her face to the west, to watch the sun as it, too, left her.

She slowly stood up, took a light jacket from the coatrack, and draped it over her shoulders. She slid on the sandals by the door and went outside.

Silence.

Autumn was descending upon the island in all its tranquility. All the crowds and commotion of the summer had vanished, replaced now by gentle quietude. The strangest summer of her life . . . After a summer of noise, of sirens, walkie-talkie sounds, crying and screaming, Deniz's classmates and their claptrap, funerary visits, now she had the quiet that came with autumn alone. She left the house and walked through the yard. Opening the little gate wrapped in vines that separated the neighbor's yard from hers, she passed into the adjacent garden.

The trees were shedding their leaves, revealing bare limbs that seemed to beseech the sky. The neighbors' yard had been bursting with flowers all summer, had flooded the air with sweet aromas, but now it was descending into autumn as well. The rosebushes were flowerless; the more delicate plants had been wrapped in nylon; the honeysuckles that had drowned the garden in their sultry, languorous scent all summer were withered on the branch; and the four o'clock flowers that made the garden a riot of color had withdrawn to hibernate until the following summer.

All the curtains were closed in the neighbors' house, and it seemed blanketed in a peaceful, deep slumber.

Berna crossed through the garden, making her way to the back of the house, and her feet carried her to the little path between the trees. Dodging the tree branches, she followed the dirt path and began her ascent. After a while she emerged from the path, covered by branches like an arcade, and arrived at the peak above the mansion. Genuine happiness spread across her face and she stretched, taking a deep breath.

I'm here, she thought to herself as she looked around. *I'm here, in this magnificent place.* Surrounded by rows of bushes and manicured grass, underneath the enormous trees shedding their leaves, stood a white gazebo, a work of master craftsmanship, tailor-made to Şener's delicate, refined taste. The sun setting directly across from her filled the evening air with its color, its bleary light filtering through the carved lattice molding of the gazebo, rippling with abandon through the last of the leaves.

Past the gazebo, a cliff descended, and from there the sea unfurled toward the wide and endless horizon, absorbing the sunlight and refracting it into a million tiny jewels. Situated at the most perfect vantage point from which to look out over the beautiful sea, the gazebo was like a sacred, sepulchral temple deep in eternal rest.

She went to the gazebo and sat on the little bench near the entrance.

From where she sat she looked out at the sea, which stretched out motionless in a wash of a thousand and one colors, which would soon draw the darkness of night like a blanket over itself. From the gazebo it looked like there was nothing else to the world but the sea, like everything had become the sea. Perhaps the only place that brought her peace after all that had happened was right there, under the gazebo.

Berna had found the gazebo by accident a few weeks earlier. Wandering like a sleepwalker delirious on sleeping pills and high on the pain of losing her son, she noticed the hidden path, and like a little girl chasing a white rabbit, she followed it, arriving here. When she saw the gazebo and its view she understood she would never be able to escape this island. From here the sea that had taken her son, the sea for which her son had been named, offered her a space to search without end. *He's out there somewhere . . . In that sea, filled with trillions of drops of water . . . Perhaps caught on a rock, perhaps drifting in the foam of the waves . . . But I know. He's there, somewhere. Somewhere so close.*

After she discovered the gazebo, she asked Şener Bey if he wouldn't mind letting her spend a little bit of time there on occasion. Benevolent, compassionate, and polite as ever, Şener Bey unsurprisingly did not disappoint her. "Of course, Berna Hanım, please, it would be our pleasure. That place has the most beautiful view from anywhere on the island. What dreams we had when we first bought the land. Neither of us really feels like going and sitting there, like having a glass of wine during the sunset anymore . . . Please think of it as your own. Use it however you like," he'd told her.

Oh, sweet Şener Bey. Oh, fatherly Fehmi Bey. What good friends, what wonderful neighbors.

She pictured the genial faces of Şener Bey and Fehmi Bey, awash in the light of the sun which by now had descended past the horizon and painted the sea a bright red. As if all its water had been replaced by blood. Watching the sunset from where she sat, Berna took a deep breath, so deep, a breath almost for two people. One for her and one for the ghost nearby.

I know it, Berna thought to herself. *I just know it. He's here somewhere*. It was the same thing she said when she played hide and seek with Deniz as a child: "I know you're here somewhere! Come out, come out, wherever you are!"

Berna knew that even if years, centuries, the infinity sign on Deniz's yearbook page, had elapsed, a trace of him would well up to the surface. Maybe one day the face of the island would totally change; the beautiful mansions would be torn down, the gardens scrupulously adorned with honeysuckle and jasmine would be razed and brand-new boutique hotels would be erected in their place. Maybe then that trace would appear ... Maybe one day an expensive, well-bred dog with long red fur would dig up the earth somewhere on the island and a missing piece of Deniz, like the T-shirt they never found, would come to light. Maybe then ...

Maybe it would take centuries, millions of years. Or maybe, who knows, it would come next Wednesday, or tomorrow.

Berna was unable to restrain herself now; a huge, satisfied grin filled her face from ear to ear. She was smiling because even though she had said so to no one, she nourished an unshakable belief that Deniz would come back to her one day. It was only here, now, under the gazebo, that she had been able to confess so to herself for the first time.

So long as she didn't see his body, she knew this feeling would last forever.

This is how God wanted it, Berna thought. *If He wanted me to believe he died, He'd have given me the body. But He didn't. That has to mean something.*

She wasn't afraid of anyone and she wanted to cry it out: *He's here somewhere. I know it. He will come back.*

Berna stood up in the gazebo and took off her sandals. Şener Bey's genteel taste was clearly visible in the gazebo's ceiling: adorned with elegant carved latticework, the roof was one of the finest examples of the art of carpentry, protecting from sun, rain, and falling leaves the cement floor, which was appointed with the most beautiful İznik tiles she had ever seen. She placed her bare feet on the cement; it felt so good to her. As if energy flowed from the stone into her feet, like millions of acupuncture needles that would heal her, ease her pain even just a little.

Her feet pressed to the warm, dry cement, Berna felt maybe for the first time in her life that she had Deniz, really had him in her grasp, because now she had waiting for him as an excuse. She would wait for him for the rest of her life. Here, standing on the cement of the gazebo until the end of days, she would wait, her eyes fixed on the waters reddened by the sun setting before her. She would wait and she would wait and once again she would wait.

Stepping her bare feet off the gazebo, she approached the edge of the cliff. Perhaps it was this waiting, the possibility that Deniz might one day come back, that kept her from throwing herself off this cliff. Because aside from examining her newspaper clippings and hatefully skimming through the yearbook, she also thought every day of jumping off this cliff, though she always managed to restrain herself.

There on the edge of the cliff, the cool wind began to blow, licking across her face, feeling to her like the caresses of a child smothering her with kisses on Mother's Day. That feeling that always ate away at her, that everyone except her was enjoying themselves at a great big party, reared its ugly head once more.

She had overlooked something, she was sure, something simple, but what? What was it? Where had she made a mistake, what had she forgotten?

Her surroundings slowly plunged into darkness. Night was approaching, crestfallen, contemplative, sad as an old lover who can't bear the pain of separation, who returns after all. Not even the chirping of the birds that filled the whole island all summer could be heard; the only sound came from the whispered waltz of the leaves falling from their trees.

God help me. Send me a sign, a miracle. Otherwise I might not be able to go on waiting for that tiny possibility, and I might throw myself over this cliff.

The rustling wind surged briefly like a wheezing breath, and the leaves on the ground brushed against Berna's feet. It was like the leaves themselves were trembling, moving as though each one had come to life.

Here on the verge I beseech you with my whole heart, with the deepest suffering of a mother. Send me a sign. What am I missing?

And in the name of all mothers who lose their children, and in the name of orphans who lose their families, and in the name of those who drink of the icy waters of grief, God sent her a sign that day, two months after she had lost her son.

Looking out over the darkening sea for which Deniz was named, Berna once again recollected detail after detail from that night, the night Deniz vanished. Their last conversation, the woman with red lipstick who tried to comfort her as she waited in Kabataş to get to the island, her journey through the choppy waves on the motorboat, the carriage, the white socks in Deniz's room, the way she knocked on Şener Bey's door, and then coming to in the chair in their living room . . . But right before that, after she had fainted and as Cem carried her to the chair in the living room, in a moment where she had only barely been conscious, she had seen something in less than a thousandth of a second before she blacked out completely.

Standing on the edge of the cliff there and in that moment, she remembered for the first time what she had seen as she lost consciousness.

The cover of the album beside the record player.

A bolt of lightning broke across the horizon opposite the cliff's edge right as the title of the album flashed up suddenly, clearly, in her head:

FLASH!

How Beautiful the Sea.

That was the name of the record.

The night her son had vanished, her neighbors had listened to that song. Why?

A strange feeling came over Berna, a feeling that hadn't even crossed her mind. It was a feeling quite like the one her neighbor experienced months ago, when he realized that his husband, eating the fabulous blackberry tart he baked, had smoked weed; it was a feeling like a key clicking into a lock. Its name was doubt and by virtue of the album cover she had remembered, *How Beautiful the Sea*, it suddenly began gnawing away at Berna.

Berna slowly began piecing together vague recollections of the two old men waiting in the wings like silent ghosts, remembering how they had acted from the moment she had arrived to the island through Deniz's disappearance and up to the point when the search concluded.

Fehmi Bey, always appearing in the backyard whenever Deniz went out to play soccer . . .

That discomfiting smile on Fehmi Bey's face the night of the ball, and the way Şener Bey remained silent for the rest of the night . . .

The expression that crossed Şener Bey's face on the veranda the day they saw that Fehmi Bey had shaved off his mustache . . .

The terror in Fehmi Bey's eyes as he waited by the stairs when they knocked on the door that night . . .

Şener Bey's ire when Captain Ziya asked about the nature of their relationship . . .

All of the glances they exchanged, the uncertainty in even their most delicate of expressions, gestures, and manipulations—Berna suddenly saw them all so clearly.

The doubt welled up in her and she continued taking stock of all the small oddities in their actions, the fear in the depths of their eyes across so many moments since Deniz disappeared.

The lightning on the horizon had grown closer, bolting across the sky over Istanbul's distant hills.

Berna spun around and began running, paying no heed to the pain she felt from the pine needles piercing the soles of her feet. Having waited tirelessly for the smallest possibility of her son emerging from the sea, Berna and the doubt overtaking her would not wait even one more minute.

As Berna ran home to make the necessary calls, the old mansion with the most beautiful garden on the island had plunged into autumn, readying for the quiet of a deepest sleep.

GOODBYE, MY LOVE

Anchored in the port of Karaköy, the Queen Mary cruise-liner with its broad observation decks looked over the majesty of Istanbul.

With more than twenty million people, the city had grown beyond its capacity, and now, like an untreatable tumor left to its own grisly fate, it continued growing out of control. People disembarked from the cityline ferry at the pier, carrying packages, bringing food home, meeting lovers, ending marriages, treating sicknesses, fulfilling pregnancy cravings, carrying out vows of revenge, kissing, saying goodbye, and reuniting once more.

Sarayburnu, where so many princes were hanged with silk ropes and tossed to sea ... Topkapı Palace, the ineluctable home of a thousand and one intrigues ... the Yeni Cami Mosque's holy minarets ... the solemn beauty of Sultanahmet ... the breathtaking immortality of the Hagia Sophia ...

The board of the Queen Mary was filled not just with postcard images of Istanbul, but also with all the sounds that made the city a city. Screeching seagulls, cheeping children, howling crowds, blaring horns, the flapping of pigeons' wings, ambulance sirens splitting the city in two, police cars speeding from a crime at one end of the city to another . . .

Motorboats on the Bosphorus, hawkers on the street, pontoon boats selling fish sandwiches on the waterfront, peddlers of fake perfumes, pickpockets, pimps, drug dealers, cab drivers . . .

The Constantinople of the twenty-first century was brimming with the spirit, the energy, the suffering of so many people, all living through another ordinary day.

Except two people waiting for the Queen Mary to embark.

For them it was not such an ordinary day.

Approximately an hour and a half earlier, wearing their sunglasses, they had gotten out of a taxi, and, offloading their luggage to the young porter, they boarded the ship. With the first-class tickets they'd purchased weeks earlier, they would occupy one of the suites that had a living room, a dining room, and a private balcony.

These two men climbed aboard the Queen Mary during its brief stop in Istanbul on the world tour it had embarked upon six months earlier, and, after entering their suite, they spent quite some time putting all their things in order. Then they rested a bit and, with the unspoken understanding that only comes from being together for many long years, they left each other to their private time and parted ways.

Both of them had personal business to attend to.

Leaning against the railing of the ship's upper deck, Fehmi was observing Istanbul, its crowds, its circulatory system, its many strangers leading their lives like sewage disappearing underground before bubbling up again; he was also talking on the phone to his closest friend, Halit. Though the two men had been talking for nearly ten minutes, neither of them could quite bring themselves to say farewell.

Halit was sitting in the office of his engineering firm, his tie still unloosed, while on the other end of the line, in his linen suit, plain socks, and a fedora on his head, Fehmi looked like a true French gentleman. "Isn't this trip rather sudden?" Halit asked. "Seems like it's a long one, too, far as I can tell. Out of nowhere . . . Well, what do I know?" There was sadness in his voice.

"I know, Halit, it is rather sudden, but you know of course about everything that happened this summer. The whole process wore us out, so we decided to go on a trip like this."

"Are you going to come back?"

Fehmi gulped. "It's not too wise for people our age to make long-term plans. Nobody knows what tomorrow will bring. Maybe something'll happen after we go, and then . . ."

"Good God, Fehmi, don't say such things."

"No, it's just an expression. This summer really taught us a lesson. Şener and I both want to live a little differently. Life is short. So short! That's why we're not planning anything

316 • YİĞİT KARAAHMET

anymore. Maybe we'll enjoy the trip a lot, maybe we'll take another afterward. We don't know yet . . . Maybe each of us will find new lovers at every port." The two of them laughed, then Fehmi became serious. "By the way, if it's no trouble, I need to ask something of you, Halit."

"Of course, tell me."

"We're leaving, but we didn't manage to sort out all our affairs. Sales on some of our real estate haven't gone through yet. I'm going to leave a note with my lawyer giving you power of attorney. I'd like to ask you to take care of all the paperwork for these sales. My lawyer, Ömer Bey, can give you the details."

"I'd be glad to. So should I then deposit the money in your account?"

"No, hold onto it, Halit. I'll get it from you."

Fehmi was never going to collect the money from those sales. He was leaving that money, which Halit would under no other circumstances accept, to Halit's two daughters.

Halit muttered into the phone, "So . . . seeing as you're selling all your property, it really does seem like this is a one-way trip. I wish we could have had dinner, you could have come over . . . Leaving in such haste . . . How is Şener Bey? Is he well?"

Hearing Şener's name on the phone, Fehmi glanced around the deck. When he left their suite for the phone call, he last saw Şener placing his creams in front of the bathroom mirror. Scanning the deck, Fehmi didn't see any sign of him.

"He's well. He says hello and sends kisses to Ayşegül.

Halit, I've got to go. Şener and I have to take care of a few more things. Take care of yourself. See you, my dear friend."

The silence on the other side of the line was meaningful, masculine.

"You too, brother, you too. May God take care of both of you."

Before hanging up, Fehmi couldn't stop himself; he struggled to get out his final words: "Halit . . . I'll miss you."

He felt like he heard a wavering breath on the other end of the line, but Halit pulled himself together. "Me, too, my friend. I'll miss you too," Halit replied. And they hung up.

Fehmi used one hand to wipe away the tears pooling in his eyes and began wandering the deck in search of Şener.

Every time he crossed paths with the staff scurrying around the ship, he greeted them respectfully and stepped out of their way. Preparations were underway for the dinner that would be served after the ship departed Istanbul; crystal glasses were carried carefully to the dining salon and stark-white tablecloths were draped over tables.

The passengers were mostly people past middle age, but a few young couples caught his eye. They were happy newlyweds, opting to spend their honeymoons divvying up tropical islands between them. While the young people spent the cool afternoon in Istanbul swimming in the pool on the ship's topmost deck, the older passengers took their places on chaises longues in the shade or else in hammocks that offered a view of the city from the sea. These many rich people relaxing, swimming, partying, and tanning all carried strong drinks from one of the five large bars scattered across the ship.

Wandering through the crowds of people somewhat weary of their world tour but uncompromising on their pleasure, Fehmi tried to find Şener.

He saw what he was looking for in the distance. Şener was seated in a wicker chaise on one of the viewing decks that overlooked the pool.

There he is . . . The man I am in love with. Half of my whole life. My beloved, as much blood on his hands as on mine.

Şener wore a stunning white kimono, so fine its quality was apparent from the opposite end of the ship. Though he usually dressed his delicate body in raw cottons, this time he garbed himself in silks; in his hand he held the last dregs of a drink as he watched the couples swimming, playing, kissing one another in the pool.

Fehmi walked toward Şener with steps as slow and trepidatious as the ones he'd taken so many years earlier when he'd first seen him at Bananarama Bar. That first time he laid eyes on Şener, his body language was marked by shame, by the uncertainty of not knowing what to call what he felt, but after so much time had passed, those first steps now lost their reticence. Lying on the terrace of the Queen Mary, the man in the white silk kimono that Fehmi approached knew every last bit of him. His most private places, the rosy spot underneath his little toe, the tiny birthmark in the crevice of his buttocks, the exact baby-soft spot behind his ear to place a kiss . . .

That man in white silks, wanting to protect his delicate skin from even the palest rays of the autumn sun; his accomplice in the gravest sin, another elderly fugitive ready to abandon the home they built together.

Fehmi grazed his hand over Şener's shoulder, and Şener jolted in terror, turning to look at Fehmi. When he saw Fehmi, calm returned to his face.

"Ah, Fehmi, darling. Was that you?"

"I'm sorry, my dear. I didn't realize you were lost in thought. Did I scare you?"

"No, no. I was just out of it for a moment."

Şener finished the rest of his gin and tonic as Fehmi sat on the other chaise, taking Şener's hands into his.

"We're leaving, my love, not too long now. Not too long at all. Please just be patient a little longer. We've gotten through so much together, we can get through these last few minutes."

"Yes, of course . . . But I feel strangely worried, Fehmi. I don't think I'll be able to relax at all until the ship embarks." He downed the last sip of his drink. "Anyway, let's not think about it now. It spoils my mood every time. Did you talk to Halit?"

"Yes. He was sad."

Şener took his hands out of Fehmi's palms and took Fehmi's hands into his own palms instead. "This is the way it has to be. Call it fate . . ."

The two lovers sat in silence, surrounded by the cawing gulls, the laughter echoing from the pool, the clinking of drinks together. Şener handed his glass to Fehmi.

"I have to call Nil, too, Fehmi, darling. But if it's okay with you, I'd like to talk to her alone. Would you mind getting me another drink in the meantime?"

Fehmi took the glass and handed the burner phone to Şener. "Of course. But will Nil pick up a call from a number she doesn't recognize?"

"Like any real star, Nil Erkutlar would of course never answer a call from a number she doesn't recognize, Fehmi. That's why I'll call her landline."

Fehmi leaned in and placed a kiss on Şener's cheek. "Good luck, my dear," he said, disappearing into the bowels of the ship.

A difficult conversation was awaiting Şener. At least, it would no doubt be more difficult than Fehmi's conversation with someone as understanding and nonchalant as Halit.

Nil Erkutlar simply couldn't bear losing what belonged to her, and she would not react well to their departure. Not to mention that according to the papers Şener had chanced to read all summer, Nil had recently broken up with her young lover, a boy she had seen in a fashion magazine. After leaving Nil Erkutlar, her young lover had succeeded in using his fifteen minutes of fame well, nabbing a supporting role in some new television show. Worse, in a cruel twist of fate, the ratings on that awful period drama had shot through the roof. Nil Erkutlar's gigolo was the envy of every young man in the slums of the city, and stood at the beginning of a bright, rich career in television. Everything had happened because of Nil, and now Nil was out of the picture. And so while the boy's pictures decorated the phone wallpapers of so many girls, Nil Erkutlar was left an obscure, forgotten, faded poster on the city's drab concrete walls.

Not to mention that in this her hour of need, her closest friend had given all of his attention and support to another blond woman, the bitch next door on Büyükada, and had neglected Nil all the while.

Nil Erkutlar was sad, disappointed, angry, defeated.

The call from the Queen Mary cruiseliner was answered on a landline in a bedroom with tightly drawn curtains in a villa in the hills of Tarabya. Lying in her satin sheets, Nil Erkutlar spoke in a throaty voice, answering with a curt "Hello."

"Nil, darling. It's me, Şener. I hope I'm not bothering you."

The enemy Nil Erkutlar had been waiting for finally appeared before her, and just as it would be had she crossed paths with Ajda in a club one night, her eyes filled with vengeance as she jolted up in bed.

"No, sir, you're certainly not bothering me one bit. To the contrary, I'm absolutely overflowing with gratitude. You finally came to your senses and managed to remember your oldest friend in the world."

Şener gulped quietly. "Nil, darling . . . Nil, baby. I wasn't able to return your calls. I'm so sorry, but, you know, we had a strange, mixed-up summer. I just couldn't find the time," he said, offering a first salvo against her ire.

Sitting in bed wearing nothing but a miniature nightie, Nil Erkutlar leaned over to her bedside table and, at jet speed, took a cigarette, lit it, and filled an enormous glass of whiskey from the decanter she kept by her bed. "I was heartbroken. Truly. I thought you'd forgotten me, just like everyone else has."

"Come on! Forget you? How? My love, you are the great Nil Erkutlar. Even if I wanted to forget you, history would never allow it."

Nil Erkutlar giggled. "Ugh, Şener, you're always like this. Where do you come up with this stuff?"

A sad smile crossed Şener's lips. He knew Nil, his closest and oldest friend, all too well. No matter how bratty she became, all it took was a few sweet words to win her heart back.

"What are you doing, Şener? It sounds like there's a piano playing in the background. Are you at home working on a new song for me?"

Şener turned his eyes to the young man playing the piano by the pool, trying to entertain the guests. "You really don't know me at all, Nil. You think I play piano that badly? Shame on you."

They both laughed loudly. The sounds of Nil refilling her glass with a second whiskey at her home in the hills of Tarabya echoed through the phone line as Nil asked, "So then, where are you, my love? Are you and Uncle Fehmi having a romantic evening at the cabaret?"

"No. We . . . we're on a ship, Nil. We're about to leave on a cruise. That's why I called you. To say farewell . . ."

"A ship? Farewell? Where do you think you're off to in such a rush?"

"Like I said, it's a cruise, it all happened very quickly. We made the decision suddenly."

The silence from the other end of the line in the telephone in the hills of Tarabya was palpable. Şener could practically smell the whiskey as she took a heavy gulp and the cigarette as she exhaled its bitter smoke.

"Aha, so you're going on a cruise. How interesting! What gave you the idea for that, sweetie?"

Şener winced at the injured tone of Nil's voice. "Um, well, Nil, darling . . . It was a sudden decision, like I said before."

"And we all know you're someone who often goes on sudden trips like this. Aren't you, Şener?"

This time the silence came from the pool terrace on the Queen Mary.

"Come now, Şener, how many years have we been friends? It takes you three days of thinking about it before you decide to leave the island for Bostancı. You really want me to believe you decided out of nowhere to go on a cruise?"

The whiskey was done, the cigarette was done, but Nil's detective work was only just beginning.

"Didn't you always say cruise ships were vulgar? Remember when I said years ago let's go to Karayipler, and you lectured me for days about cruise ships and how miserable the people on them are."

"No, sweetheart. This is a luxury cruise liner. We have a fabulous suite."

"You, the biggest cheapskate in the world . . . in a fabulous suite . . . deciding to go on a cruise. Interesting!"

Nil's voice took on the wrathful quality it had whenever she felt like she was being lied to about something.

"For the love of God, come on! I get it, you're going on a cruise, but for what reason? Enough with the ruse that this was a sudden decision, okay? Every time you insult my intelligence with your lies it only pisses me off more."

The ice in her drink clattered with a peevish malaise.

"Wait, let me tell you what I think it is . . . Şener. Might this cruise of yours have anything to do with the missing kid from the house next door?"

Şener jolted up in his chaise. "The missing kid? Where'd that come from? What does that have to do with anything?"

"I don't know, Şener, darling. I ought to ask you."

Nil audibly refilled her whiskey before continuing on her warpath: "Don't act like I'm stupid. This summer on Büyükada, in the house next door to you no less, a handsome boy goes missing; I saw his pictures in the newspaper, I had them delivered to read the news about my old flame, God damn that bastard, I hope he falls in a well, rots in a pit . . . Anyway, the boy next door to you goes missing, he's never found, and suddenly you decide to go on a cruise. Doesn't seem like much of a coincidence to me."

Şener gulped. "You're being ridiculous, Nil. Don't exaggerate. Yes, if you're curious, it did have an effect on us. We were so worn out, so torn up by it . . ."

"Yes, *so* worn out, *so* torn up . . . Mmhmm . . ." Nil trailed off. Then she raised her voice: "Tell me the truth," she yelled, "or else I'm hopping in a cab and coming to that ship, and we'll have this conversation there."

Imagining the scale of the scene Nil Erkutlar would make on the ship sent a shudder down Şener's spine.

"So then, Şener, I'm listening. What's the deal with this cruise?"

"Fehmi has cancer, Nil."

Knock. Knock. Knock. Şener rapped his knuckle quietly three times on the wooden edge of the chaise.

"What? How?"

"Yes, he has cancer. We just learned last week."

"How could that be? So suddenly. What kind of cancer?" Nil Erkutlar asked.

Şener thought a moment. "Prostate," he said. He chose that organ because he supposed Nil would take less interest in an organ she didn't have and because she wouldn't know as much about it.

"Oh, that's awful. My ex-husband had that too. Serges. How is he doing?"

"As well as he can. He was upset, but there's nothing else to do. He wanted to go on the cruise, and I didn't want to disappoint him. It's not some silly reason like you thought. I have no idea how you came up with that, Nil, darling."

Nil was sobbing into the phone. "Of course, of course. I was just talking. It was tactless of me, when you're dealing with so much. I'm so sorry."

Nil's weeping made a lump well up in Şener's throat. Nil knew Şener would never, ever tell a lie like that about Fehmi, so she didn't need any more persuading. Love is sometime a profoundly dangerous weapon. Şener had tested it extensively all summer long.

"Give the phone to Fehmi. I want to talk to him," Nil said, still sobbing.

"Fehmi's in the suite, Nil. He didn't want me to tell anyone, he doesn't want to talk to anyone. You know Fehmi, he's so closed off about these things. He keeps acting like he doesn't have any illness at all. He doesn't even know that I'm talking to you."

"So I won't even be able to talk to Fehmi? My God, what on earth? Here I am, pitying myself over my ex-boyfriend, and you, my dear, what awful things you've been dealing with."

Nil continued weeping on the other end of the line. Şener tried to comfort her. "Yes, Nil, it's unfortunate. But given our age we have to be prepared for these kinds of things. He's in good condition for now. The doctors want to keep observing him and then they'll decide on a course of treatment. They said for him to keep his spirits high. When we got the news we decided to go on the trip we always imagined," he said. Everything Şener had said to her up till now was a lie, but then he said perhaps the only true thing in their conversation: "It was a hard summer. Hard and full of pain. Fehmi was so upset over the missing boy. Taking some distance from here will do him good."

"Of course, of course. You're so right. Go and relax a bit. When will you return?"

"I'm not sure yet. Maybe in three months . . . Maybe a little later."

We might not return at all, Şener thought to himself. The tiny accident they'd caused hadn't just upended their lives: it now sent all their loved ones, their home, the city they lived in, toppling like dominoes.

"Do you know what saddens me the most?" Nil asked, after a brief but heavy silence. "I'm completely alone in this world, that's what saddens me the most. Just look at the two of you, how beautiful you are, you've been together for so many years. Even in the hardest of times you stand by each other. But what about me?" Then she fell silent. The sobs continued. "I'm completely alone, a washed-up diva. Sitting in this enormous house, buried in memories, waiting to die all by my lonesome." She was overcome by her tears.

Because she was right. Despite her allure, her fame, her money, her jewels, Nil was alone, as she said, truly alone, and she was old now too. The older people get, the worse they feel when they're alone.

"Don't say that, Nil, darling. You're Nil Erkutlar. Your name's emblazoned in gold letters all across Turkish pop music. Stars are always alone, Nil, baby. And you're one of the highest of them all. Plus, your fans are your one true love. There are millions of people watching your every step."

"No, Şener. That's over now, too, I know it. My golden age has come to an end. The youth now listen to entirely different people, while aging stars like me are simply leaving this world behind. Every passing day another fan vanishes.

The millions have dwindled to the hundreds of thousands, and they too will fade soon enough. The day will come when there's not a single person left around me and I'll die completely alone and they'll bury me in a potter's field, a grave for the forgotten."

Şener interrupted her, a firm tone in his voice. "Only those who deserve to be there are buried in a potter's field, Nil, baby. As your oldest friend, as your colleague who discovered your value, and, most importantly, as a fan of your magnificent voice, I would never stand for it."

Nil had gotten caught up in the fear of being buried in a potter's field. "How are you going to do that, Şener? On a luxury cruiseliner, taking care of Fehmi's prostate, how will you stop them?" she sobbed.

Şener smiled. "We'll write you a song. Or rather, we'll have you re-record an old song. With your wonderful voice and your wiles you'll have them in the palm of your hand by the millions. And ta-daaa! Nil Erkutlar will once again be at the top. Trust me."

The excitement with which Nil leapt out of bed was so strong Şener felt it from dozens of kilometers away. "What do you mean?" she asked. "What song?"

Şener stood up. The sun beat down on the deck, and the crowds on the edge of the pool quivered with happiness. "Nil, do you remember 'Let Me Give You, My Love?'"

Nil was by now drunk as a sailor; she wouldn't even remember her own name at this point. "Oh, wait. Damn, I can't remember. How'd it go? Sing the words for me."

Though Şener hardly ever used it anymore for singing, his crystalline voice still had command over the notes, and he began singing the chorus:

"Let me give you, my love, what you desire
A life as festive as dancing fire,
A spring as bright as hyacinth and aster,
A world that turns and dances faster . . .
Do you still not remember it, Nil?"

Nil was overcome with laughter. "Of course I do! Let me see, how did the rest go . . ."

With the voice that had left her name emblazoned in gold across Turkish pop music, Nil Erkutlar began singing the song that would rocket her back to stardom, accompanied by a man she had met in the lobby of the Hilton many years ago, a man who now stood on the deck of a cruise ship. *"Let me give you, my love, what you desire, cranes in the sky soaring higher . . ."*

This was their first duet in many, many years; it had also been the last song they sang together before they broke their act up. The place for her in the potter's field now awaited a different washed-up diva.

Despite its crowds, its ugliness, its chaos, Istanbul has the most beautiful sunsets in the world. If they held a poll and asked everyone what the color of Istanbul's sunset was, everyone would give the same answer: blood red, with a little bit of disco glitter.

The sun had begun descending over the Golden Horn, behind the Galata Tower, painting the city the color of blood. The passengers who had disembarked from the Queen Mary to wander Istanbul were now returning. Final preparations were underway, the sailors were trying to rally, but for some reason the ship just wouldn't leave the port. As if the film wouldn't finish, as if the writer couldn't conclude his novel, as if the longer those minutes dragged on the likelier those lovers were to be caught.

The bitter scream of an ambulance pierced the air as it crossed the Galata Bridge. Sending a shudder through all who heard it, the ambulance siren reverberated across the deck of the Queen Mary. Holding his breath for the duration of the siren, Şener leapt out of his chaise. Panicked, he looked around, and a pair of warm hands found his in the air. Fehmi smiled at him from the adjacent chaise.

"Calm down, dear. It's nothing."

Like a young girl betrothed to a soldier wearing herself out waiting for his return, Şener sat down, out of breath. Waiting brought him no calm but, to the contrary, pushed him into the depths of even greater anxiety. He could feel his heart beating in his wrists. "Why aren't we leaving? I don't get it. It's half an hour past the time they said we'd depart."

Fehmi held fast to Şener's hands. "All right, Şener dear. Try to remain calm. Your blood pressure's going to make you explode." Fehmi wanted to soothe Şener, but he was worried too. A voice inside his head spoke. "Did someone perhaps call the ship and delay its departure?" it whispered to his conscience. Fehmi immediately suppressed that malicious, wicked voice.

Because the two lovers sitting there were not just awaiting the boat's departure, but also their fate. They were as they had been from the beginning. As they had been from the moment they first met at the Bananarama Bar up to the point where they sat in chaises on the deck of a ship . . . Always hand-in-hand. Still and forever hand-in-hand. One hand on an iron, one hand in the lap of the silk kimono . . . Covered in both liver spots and blood, these hands had never parted.

But killing time was killing them.

These two men had been waiting for many years of their lives, and yet the waiting only felt agonizing now. As if the curse of some dead body would rise from the grave, cross the seas and the hills, and find them on this ship.

The rhythm of the piano beside the pool had picked up, setting into motion all the unknowns of the setting day and the coming night. The members of the orchestra stood perfectly at the ready onstage, waiting for the ship to depart in order to begin the night's festivities. The languor aboard the ship all day was slowly replaced by the sounds of blithe merriment across every deck.

Fehmi turned his head to Şener and looked at him a moment. He'd been keeping a question to himself for some time now, but didn't want to leave without asking it.

"Do you regret it, Şener?"

Şener turned in an instant. His gaze assured, he didn't

hesitate a second in his reply. "I have never once regretted loving you, and that's the only thing that matters."

Fehmi nodded silently and brought Şener's hands to his lips to kiss them. He was no longer afraid. He was ready to pay the price, whatever it was. If there was an end to this, it would be an end for the both of them.

A police siren droned shrilly in the distance, making its way toward Karaköy.

The sound was still so far it could only be heard by sensitive ears, ears that expected to hear a police siren. But it was approaching. Approaching in order to capture a thousand and one murderers, thieves, drug dealers, pimps. Approaching the pier. Approaching lovers, beloveds, fugitives.

"Please, come on already. Let's get moving. Let the story end already," Şener said, his eyes fixed on the pool.

Fehmi squeezed Şener's hands, and the two lovers' eyes met.

And the Queen Mary sounded its horn three times in a row. Seagulls scattered from the ship's stacks and the engines began rumbling.

The three blasts of the horn echoed across the historic peninsula, against the walls of the Yeni Cami Mosque, through the minarets of the Süleymaniye Mosque, over the ancient dome of the Hagia Sophia.

At those three long blasts, the spirits of concubines who lived trapped over the centuries in Topkapı Palace ran to the windows. The ghost of a page boy playing hide and seek in the palace garden was startled by those three blasts, and found refuge behind a timeworn plane tree.

The handsome pianist at the edge of the Queen Mary's pool ran his hand over the keys of the piano, playing them all before striking a final, single note and silencing the piano for good.

The passengers gathered around the pool as waiters percolated through the crowd, carrying trays of cocktails in every imaginable color. Athletic young men in speedos jumped into the pool, which had warmed over the course of the day. Lovers locked in embrace danced in rhythm with the music across the deck.

"Champagne!" called a smiling old man from one of the chaises on the deck. In the setting sun his white hair looked platinum. He lowered his sunglasses and, looking at the handsome, swarthy lover who sat by his side, erupted in laughter. "Please bring us your most expensive champagne. We're celebrating!"

The young waiter understood the word champagne, the most universal word in the world, and was already in motion.

Şener got up from his chaise, sat beside Fehmi, and placed a long kiss on his lips. A kiss feverish as the first day, faithful as their forty years.

With gratitude, with longing, with adoration, "I love you," he said. "I love you more than anything else."

The bottle of champagne burst open behind them, its pop sweet and sexy as the cry of an orgasm, and two flutes were filled for them. The two lovers clinked their glasses together as the crowd assembled in dance by the pool began applauding at the end of the first song.

The orchestra continued without rest, beginning the next song at the same tempo. The ship waved farewell to the whole city, and as it silently left the Bosphorus behind, the orchestra's song began filling the deck with the imaginary scent of coconuts from a faraway tropical island.

The Queen Mary passed through the open waters near Büyükada, and the two lovers, champagne in hand, looked among the hills for that place from which the sea looked most beautiful. The setting sun's reddening rays brightened that little peak, enveloping it in the loving arms of endless sleep.

Şener pulled Fehmi to himself. "Come on, let's dance," he said. Embarrassed, Fehmi looked around. Dance? It had been such a long time since they'd danced together. Şener stared insistently into Fehmi's eyes. "Come on, please? Let's dance as well. There's nothing left to bring us down."

Smiling, Fehmi stood up, and the two lovers walked hand in hand, splitting the crowd on their way to the edge of the pool. Everyone made way for them, greeting them with smiles, raising their own glasses to Şener and Fehmi's.

It was the first time they had ever held hands in a crowd. After forty long years, they no longer had any reason to fear, to hide, to run away.

In that moment something came to Fehmi's mind, and he stopped Şener, who was pulling him onto the dance floor. A melancholic expression appeared on Fehmi's face.

"There's just one thing I left behind that I feel sad about, my dear," he said.

Şener took Fehmi's face into his hands. "Oh, come on, you can't be sad about anything now. What is it? Tell me quickly so I can kill that too," he replied.

Fehmi pulled his face away from Şener's hands. "My God, you're insane! Do you even hear yourself? I'm sad about the play I was translating, love. It was going so well. I wish I could've finished it."

Şener smiled and held Fehmi's hands tight. "Don't be sad about anything, Fehmi, darling. That's in the past. Now it's time to turn a brand-new page in your life. You got English out of the way, believe me. You're a wonderful translator. Now it's time to learn French," he said, winking at Fehmi mischievously. "In fact, let's learn your first French sentence now."

Fehmi smiled. "What's that?"

Şener looked back at Istanbul, at the city they left behind. He raised his glass of champagne and replied, "Adieu, mon amour."

The ship moved farther and farther and farther away from Istanbul. All the seas, the hidden docks, the straits, the mosques, the graves beneath the wind, the lamentations of mothers, the unhappy dinners, the betrayals, the furtive kisses—all of it was left behind.

And the Queen Mary, already a tiny point on the endless, beautiful ocean, vanished.

ACKNOWLEDGMENTS

A month before the first edition of this book appeared on shelves in Turkey, I wrote an acknowledgments section for the book, which began with the sentences, "This book has undergone so many adventures from the moment I first started writing it until this very moment, when you hold it in your hands. There are a number of people who have dedicated so much work to make this possible, and I can't go without acknowledging them."

There have been so many more surprises since the book was published. In a country like Turkey, where the homophobia runs bone-deep, the book was received with a care and attention that far, far exceeded my expectations, reaching places that I could never have even dreamed of (your hands, for instance!). And, most important of all, it helped me discover what I wanted to do with my life after I turned forty. In fact, I realized, I had been doing what I wanted to do all along. This book helped me see that.

Now, as this book undergoes preparations to meet readers in other languages for the first time, I decided that I wanted to update my acknowledgements. Because yes, the book has undergone many adventures "until this very moment," and indeed, so many people have dedicated so much work to make this possible and I certainly can't go without acknowledging them:

First of all, to my readers of every age, profession, and gender, who I believe raised me up and brought me to this point, for helping me overcome the question of belonging that plagued me all my life, for allowing me to feel like I belonged somewhere;

To 6:45 Yayın, my publisher in Turkey, with whom I have the greatest love-hate relationship, for constantly getting on my nerves and always treating me like a queen;

To the team at Anatolia Lit and Amy Spangler, for doing everything in their power to carry me and my work to your distant hands and distant language;

To the entire Soho Press team, and especially to Taz Urnov, for all their grace in the process of publishing this book in a new language, for the efforts they put into including me in the process and for giving me in spades the editorial support I never got for the book in Turkish;

To Nicholas Glastonbury, this book's godmother, who has been a wonderful translator through this whole process and whom I now consider to be a dear friend, for loving so many of the jokes in this book as much as I do and without whom none of this would have been possible;

To Gencay Ünsalan, for loving this story at least as much if not more than I did from the first moment, when it was just a tiny idea, and for constantly motivating me to finish the book;

To Deniz Yurdakul, for her unwavering material and emotional support over the course of writing the book;

To Tarık Bayazıt and Savaş Ertunç, for setting aside their valuable time to offer me their impressions of Büyükada and their suggestions for some of the meals in the book;

To Elçin Yahşi, Muammer Brav, Cem Tunçer, and Arda Yaman, for their ideas and support in reading, editing, and publishing the book;

To Halid Ziya Uşaklıgil, Nahid Sırrı Örik, Truman Capote, and Patricia Highsmith, for always whispering into my ear what needed to happen on those nights when I got stuck;

and to my grandmother, Leman Yolasığmaz, for nourishing me with her homecooked meals when I retreated to her home in Giresun to write;

I offer my deepest thanks.

If not for these people this book would not exist.

With endless gratitude and appreciation . . .

Yiğit K.
November 2024